THE
LODESTONE SAGA

THE LODESTONE SAGA

BOOK ONE
THE SWORD OF VaLor'

ROBERT LOUIS ENGLEMAN

The Lodestone Saga: Book One

Copyright © 2018 by Robert Louis Engleman. All rights reserved.

No part of this publication may be reproduced, stored in a retrieval system or transmitted in any way by any means, electronic, mechanical, photocopy, recording or otherwise without the prior permission of the author except as provided by USA copyright law.

This novel is a work of fiction. Names, descriptions, entities, and incidents included in the story are products of the author's imagination. Any resemblance to actual persons, events, and entities is entirely coincidental.

The opinions expressed by the author are not necessarily those of URLink Print and Media.

1603 Capitol Ave., Suite 310 Cheyenne, Wyoming USA 82001
1-888-980-6523 | admin@urlinkpublishing.com

URLink Print and Media is committed to excellence in the publishing industry.

Book design copyright © 2018 by URLink Print and Media. All rights reserved.

Published in the United States of America

ISBN 978-1-64367-070-6 (Paperback)
ISBN 978-1-64367-071-3 (Digital)

Fiction
18.10.18

Contents

Introduction 7
1 A Meeting In Time..25
2 The Grotto 29
3 The Smithy 40
4 First Battle..47
5 The Blue Keep 61
6 The Portal 81
7 Mero Wood 89
8 Of Dwarves and Bones 107
9 Val 119
10 Allece 126
11 Old Home..136
12 The Watchers 148
13 The Wyrm and the Sword..................................159
14 Coming Of The King 165
15 Planing and Parting 178

16	Road To Maldor	190
17	Battle of Catch Mountain	204
18	Maldor	213
19	The Gathering	225
20	The Final Battle	240
21	The Magic	250

Glossary 259

Book two: The Tiara of Thann, Sample 261

INTRODUCTION

For their pleasure, the Gods created an "inter-dimensional reality" which they called the Eight Sister Worlds. They made them all geological reflections of the original, Sithia, though each one was topographically different in ways that pleased them. Each world lay in its own dimension and time. They placed a variety of flora, fauna and beings upon the worlds that they might enjoy the resulting interaction. The beings were precious to the Gods, for they had made them in their own image. The Gods gave the beings strength that they might endure, desire that they might strive, hearts that they might experience joy, sorrow and love; and finally, intellect that they might choose for themselves. And they gave each world Magic as pleased them, this to one, that to another.

To prevent their creations from falling into complete darkness, which one of the Gods favored, and knowing there must be opposition in all things, they set in place, the Blue Keeps in each of those worlds, the Lodestone and the shards of the Stone that were to become pendants for their chosen warrior Knights of the Stone. When they were done, they called it the beginning, the Year of the Stone.

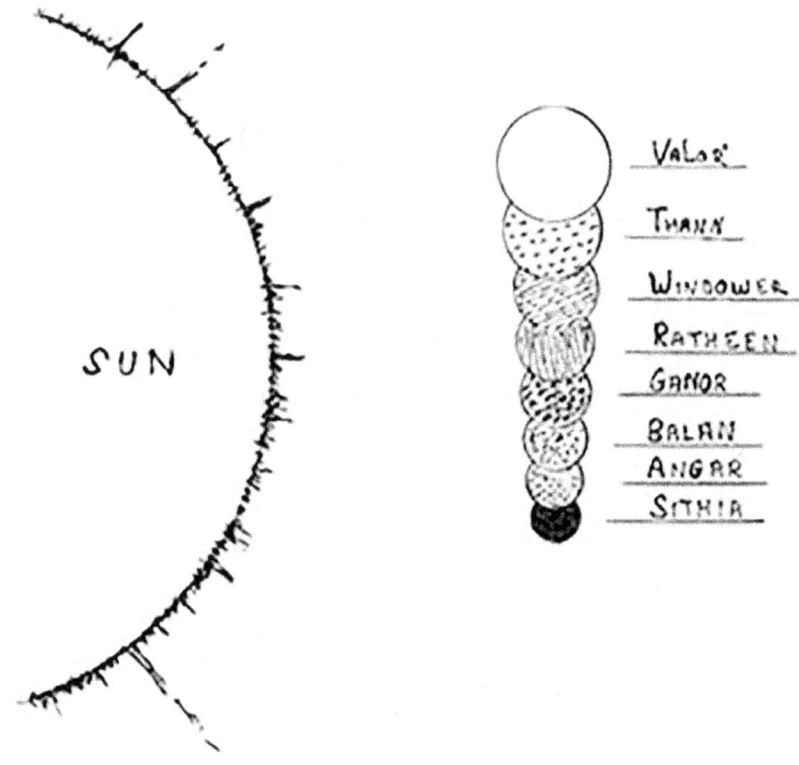

Herein are stories of two of those worlds, Ganor and Valor'. But to begin we look at the developing of the great Evil, this takes us to Sithia, the eighth world.

5223 AS (After the Year of the Stone)
SITHIA Eighth Sister World
DEMON SORCERER

The sorcerer Korshan stood wrapped in thoughts as dark as his robe. Here within the deepest bowels of this ancient, long dormant volcano, he was the undisputed ruler, the master, the King. Here he ruled absolute, but what of the surface of this land known as Sithia? What of the millions of people, who lived in the light on the surface, and what about the other seven worlds? He must rule them all at any cost! His mind cried out with the need to hold it all in his grasp. With the power that was soon to be his, he could destroy what remained of the Brotherhood of the Stone, those second rate wizards and their handful of slightly gifted fools—they would not stop him this time. Now he would bring an age of endless, blissful darkness to the surface and turn loose the hordes of the void. His ethereal army would crush all resistance, would turn the peoples of the surface into slaves, food and playthings. Then, one by one he would set his minions to work on the other worlds and draw them slowly but surely into his grasp. But first he must meld with the Demon Thantox, lord of the void. Only then would he have the necessary power.

His spell had to be just right.

This far beneath the extinct volcano's throat nothing lived, not insects, not even mold, nothing. It was a totally sterile environment, a necessity for his spell. His eyes glowed faintly red with his infravision, the only light in, otherwise, total blackness. He began by slowly tracing an octagon on the smooth granite floor. Then, from a pouch that he drew from within his voluminous robes, he dribbled yellow phosphorescent powder around it in a continuous stream. Once completed, the Octagon produced a soft shimmering light. The walls of the small natural cavern were barely discernible in the subdued glow of the powder. Ceremoniously, at each of the octagon's points he materialized and placed a single waist high candle stand with a foot tall candle secured in a large earthen bowl. The only difference in the eight points was the bowl at the north point being half again bigger than the other seven. Standing in front of the northern tip he shuddered, then, shrugging off any doubt, hummed a single low note as he reached out and touched the wick of the candle before him. The candle leapt afire; the room saw real light for the first time ever. Slowly, humming the single tone softly, he walked around the octagon touching each candle bringing them to life as he went. The chamber walls now shimmered. Shadows moved about the walls, a result of the displacement of the air on the candles as he walked. Again standing at the north point, he brought forth from his robe a needle sharp, finely honed knife about eight inches long. In a high singsong voice he began to chant. Careful not to step into the octagon, he slowly walked around its perimeter. With great ceremony he pared off a single bit of fingernail at each point and dropped it into the earthen bowl. Returning the knife to his robe he again walked around the octagon chanting and placing bits of dark leaves into each bowl. He went around a fourth time dropping a single large, drop of spittle into each bowl. On the fifth round he placed a small scrap of parchment with a rune written on it into each bowl. And a sixth time around he placed a large pinch of mineral ingredients from a small leather pouch into each bowl. On the seventh trip he laid a single hair from his head and a single piece of quartz stone about the size of an egg into each bowl being sure to place the hair on top of the stone. The large north bowl received the biggest stone. Finally, he once again drew forth the dagger and deliberately, deeply sliced his finger with his knife. Still chanting he walked slowly around the octagon, dripping precisely eight drops of blood into each bowl. Once again at the north point, and still chanting, he laid the knife on the floor before him, healed the cut with a single word and slipped the robe from his frail nearly emaciated frame. He laid the robe carefully next to the knife outside the octagon, standing with only a light cotton wrap around his loins. With increasing intensity his chanting echoed off the cavern walls. Hurriedly, he stepped into the octagon. With a flick of his wrist, at a particularly high note in his chant, he gestured at the candles. Their brightness increased eight times, shattering the gloom that had lain heavily over the chamber. Lightning leapt from his fingers and flew about the octagon. His chanting grew stronger. The acrid smell of ozone filled the air. One by one he faced the points of the octagon and, gesturing, the bowls began to steam. All around him lightning danced, burning the octagon deep into the granite floor.

Directly in the center of the octagon a mist began to take form. With several distinct commands a large head could be seen to coalesce out of swirling clouds of purple mist. Shoulders and torso soon followed.

Thantox, the Demon Lord, was not happy. "Why do you summon me mortal?" the voice thundered with obvious disdain, ear shattering within the chamber.

The sorcerer's voice droned on.

"Fool!", roared the demon, "What magical tricks do you attempt now?"

The sorcerer stood fast, chanting even louder, his frail body seeming to quake at the demon's voice.

The demon sneered, "By entering into the casting lines you have placed yourself into my realm. Perhaps it is now time for me to destroy you and stop your endless meddling into mysteries you cannot begin to fathom."

The sorcerer suddenly stopped. Sweat oozed down his forehead turning to icy rivulets that ran down his face in the chill of the cavern. In a determined tone that gradually grew stronger, he looked full into the eyes of Thantox and said, "I have decided that the only way I can conquer the eight worlds is if I become the Lord of the void."

Fully fifteen feet tall and nearly completely solid now, Thantox could easily squash the small man, if he could move, which he could not until he was completely solidified. "How do you propose to do that little man?"

"I have already done it. With just three more words and two gestures, you will meld with me and we, together, will rule both the abyss and the eight worlds. That is, of course, if you allow it. Should you choose not to however, I merely change one word and you die, immortal or not."

"There is no such spell," thundered the demon.

"Perhaps there wasn't, but now there is and it will work."

"I don't believe you!" roared the demon.

"Then, I guess I will just have to destroy you and deal with your successor." With that he raised his hands and began to gesture. "Let me know if you change your mind." He spoke one of the words, a long complex thing of many syllables. Gesturing he began the next, long, long, long word.

The demon was nearly solid. Sweat had formed in tiny beads over his entire body now and he shivered slightly as a chill set into his flesh.

Thantox suddenly became aware of his life force beginning to shift, a feeling he had never before experienced. Something was wrong; he felt weak and sickly. Could it be true? He had never felt weak or sick before.

"Hold," shouted the demon.

The sorcerer looked up.

"What do I gain out of this….ah, arrangement?"

"You and I will become one being. We will be the most powerful being in all of the eight worlds, but my intellect will rule the combined body. You will, however, live on, which will be better than the alternative. Choose quickly, the time is running out as is my patience."

"You lie human!" The demon spat the words out in obvious contempt. "This has never been done before."

"Then you have nothing to fear."

Once more the gesturing began. Once more began the feeling of being torn apart from within. The demon felt sick. Demons don't feel sick! He knew now that the sorcerer had won. "All right," he whispered, defeated for the first time. This was a terrible, degrading new feeling, for when demons are defeated they become little or nothing to the rest of the demon world. "But now that I am defeated who will follow me….us?"

"Take heart Thantox. Combined, we will be far, far more powerful than you ever could have imagined." With that the Wizard spoke the last very short word and relaxed in anticipation. All at once he could feel himself beginning to disintegrate into thick, purple, mists, his body cried out in terror, his mind raced with questions, then his screams mingled with those of the demon, echoing up the winding corridors toward the upper chambers of the long dead volcano.

… A small, bearded figure in a bright yellow robe darted out of its hiding place in a low narrow passageway and ran quickly to the octagon. In a fluid motion it threw a handful of leaves and flower petals into the swirling mists, then scurried back to the safety of the passageway and fled, screams echoing in its ears as it hurried away …

Blackness surrounded the sorcerer. He felt strange, as though his skin no longer fit. A thick, acrid taste sat heavily in his mouth and a smell like rotting flesh assailed his nostrils. Slowly he moved. Everything felt strange. His head throbbed. With a simple spell he quelled the ache in his head, then willed a light to appear above. Dim though it was, it caused his eyes to blink in discomfort. He lay in the center of the octagon, now a still smoking line, etched deep into the stone floor as though acid had cut its way down into the granite. Struggling to rise to his feet, he could see that the spell had indeed worked. He stood nearly fifteen feet tall. His skin had a decidedly gray cast and was hard and scaly. A wave of his hand turned the air before him into a solid shining surface in which he could see his reflection. He couldn't prevent the reaction; he flinched back in disgust. The face reflecting back had a definite resemblance to his own, but it nestled in a head with wild green hair, horns that turned forward over small pointy ears and fangs that stood out in a mouth that seemed to hang slightly open. Uncontrollably, he shivered.

"What did you expect, a fairy prince?"

The voice had come from within his head.

"Surely you didn't expect I would be totally gone?"

"I wasn't sure how your half would influence me. I only knew that it must be done." His voice was strong and thundered through the cavern.

"It isn't necessary to shout, I can hear your thoughts you know."

He stumbled cautiously to the edge of the octagon, and hesitantly stepped over it. Relieved that it hadn't held him inside, he stooped to retrieve his robe. He gestured and it grew large enough for him to wear.

"Must I be forced to wear these distasteful rags? At least allow me to be garbed in something more regal." There was a flash of light and the familiar black robe had changed to bright purple fringed in orange and green.

The sorcerer was shocked. He hadn't expected the demon to have any power other than through him. As soon as the thought struck him the voice said, *"What? Was I to be a silent and obedient servant? It seems that I am more of a reluctant, possibly troublesome, partner."*

Korshan made a quick mental shift, blocking the demon out of his thoughts; the demon must not be allowed to penetrate his plans too deeply.

"Now, that wasn't nice. How are we to work together if we are separated in this manner?" There was definite sarcasm in the thought.

Once more he brought forth the shining reflective surface. Actually, he made a rather imposing figure. "Enough of this, there is work to do and I am anxious to be about it. If you can contain yourself long enough we are about to bring a new order to the world above." Almost casually he walked around the octagon and picked out of each bowl a flat, blood red, amulet about as big around as a chicken egg and flat as a coin, all that was left of the ingredients he had put in the bowls. Finally, out of the largest bowl he removed one nearly twice the size of the others, saying as he did, "And one with which to control the others." From within his robe he produced a golden chain, which he sealed to the amulet with a simple spell, and placed the chain over his head. Finally, he turned and strode purposefully toward the passage that would take him…them to the surface.

"I think we are more Thantox than Korshan, so we should be called Thantox."

"But it is I, Korshan, who is in control."

His long, rather heavy and heretofore unnoticed tail suddenly got in front of his left foot causing him to trip and fall forward. Only a quick, reflexive spell kept him from hitting the ground and getting a bruising. He stood up straight, and took a swipe at his robe as though he were dusting himself off, "All right, all right, how about…ah…Kortox." A lack of response signaled at least a temporary acceptance.

THE LODESTONE SAGA: THE SWORD OF VaLor'

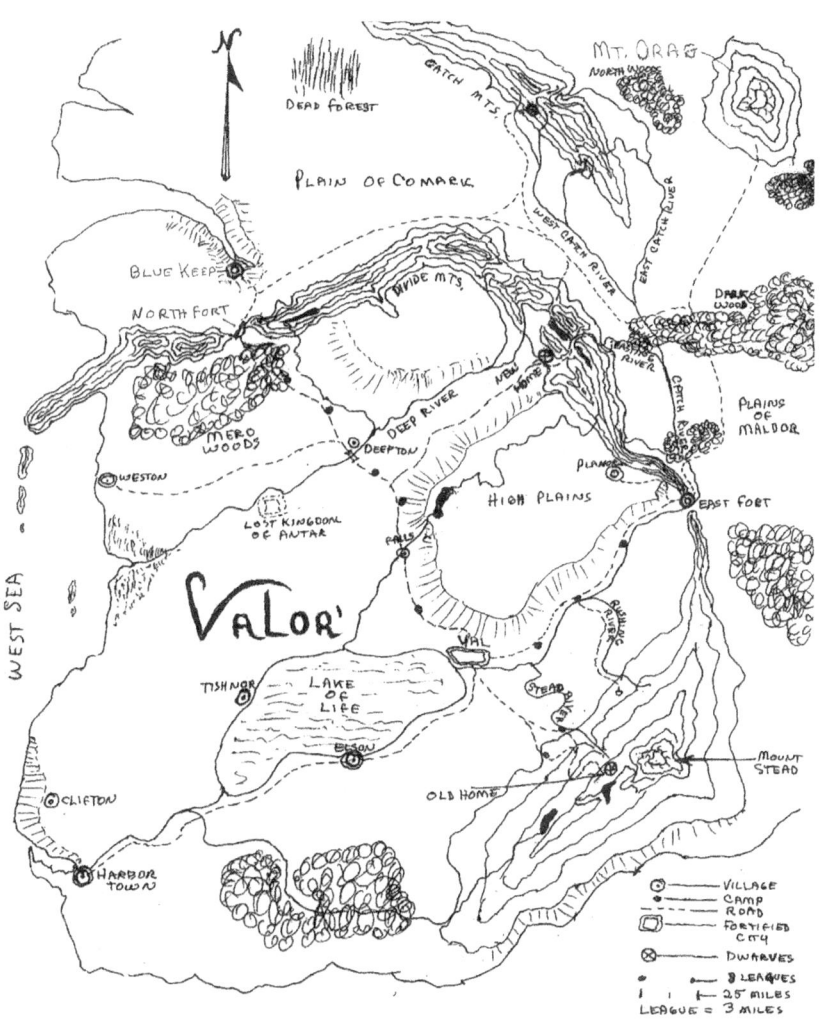

PROLOGUE

5207 AS, VaLor' *First Sister World*

The Great War stopped. It wasn't won by anyone. It just stopped. It just ran out of fuel, manpower, blood, will, and of course—magic, the excessive use of which nearly destroyed their world. Both forces had returned to their own lands to rebuild and prepare for the future, a future that both knew would again bring war. Two wizards remained of the many that had guarded VaLor' and they knew that sooner or later Xzuron, the evil sorcerer, and his armies of darkness would come again. The writings of the ancient prophet, Orn, assured them it would be so. Without hesitation the wizards set about preparing for that day.

5507 AS, **World of VaLor'**

Three hundred years had passed since Xzuron the sorcerer had returned to Mount Orag without victory. There he had plotted, planned and gradually regained his former strength. He had been reduced to a shadow of the powerful being that had brought his armies against the VaLor'ians at North Fort. The cost of the war had been great to both. The armies of VaLor' had nearly perished in the battle. During that battle, great amounts of magical energy had been released, leaving the plain of Comark barren and lifeless still, three hundred years later.

In the huge cavern, deep within the heart of Mount Orag, lava bubbled in slow flowing streams. Fire danced and fumes leapt high into the air mixing with gasses and ash. Up it swirled, lifted by the heat, up the great chimney that was the throat of the long slumbering volcano. As the heat rose up the chimney, fresh air was drawn into the cavern through the many tunnels that led out into the world of mankind. But here, within the volcano only one man dwelt—Xzuron; Xzuron the Great, Xzuron the Powerful, Xzuron the Magnificent. He stood, cloaked in black, his sorcerer's hands tucked into the sleeves of his night black robe. The other occupants of this oppressive environment were his subjects. Satros who had once been human, but their greed and avarice led them into Xzuron's lair and, inevitably, his total control. The other beings were morags, beings formed from the elements of the earth and slavishly under the control of Xzuron and his satros. Xzuron, stared with satisfaction at the forming platform below him. Eight of his sixteen faithful satros, knelt with one hand on the ground and the other pointed at the platform. Dust and molecules would gather, charged with the life and soul of the earth and every few minutes a figure, a head taller than a tall man and much broader, would form. A new morag warrior had been created. The new warrior was then pulled aside, clothed, and armed. Finally, its training would begin, and another morag warrior joined the throng assembling on the floor of the huge cavern, Any of the new life forms that appeared less than acceptable, too small, too badly misshapen, not enough arms or legs, were thrown to the rapidly increasing throng and were torn apart and eaten on the spot by those that were more … acceptable.

The satros, once human, now composed of evil and power worked on, nonstop. Eight of them were captains and eight were lieutenants, they working together under the discipline and censure of Xzuron. They were a head shorter than the morags and were cowled and robed in black just like their master. Their eyes showed an unnatural red from within their hoods, a red the color of blood and of the hot lava that flowed in the veins of the mountain. Around their necks on thick gold chains, each wore a flat blood red stone about the size of a small chicken egg but as thin as a coin. They showed no emotion. They acted and moved as extensions of Xzuron. Eight attended the platform, a steady stream of energy flowing from the solid rock floor beneath them, to the stones around their necks and on to the platform, giving life and shape where there had been nothing but air. The other eight satros stood beside the dark figure of Xzuron as he gazed with pleasure at his rapidly growing army. After an hour, the satros would change places and the standing eight would take up the forming of the large gray beings while those that had been forming would assume the positions next to their master.

Tordaqs, great bat-like creatures from a different age, soared through the smoke and fume laden air of the cavern. These were the mounts of the satros, and they fed freely on the teeming mass of morags that swarmed on the immense floor of the cavern.

Xzuron smiled within his hood. Soon now he would again invade VaLor'. This time he would succeed, he would be repaid for his lack of victory on the plain of Comark, that great desolate area where so much power had been expended in battle, that even now after three hundred years, very little lived. He had plotted this day alone, until about a hundred years before when Kortox, the Demon sorcerer of Sithia, had come to him, sending his essence between worlds through the void. Kortox had given him the blood red pendant he now wore beneath his robe and taught him how to conjure other pendants for his officers. It was then easy to obtain the fools that would sell their lives for the power he would grant them. Yes, this time he would succeed. This time he had the pendants and the power of the demon sorcerer Kortox to aid him. He reverently touched the blood red pendant he himself wore beneath his robe. His new power would prove more than sufficient to handle the two weak wizards that had survived his last war.

PART ONE

CHAPTER ONE

A Meeting In Time

5507 AS, Village of Downfelt, World of VaLor'

The inn at the heart of the village of Downfelt was small but clean. Heavy, dark, hand-hewn timbers, low enough for the average man to easily reach up and touch, supported the apartments above the common room. Kegs of mead lined the wall behind the cleaned and polished bar. Fresh rushes covered the plank floor and smokeless, hanging, lanterns cast pleasantly shifting shadows onto the tables and into the booths that lined the outer walls. The aroma of stew, fresh baked bread and a heady smell of rich mead filled the air, tempting the appetites of the few patrons engaged in conversation here and there about the room.

In a corner booth two travelers, cloaks open and cowls thrown back, slowly finished a large meal of tasty stew and fresh bread, then topped it all off with great helpings of berry cobbler and honey mead. Finally, sitting back with a visible show of satisfaction, the shorter man (four feet eight inches tall in his boots), the one who had eaten the most by nearly twice, brought forth a small, fine, long stemmed ceramic pipe with a well-used bowl. Carefully, almost reverently, he filled the bowl with a sweet smelling mixture while his tall companion looked on. Glancing around the room conspiratorially to satisfy himself that no one was watching, the shorter man snapped his fingers over the pipe bowl and smiled as it began to glow. Carefully savoring it, he drew on the stem. Releasing the smoke with a sigh of pleasure he looked up at his smiling friend. His voice, deep and full as it had to be, emanating from that broad shouldered, deep chested, dwarfish frame. "Suffer me this small vice old friend. I don't inhale and I love the taste, especially after such a fine feast as this one." His coal black eyes twinkled under heavy bushy brows and it was difficult to see his mouth and tiny sharp nose in the heavy, wavy, gray beard that hung down to his belt. The hair which rimmed his shining pate was reddish brown with just a touch of gray in the thick sideburns which blended full and bushy into his beard.

The tall man's closely bearded, finely chiseled features broke into an even broader grin, "It's been many a turn since we sat together over such fine fare. But tell me, why have you called me here, or is it still too soon to ask?"

The Dwarfs eyes gleamed, "E'Alam my young friend, how long has it been since our calling was held by just we two? Three hundred turns? More? I have trouble remembering. But times are changing. I feel that the powers are shifting … that soon the Stone will be calling new members to our order. Since I must stay here, could you attune yourself to help the neophytes find their way and help them avoid the ease of the path of darkness? As you know, the evil ones will also feel this shift and they will try to draw them into their employ. It is strong, this call of the Stone. Its urging is even now emanating in at least three, possibly four, of our sister worlds. Perhaps now, finally, we will see the resurgence of talent necessary to free your own world, Sithia, and hopefully in the not too distant future. As for why we meet here isn't this more pleasant than standing on some windswept ridge high in the Divides, or huddled in one of my people's unused caverns deep in a mountain?"

"Truly that is so," assured the Dwarf's companion. "I, too, have felt the call of the Stone. I feel its urgings and I hear its voice. I hope that it has found, or formed, talent enough to aid our fight against the darkness, for surely, shadow grows in all of the worlds as it does here."

The Dwarf leaned back enjoying his pipe. Finally he spoke again, "I must return to my vigil, friend. I only pray that the Stone works fast enough to help us here in VaLor', for the darkness is gathering in the north. Surely it is time for the King to return."

"Keep listening here on VaLor' old friend and I will attend to the other worlds, where the darkness is trying for a foothold and the Stone is stirring".

Together they stood and strode to the heavy oaken door. For now, they must be patient. Sithia would have to wait.

When darkness threats Sister Worlds anew,
The Stone will, call fresh hearts born true.
And soon they'll stand to join the fight,
To turn the pending endless night.

Excerpt from the prophesies of Orn the Seer

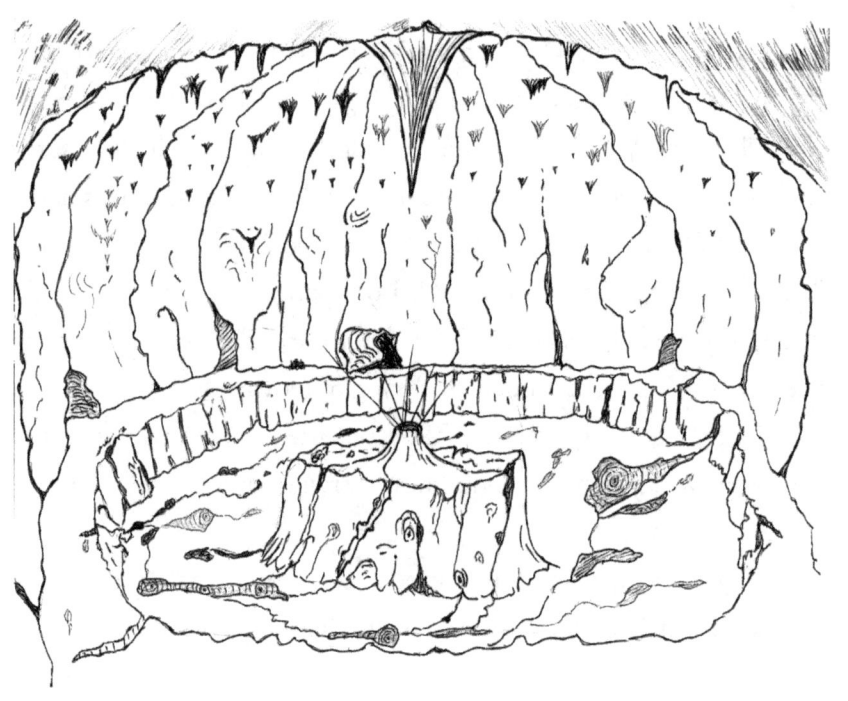

CHAPTER TWO

The Grotto

5517 AS, GANOR, 5th Sister World,

Leon sat on the rickety old bench staring at the smoldering ashes, just a few yards away, that were all that remained of his home. It hadn't been much, just a small single room—sheep herder's hut—with rock walls and a thatch roof. But for all twelve years of his life it had given him comfort in an otherwise lonely existence. Tears etched a path from his gray-flecked, blue eyes through the dirt on his face. His hand scratched through blond unruly hair then rubbed absently over the scared old bench Grandfather had built and placed here beneath his favorite tree.

He looked up the hill at the three graves: Grandmother's, she had died long before he was even born; Leonetta, his mother who had died just six months after his birth; and Grandfather's, who had died when Leon was ten. Grandfather had told him that he was the son of a raider who had brutally taken his mother when she was just a girl, then left her for dead. Grandfather had raised him, becoming his parent and companion, gradually teaching him the skills he needed to care for himself and tend their small flock of sheep. Eventually, when it became necessary, Leon helped his aging and ailing Grandfather until he too was gone.

Just that morning Leon had been happily playing on the ridge that overlooked the fjord with three boys of the village. This didn't happen often because not many parents would let their children play with a raider's child. And then there was the fact that the women of the village felt that his mother and grandmother before her had some strange, indefinable powers. No one was sure what those powers might be; perhaps it was just that they chose to live away from the village with grandfather and his sheep that made them seem different.

Up on the ridge from where the boys were playing stood the Blue Keep, named for the strange blue lights that sometimes danced about its tower. No one knew how long the ancient fortress had stood on the ridge, but all who lived in the village knew that it was the home of their mysterious Guardian. It was rumored that he was a wizard who had moved here after his own world had been destroyed.

Now, it was spring and the air was full of the heady smells of new grass and blooming wildflowers. Insects hummed with the vigor of the season and the boys ran and tumbled and shouted like so many puppies on a holiday. The sun was warm, and the bright blue sky was dotted with small fluffy clouds scurrying on to some rendezvous far to the east. At times like this Leon could forget the loneliness he felt, and just enjoy the companionship of his friends.

Suddenly, the Guardian of the Keep appeared before them his long cowled robe shimmering and nearly transparent. "Flee south," he commanded as he gestured in the direction of the craggy hills and canyons to the south of the Keep. "Raiders are coming."

The boys looked down into the fjord, where they saw the sculpted bow of a large galley edging into their harbor. Its sail was down and oars pulled it rapidly toward the dark sands of the small beach. Knowing that the direction the guardian pointed was their closest safety, they turned and ran, oblivious to the fact that the Guardian had disappeared while they were looking away.

As the boys neared the rocky formations, the raiders topped the rise where the boys had been playing. A couple of men broke out of the group to chase them and the rest turned toward the village. Looking over his shoulder Leon, puzzled, noticed that the Keep seemed to have disappeared completely, leaving a huge pile of broken rock in its place. The boys, gasping for breath, ran into the protection of the canyon and paused to suck in deep gasps of air. Looking back, they could see the two raiders overtaking them. Above the vale the sky grew dark with heavy, black rain clouds, seemingly coming from nowhere. Thunder roared and lightning flashed. Rain began to pelt the fields of the vale blinding the eyes of the invaders. The closer the raiders came to the village the harder the elements fought them until they were forced to turn and flee back toward the beach. They took time to pillage and burn only one cottage on the outskirts of the village and a small hut by the vale.

Leon and his friends charged headlong into the canyon, cutting back and forth, climbing ledges and sliding down rock-strewn ravines until they felt sure they had lost their pursuers. There was very little undergrowth and no trees, just small brush and bunch grass. Cautiously they walked up a small valley keeping a sharp lookout as they went. Leon felt as though he were being watched though he could see no one. Then, like a magnet he felt his attention being drawn toward a small depression up the rise on his right. For some unexplainable reason he knew they would find safety in that direction, so he quietly signaled his companions up the slope. As they stepped down into the depression they spotted a small cave entrance. They hadn't noticed the cave before even though they often played in these hills; as a matter of fact they hadn't even noticed the depression until that day. On hands and knees they crawled in, fear pushing them and curiosity pulling as they inched forward. Before their eyes had begun to adjust to the dark they heard footsteps from the rim of the depression. They had been followed. Quietly they moved deeper into the waiting gloom, blindly feeling their way as they went. The roof of the passage tapered up slowly until they could stand. They proceeded with slow shuffling footsteps while groping the in dark before them. The walls were fairly smooth and often damp, the ground irregular. Caution was needed to avoid stumbling in the many dips and inclines or tripping over the numerous rocks and irregularities of the rock beneath their feet. The air was laden with moisture and the further they went the more moisture hung on the walls and covered the path. After what seemed to them to be a great long time, but in reality was just a few minutes, a soft bluish glow began to illuminate the darkness ahead. They moved on. Leon followed the others, for though he was a head taller he was thin and frail and seldom assumed the roll of leader in their youthful adventures. The passage began to broaden, and as it did, the light increased. They entered a large circular room about a stone's cast wide. Blue light danced and reflected off hundreds of stalactites as though the roof were covered with blue diamonds. Silently, mouths and eyes wide open, they stared in near reverence. The only sound was the intermittent drip, drip of water and the gasps of the boys. A ledge ran all the way around the cavern, a continuation of their path and easily wide enough to walk on. The edge of the path dropped off into a pit about ten feet deep, which ran all the way across the room. In the very center a natural, raised circular platform stood. It was about ten feet across, and the same height as the path on which the boys stood. In the center of the platform rose a single stalagmite with an unusually flat top, from which the blue light pulsed causing the multitude of reflections that held the boys in a near trance.

Leon recovered first. As his eyes took in the grotto before him he noticed that there were other entrances on the far side. In the floor of the pit were numerous puddles caused by the steady dripping. Tiny rivulets moved toward an opening at the side to the left, which acted like a drain. At some time in the far distant past this might have been a small underground lake with an island at its center.

A mild but insistent pull seemed to draw Leon to the source of the blue light, and almost as if they were one person the boys started seeking a way down into the pit. The sides were very irregular and easily scaled. Soon they were jumping across the puddles and climbing up onto the platform, all thought of the raiders gone. Finally, at the top they stopped and stared into a clear pool of water in a bowl shaped cavity that was the top of the stalagmite. In the center of the cavity lay a blue crystal pendant about the size and shape of a chicken egg, though flat and thin like a coin. Attached to the crystal was a heavy gold chain. It was from the pendant that the clear blue light radiated. For long seconds they stood mesmerized, unable to tear their eyes from the beauty of the pendant and its resting place. Young Kemper, the mason's son, gently put forth his hand. He found he could touch the water, but that his hand would not penetrate it. It was as if an invisible shield covered the cavity. They stood in awe. Slowly they raised their hands as though they were of one mind.

Their concentration was shattered by harsh laughter from the tunnel behind them. The two raiders rushed in with thoughts of valuable young slaves and hidden treasure. They quickly dropped into the pit and rushed to either side of the pedestal to prevent the boys from escaping. In hardly any time at all they climbed onto the platform, their huge swords swinging threateningly. Tad tried to escape over the edge but the flat of a heavy sword alongside the head left him lying bruised and unconscious, half on and half off the platform. With threatening gestures they made the boys sit down beside Tad and then turned to the stalagmite and its treasure. Simultaneously both men thrust their hands toward the pendant. Cursing they pulled back their hands and rubbed their bruised fingers. Like Kemper they had hit the unseen shield that protected the resting place of the pendant. They reached again, and again ran into the unseen but solid impenetrable field that covered the pendant. In frustration and great anger they swung their swords together at the invisible shield. A great flash rent the serenity of the chamber as their swords smashed into the protective shield over the pendant. Instantly they were flung backwards into the pit where they lay unmoving amid the pools of clear water, their swords vaporized by the power of the shield.

Silence once again filled the grotto interrupted only by the intermittent dripping of water and the boys catching their breath.

Torn between the desire to flee and the attraction of the pendant the boys stood silently for a moment as their heartbeats slowed to normal.

Leon turned to Kemper, "If you can check on Tad, I'll look to the raiders." Kemper nodded.

Leon slipped over the edge into the pit and cautiously crept to the bodies of the raiders, ready to run at the slightest movement. They lay still, not breathing. He could detect no sign of life. When he touched them, they were already as cold as the stone upon which they lay. They were unquestionably dead.

Tad had started to move and wake up by the time Leon had climbed back up on the platform.

"Maybe we should leave," murmured Kemper, staring at the pendant.

Sean, the youngest boy nodded in agreement.

"Were you hurt when you tried to touch it?" asked Leon as the two boys lifted Tad to his feet and held him up until he could hold himself.

"No, it just would not let me reach into the water." He reached out again and once more felt the resistance just at the surface of the water. "It's hard to explain but it doesn't feel dangerous. It just won't let me touch the pendant."

Again Kemper reached out to touch the water, then the rapidly improving Tad, and finally Sean, all with the same result.

Leon could contain himself no longer and warily he reached out. The water began to ripple. Light from the pendant danced around the grotto. The dripping of water took on a musical sound, and wind started to whistle through the caves. The music of the grotto grew and grew in volume. The pendant slowly floated up out of the water and settled to rest on Leon's outstretched palm. Then … suddenly … all was silent again.

"Tis' magical!" whispered Tad. The others, nodding in agreement, astonishment on their faces, eyes and mouths wide open in a sudden new respect for Leon.

Leon felt compelled to place the gold chain around his neck where it settled as though it were a part of him, as though it were an old friend returned to its rightful place. He suddenly felt warmed and comforted by its presence, though still quite confused. He was infused with a new feeling of…of companionship. He stood silent, wrapped in this new feeling. It was similar to the way he had felt in the arms of his grandfather.

Tad interrupted his thoughts, "We should go. I want to know what has happened at the village."

The boys slid over the side into the pit and approached the bodies. Cautiously they removed belt knives, small pouches of coins and a few pieces of jewelry from the bodies.

After much tugging, Tad pulled loose the final large ring and divided up the treasure amongst himself Sean and Kemmer. Leon refused anything feeling that the Pendant was more than enough for him.

With little effort they climbed out of the pit, and after pausing for one last long look at the slowly fading beauty of the grotto, they turned and made their way back into the tunnel they had entered by. Light from the pendant lit the way back up the passage. Behind them the grotto dimmed and the light faded, but it didn't die, it would remain in a subdued beauty for many years to come, waiting.

Silently the tall robed figure of the guardian entered the grotto from another passage and moved to the edge of the pit. He stretched out his hands toward the bodies. In a flash the bodies disappeared, leaving only a small trace of white ash. Nodding in satisfaction he quietly returned by the way he had come.

When the boys exited the cave the sun was shining again, the sky clear and all seemed to be as it had been before the arrival of the raiders. Leon slid the pendant beneath his shirt while securing an oath from his comrades that it would be their secret. They made up a story about how the raiders had fallen to their deaths while chasing them and as they concocted the story it became truth to all but Leon. After that moment none but Leon even remembered the blue grotto and its pedestal. Then they set off at an easy jogging pace toward the village. At the ridge below the Blue Keep they paused and cautiously looked over the edge toward the beach. There was no sign of the raiders or their galley but far out toward the mouth of the fjord a small storm seemed to be raging. Lightning flashed and the rumble of thunder echoed along the steep canyon walls to the boys.

Leon looked toward the village; he could see smoke wafting skyward from the direction of his hut and from the village. Concerned for their families, his friends barely paused as they ran past his flaming hut. The boys ran on through the vale and down the path. Leon followed.

They found the villagers cautiously returning to their homes. Seeing that all was well Leon jogged back to the ashes of his cabin. He slowly walked around the rock walls that were all that remained. Smoke curled slowly skyward from the ashes. Here and there a hinge, a clasp, a pot or some other barely identifiable piece of his life lay smoldering amidst the embers. Wearily he sat down on the bench beneath the willow tree that stood unharmed in front of the rubble that once had been his home, his refuge, his life. He lowered his head into his hands and softly sobbed. Here it was that his grandfather had told him stories of the world and taught him of his mother. Here it was that the frail old man had died. Now what would he do, what would become of him?

A faint whisper said, *"Be comforted, for we are with you."*

He looked around in confusion, seeing no one, "What? Who?"

His thoughts were interrupted by the sound of feet running up the trail from the village. Making a quick swipe at his eyes, the tears causing dirty smudges on his cheeks. Then he stood and turned toward the path still looking for the source of the voice.

Kemper came hurriedly up to him panting, "Leon, I was told to come fetch you and your things and bring you back to the village. They know about your hut."

Leon stood staring, first at Kemper, then at the graves, then at the ashes of his home. He wasn't sure what to do. Obviously, the voice had been his imagination. Hesitantly he nodded. Not many in the village seemed to like him but he had to do something. He had owned very little so he had not lost much, but he did have a certain independence, which he feared he might now lose. How would the villagers react to him? Where would he stay?

The sheep were scattered but he whistled and in a few minutes the two boys had gathered them together and started herding them toward the village. The loss of his home had a deep affect on him, making him feel more alone than ever before in his short life. Even the death of his grandfather had not affected him so, for he had seen that loss coming for a long time. With heavy heart he trudged toward the village.

From deep within the shadows of the stunted trees that served as forest along these austere coasts a robed figure watched as the boy, Leon, and his friend gathered his small flock together and began herding them toward the village. Then, silently the figure turned and made its way toward the Blue Keep. Within the cowl of his robe, the features of the Guardian assumed a satisfied expression.

Though born of sorrow, raised alone,
Still, he'll be chosen of the Stone.
For from the least, shall come the best,
Heart must be true, to stand the test.

Excerpt from Prophesies of Orn the Seer

CHAPTER THREE

The Smithy

When Leon arrived at the village the hardy independent people had already returned from hiding, and nearly every able-bodied man was hard at work helping clean up the burned out cottage. As he approached, a burly, balding man with great shoulders, huge hands and a broad, smiling, bearded face, paused in his labors and walked to meet him. Larkin, the smith, greeted him warmly with his huge right hand extended to clasp Leon's. "Son, I hear you need a new place to live and I could use an apprentice. What say you? You could bed down in the back corner of the forge room, and take your meals with Mae and me." Mae was a large woman nearly as wide as she was tall. She had a ready smile and a great beefy hug for everyone.

Leon felt a blanket of relief roll over him as he considered the offer. He had always liked the smith and his amiable wife, and now this opportunity seemed almost too good to be true. Leon nodded his shaggy blond head and gestured toward his small herd of sheep.

Smiling, the large man took him gently by the shoulders, "I'm sure we can find someone to adopt these fine friends of yours since you'll be much too busy to care for them for quite some time."

And so it was that for the next four years Leon learned the art of blacksmithing. He continued to grow, and by the age of sixteen was taller than any man in the village with arms and shoulders greater than any except Larkin. It was a good time filled with all the warmth of family that he had never known. There was abundant wholesome food, the aroma of which set his mouth to watering each day. There was hard but satisfying labor and many new skills and abilities patiently taught by the fatherly smith. Leon felt his life was indeed good and this somewhat worried him. There were still very few of the villagers who trusted him but it didn't matter when he was in the warmth of the smith's home.

Throughout the years he had always worn the pendant beneath a plain gray sleeveless tunic when he worked, which was covered by a good leather apron both of which Mae had sewn with her own hands. She had also made him two finer, sleeved tunics for regular wear on the chilly nights that frequented these parts.

One evening as they sat at the simple, but well finished, plank table eating dinner, Larkin seemed unusually quiet during the small chatter that usually attended their meals. Leon noticed the smith often staring at his plate as though in deep thought. Finally, with a long sigh he looked up at Leon. "A knight of some kingdom to the south has come to the village. He says that he has been hired to teach you the arts of warfare. He will meet you here tomorrow morning. Should you decide to accept his offer you will go with him, but it is your choice."

Leon sat in stunned silence, eyes staring in the general direction of Larkin but seeing nothing, his mind eagerly sorting through this unasked for, yet somehow terribly exciting news. In this age a warrior was one who always had a profession, and though it was a hard and often uncomfortable occupation, there was glory attached to it that drew the imagination of most young men … and the prospect of actually being trained by a knight….! If he proved good enough his deeds in battle might lead him on the path to knighthood. Certainly there was no nobility in his background and that was the usual path. All boys wanted to be knights; it was their greatest dream. Then why was it that he hesitated now when it might be within his grasp? What was it holding back the response he wanted to spill out? Why was it that he hesitated? His hand went unconsciously to the pendant beneath his shirt, and he knew. The security he had come to know at the smithy, and the love he held for these gentle people were now the anchor of his life. How could he break this tie, this feeling which bound him to them?

"Understand, we are not asking you to leave," Larkin continued. "Perhaps you could train during the morning hours and still find time to help around the smithy, and of course you would stay here with us regardless. We have grown very attached to you, and we are grateful you have stayed with us here for a time. You have filled a void as the son we never had. But we know, even a son must find his own niche in the world. We also know it is within you to be a smith, a warrior or anything else, if it is your wish. We will support you whatever your decision may be."

Leon's heart was full and his eyes moist, as he looked, first to the smith and then to gentle Mae. Their kindness and understanding had filled a great emptiness in his life and he would be forever grateful. Being trained at arms could only be an asset to him in the years to come and so he nodded in assent. Dinner proceeded more normally thereafter but by the time he headed off to his cot he could hardly sleep because of the excitement he felt. And so, long into the night, he lay restlessly drifting in and out of sleep. Strangely he found himself floating above his sleeping body. Then he floated in the Blue Grotto. He ghosted through a never before seen castle. Next he saw a strange land like nothing he had ever seen before. The people were different in that land, some short with broad shoulders and long beards. Others were tall and slender with pointed ears that reached nearly to the top of their heads, and he saw a banner with a dragon on it, then…

An urgent thumping on the large barn-like doors of the smithy brought Leon suddenly awake. He jumped up and wrapped his light blanket around his shoulders, then at a run he hurried to open the small man door in the large barn type doors. There in the first glimmer of morning light, astride a great, black war-horse, sat a knight in full battle armor, complete with lance. His visor was raised, and bright brown eyes and a bushy brown mustache streaked with gray were plainly visible in the slight shadow of his helm. Leon stepped back, "Welcome Sir Knight. How may I address you?"

"Sir Knight will do nicely. Art thou the boy Leon?"

"Aye Sir, I am. Would it be improper for me to ask, who it is that has sent you to me."

"This ye shall learn in time if thou dost decide to follow this path. Now, ye must make the choice. Come if thou wilt, but if thou comest be prepared for a year of the hardest training thou couldst imagine. I shall wait a few minutes for you to dress and follow." Leon quickly ran back into the smithy and slipped on a fresh long sleeved tunic, trousers and boots, gathered his worn coat from its hook, and hurried quietly into Mae's kitchen where he stuffed an apple and a large chunk of jerky into a pocket of his coat and returned to the smithy. He closed and latched the door, then followed the Knight who was slowly moving up the path toward the vale that had once held Leon's home.

In the vale they met a young, dark haired man who patiently awaited their arrival. His tunic and trousers were well made, sturdy, light blue in color and he sat upon a fine, gray gelding and held a lead line to an equally handsome chestnut gelding packed high with supplies. The Knight gestured, first toward Leon, and then toward the stranger, "Leon, this be Fallon, my squire. The lessons he would teach thee are oft of more importance than mine. Harken, to all he has to say. Thou art a large one but size and power be of little use when it comes to courtly things, for this, a keen mind and a quick wit will serve thee better. Fallon here can teach thee better than I in that quarter."

Fallon was a year older than Leon and had about him a certain dignity that hinted at good breeding. "At your service," he said with a slight bending at the waist and a flourish of his arm. Upon dismounting he stood as tall as Leon but was slighter in build and looked to be quite athletic which proved to be the case in the following days. He had brownish green eyes and light brown hair that hung comfortably down over his shoulders. Fallon was the youngest son of the king of a poor but honorable kingdom in the southlands and had been squired to the Knight so that he might gain through knowledge of arms, that which was not available to him by right of birth. In some ways he was of a gentle nature but his skill was great in the arts of war. And so, he became Leon's sparing partner, teacher and friend as the days passed. While Leon learned the use of sword, mace and lance, he was also tutored in the subtleties of the court. Sir Knight was adamant that no aspect of his education be slighted. The horses they used were much smaller than the war-horse of the Knight, but much larger than the ponies that were prevalent around the village, they were more than adequate to teach him of horsemanship and the care and feeding that he must know in order to travel the byways of these lands or any other. Learning to ride, however, gave him much discomfort in the general areas of his inner thighs and rump and that took weeks to get accustomed to.

The first few days were spent upgrading a small house that had been made available to them in the village, and building a simple stable for the horses.

Then the real work, that of his training, began.

Leon's tutoring went on throughout that year and into the next. The years he had spent working in the smithy had given him strength and endurance not often attained by those who sought after the arts of war. When the weather was too stormy for arms practice, courtly manners, letters, numbers and etiquette were taught. When they grew tired of that, Fallon was an expert at the use of hands and feet as weapons not to mention a preference for throwing knives, which he always carried, secreted here and there about his person. There was always something to learn. And learn he did, from first light to well into the afternoon. Still, Leon managed to find some time each day to help Larkin at the smithy.

After the first day Sir Knight seldom wore his full armor, unless he was demonstrating its use. Instead, he wore light protective clothing of chain mail and leather similar to that which any soldier of the realms might wear. He spent his hours supervising the training, never seeming to be quite satisfied at the degree of proficiency that Leon had achieved. He was just slightly taller, half a hand, than Leon at that time but heavy in the upper body and quick and sure when it came to handling weapons.

The days passed swiftly, however, and by the time Leon was well into his seventeenth year his skill was such that he seldom received new bruises from the practice wands, but rather frequently bested Fallon and infrequently even Sir Knight. He now stood a full hand taller than Fallon and was equally as swift. His nearly white-blond, hair, no longer unruly, hung in gentle waves down to his shoulders, held back by a woven leather band around his forehead. The special throwing knives made for him by Larkin seemed to leap out of their hiding places of their own accord and wing with sure accuracy to their targets. Now, according to Sir Knight, Leon had reached a degree of comfort and familiarity with weapons that few in the land could match. And as his abilities grew his closeness with his teachers also grew until it was more a relationship of comrades than of teachers and student. Sir Gallan, was the Knight's name and he now gave it freely, for Leon had earned his respect through hard work and a never-ending effort toward perfection.

From ashes to a life that's true,
He'll grow in mind and body too.
Tho none shall know the Stone's true plan,
Twill guide him forth from boy to man.

Excerpt from the prophesies of Orn the Seer

CHAPTER FOUR

First Battle

5522 AS

As the three comrades crouched, drawing in the dirt with sticks, discussing possible tactical moves, a cowled figure appeared standing silently behind Fallon. The figure was nearly transparent and shimmered, almost rippling, like a reflection on water.

With a start, all three stood and turned to face the figure. Leon had his sword out and leveled in an instant.

Sir Galan laid his hand lightly on Leon's arm and cautioned, "Gently, friend. Thou knowest not what thou doest. Thou couldst not bring harm to this apparition in any case."

With that the cowled figure nodded slightly in recognition toward Sir Galan, then turned to face Leon, "I am E'Alam, Guardian of the Keep. Once again I bring you warning of peril approaching your shores. The raiders return. Since I am unable to be there in person, perhaps you could arrange a little surprise for them, one unlike the easy spoils they hope for."

Leon stood as if mesmerized for a moment as he remembered the time five years before, when the Guardian had sent him and his friends scurrying into the hills barely ahead of the raiders. Snapping out of his reverie he bowed in respect as Fallon had taught him. "Please excuse my sword. It seems to move of its own accord lately," Leon said apologetically as he slipped his sword back into its scabbard.

A tight smile had crossed Sir Galan's features, "Aye friend Wizard, thou speakest truly. Perhaps we will prepare just a little surprise for our visitors." As Sir Galan's eyes wandered across the vale in concentration the image of the Guardian shimmered and disappeared.

Leon stood in confusion. He had heard of wizards, and there were those in the village who said that the Guardian from the Blue Keep was such, but he had never actually put that together with the robed figure that had helped him in his youth. He couldn't begin to imagine how a person, or a wizard for that matter, could be in two places at the same time.

"Close your mouth Leon," laughed Fallon. "He is just another person, except that he handles things a little differently than we do."

Sir Galan gestured for them to follow. "Come, we must make preparations."

Raiders were known for working in small groups of thirty to sixty men per galley, except for major raids when several of their chieftains combined efforts to assemble a force large enough for a major expedition. In such times a number of galleys traveled together. Their home ports were much farther to the north and they came south pillaging the isles with little or no interference. As warriors they were fierce fighters who asked no quarter in battle; and often as not would die rather than be captured. Every few years they would return to these small villages of the northern isles in search of supplies with which to stock their ships for expeditions south to the more wealthy areas where plundering was more profitable. They seldom destroyed these small villages, preferring to keep them alive as supply points for the future. They did kill a few inhabitants, take a few slaves, take their pleasure with the women—when the women could be found—and always burned a few huts. This was done chiefly to maintain the proper state of fear in the inhabitants so, when they came, they seldom encountered any resistance. Usually the people ran into the surrounding country leaving their homes to be ransacked.

In the village beneath the Blue Keep, however, the people had the help of a rather powerful Wizard to ward off the unwanted intents of the warriors from the north.

For years the villagers' defense was simply not to be there when the raiders marched into the village. Few of the village men had any experience at arms, and those who did were old or handicapped from the service they had seen. When the warning was given, they gathered most of their valuables and either carried them away, or hid them in secret chambers beneath the floors of their homes along with the bulk of their food supplies. The plan was to leave enough supplies out to prevent serious searching. Then, with the aid of the Wizard, the raiders were usually turned away without too great a loss. So it had been as long as memory served. This year was different. There were three well-trained and mounted men-at-arms, one of which wore full armor and sat astride a huge armored warhorse. This year might prove to be a bit more challenging for the raiders.

The knot of rough looking men coming over the hill from the beach below was a combination of crude, dirty and disorderly rogues dressed in animal skins, fur and minimal armor in the form of breast plates, arm bands, shields of metal or hard hide, and metal or hard leather helms. There were two who, combining a defiant flamboyance of jewels and fir, achieved a certain air of authority. The raiders' weapons were an assortment of axes, swords and spears, and since they expected no resistance they moved along the path with swaggering bravado, more like a rather disorganized mob than a fighting force.

About a long arrow's flight from the village was a draw just deep enough that once at the bottom neither the village nor the vale could be seen. Here it was that Leon, armored in chain mail, rode over the rise from the village toward the brigands and stopped. "I come to warn you to leave this village or pay the price with your blood," he shouted.

For a second the group of men halted. Then, with a whooping yell of defiance they began to move once more toward the village. Almost immediately they become aware of the sound of hoof beats thundering down on them from behind. Before they could brace themselves Sir Galan in full armor and swinging his mace, smashed into them charging through as though they were sticks of straw. As he blasted through the startled band of men and started up the rise toward the village, Leon and Fallon with shield and sword, charged down around the knight and crashed into the confusion Sir Galan had left. Like Sir Galan they were through the raiders and up the rise toward the ridge above the beach before the raiders could form any effective resistance. As Leon and Fallon turned their mounts Sir Galan smashed into the raiders again, this time halting his mount to stand and swing his mace with deadly effect. Leon and Fallon reentered the battle. The odds, which had been nearly ten to one, were now considerably reduced to knots of men here and there on either side of the path. They charged their mounts into the men swinging their heavy two handed battle swords easily with one hand, thus dividing the groups again with terrible killing efficiency.

    Strangely exhilarated Leon swerved into yet another knot of men, sword cleaving first one then another. Suddenly his horse went down. Leon landed hard on his left side barely managing to kick free as his mount hit the ground and rolled up onto his feet. His left leg hurt but it held him. He turned to find himself face to face with three of the enemy, all large men. The nearest one, a look of glee on his face and a wild yell swung a great double-headed axe at Leon's head. With the ease and quickness of youth Leon dropped to one knee and brought his shield up to deflect the axe. Then, as though it were a continuation of the same fluid movement, he drove the point of his two hand sword up under the man's breast plate and deep into the chest of his attacker. With a look of surprise and disbelief the body crumpled backward. Leon let loose of the heavy two handed sword, came quickly to his feet and spun away from the bodies of his horse and his dead foe. As he spun he drew his belt sword. Lighter and better balanced, it moved gracefully in his hand. At the same time he was seeking good footing and looking for other possible dangers. He braced himself as he turned back to the two remaining raiders. Automatically he checked the action around him where he could see two other small groups of combatants, but then he quickly shifted his attention fully to his opponents. The first was a great burly fellow with a full red beard and scarred face that grimaced cruelly from under a hard leather helm. His eyes went suddenly wide and he stepped back and to one side gesturing at Leon to his comrade who then turned his full attention to Leon for the first time.

Leon gasped in confusion and stumbled back as he looked full into a nearly exact image of his own face. Although it was middle aged and wore a bitter, hard expression, it was like looking into a mirror of the future at his own scarred reflection. The man wore partial body armor fringed with rare white ermine furs. Gold adorned his thick throat and muscular arms, while jewels glittered from his armor. He was obviously the leader, and without hesitation he yelled at the huge red bearded raider who then charged at Leon with sword swinging. Stunned by the sight before him Leon barely recovered in time to deflect the swiftly falling sword with his shield; his full attention shifted to staying alive. The great strength of the man would have instantly crushed a warrior of lesser strength and slower reflexes, but Leon's prowess as a swordsman was such that he easily sidestepped the bullish rush of his opponent. Then, before the man could collect himself, lightning quick moves of Leon's blade had the bear-like ruffian bleeding from several wounds. The blond leader moved to Leon's left to begin an attack of his own. Leon was hard pressed with red beard's strength to his right and the leader circling to get behind him on his left. He knew he could not last long. In a desperate gamble he drove in on red beard, taking a blow on his shield as he shifted his sword to his shield hand. Then, nearly in the man's arms, he drew his belt knife and thrust it into the brute's chest clear to the hilt. With unexpected persistence the bearded man grabbed him in a bear hug then slowly pulled Leon over on him as he fell. Leon squirmed to free himself knowing that his back was vulnerable. The huge man shuddered his last and Leon pushed back with strength that he never could have found under normal circumstances. As he broke free he rolled swiftly to the side and stopped as he looked up into the cruel eyes of the man who wore his face, then watched as the man raised his sword for the death stroke. With a look of contempt and using both hands, the man, slowly pushed the sword toward Leon's heart. Leon closed his eyes waiting to die. Abruptly a humming sensation began to fill his being.

"Fear not. We will protect you." The whisper resonated with the humming.

When the sword didn't pierce his body Leon looked up to see the warrior pushing on the hilt of the sword, which had stopped a thin fingers width above Leon's chest. The man pressed harder, sweat beading on his brow, evil determination in his features. The humming grew. With a strange look of surprise the leader's eyes glazed over and he fell forward. The still poised sword slid harmlessly to the side and Leon found himself pinned beneath the dead weight of the man who had surely been his father.

As Leon struggled to push the body off, it was lifted and dropped aside.

Fallon reached down and grabbed him by the wrist and pulled him to his feet. "Sorry to stop your fun friend, but you seemed to have lost interest in defending yourself, and that's a sure way to end an otherwise promising career."

"Thank you," Leon said softly, then, "Look at him."

Fallon jerked one of his throwing knives from the neck of the body then rolled it over. "I see. You do know he would have killed you. It just had to be done. At least it wasn't your hand that killed him."

"For that I truly do thank you my friend." Leon turned and walked away from the carnage. All of a sudden the smell of death, the blood, the gaping wounds, the viscera, the sweat, the torn earth and grass, all left him feeling as though he was going to be sick.

Leon was bone tired and somewhat confused by the events of the day, but he was also strangely exhilarated and relieved at the same time. He had fought his first real fight and done well, but most important … he had survived. After a short time his mind and body relaxed and he walked back to the scene of the battle. He found Sir Galan and Fallon discussing the fight as though it were merely another training session in the vale.

As he approached, Sir Galan gestured for him to come and join them. "Ah, Leon my young friend, thou hast done well this day. But, we be not yet finished."

The boat was beached on the sand where a handful of men stood a careless watch. They laughed and gestured at the small plume of smoke that could be seen rising skyward in the direction of the village, not even suspecting that it was a haystack deliberately set by the villagers to mislead those guarding the boat.

Leon and Fallon, no longer wearing their armor, crawled toward the boat carefully, carrying clay pots of live coals with long leather thongs attached. They had approached the beach from further downriver, away from the path to the village. Now they lay in position concealed by low sand dunes about fifty steps from the boat.

The laughter of the guards was interrupted by the long mournful call of a battle horn from up the path in the direction of the village. At the crest of the high sand bank Sir Galan, in full armor, rode his great charger slowly at a walk over the ridge and down the path toward the beach. From the first wail of the horn all eyes turned toward the top of the rise where they stayed, as though glued in disbelief. They had never confronted a mounted knight and weren't quite sure how to handle this one.

From the moment the horn sounded Leon and Fallon moved quickly and silently along the edge of the water toward the boat. With a quick motion of the wrist they loosed the lids and, using the thongs, hurled the clay pots of live coals into the boat. Just before the pots landed they let out a great yell and threw a handful of rocks at the raiders. Turning, they ran back the way they had come with a couple of raiders in pursuit. They ran back down the beach about a hundred paces, stopped, picked up their swords and shields and turned to meet the raiders. With shouts of surprise the two would be invaders turned back toward the ship to get away from the newly armed men who now pursued them. With concerted effort the raiders put their shoulders to the prow of the galley and pushed it off the beach, quickly climbing aboard as it slid into deep water. Oars hit the water and began churning the boat back away from the beach. By the time the galley was a long stone's throw from the beach smoke and flame was billowing from the deck of the boat. Shouts were heard and frantic activity could be seen on the deck as fire quickly spread across the dry tar and pitch calked deck. The only escape for the raiders was to swim back through the ice-cold water to the beach. Only two accomplished the swim and they surrendered without a fight. They were young and not so fierce as the warriors that had been in the battle of the vale.

It had been a long day. The companions herded their captives up the path toward the village stopping at the crest of the hill to look back toward the setting sun and watch the last moments of the galley as it sank, steaming and belching smoke, into the deep, clear, cold waters of the fjord.

The villagers were busy cleaning up the battle site and a row of fresh burial sites could be seen on the ridge above the vale. The invaders had carried more gold and jewels on their persons than these humble villagers would normally see in a lifetime. Still, they offered it all to the companions as reward for the battle well fought. Sir Galan gave most of it to the villagers and sent them to their homes to contemplate somewhat brighter futures. Then he and Fallon divided that which he had kept, giving to Leon a leather pouch which held all of the gold and jewels that had been on the body of his father.

Leon stood, leather bag in hand, staring down at the village. It was nearly dark and lamps were being lit. Smoke curled from the chimneys and the smell of cooking soon reminded them that they too must eat. Fallon and Sir Galan had stood silently beside Leon allowing him the time he needed to sort out the events of the day. The great warhorse cropped grass at the side of the path, Fallon's smaller gelding close by. Leon's own mount had been killed. Leon felt as though a chapter in his life had been completed, and now the uncertainty of the future brought him both excitement and trepidation. The broken strands of his parenthood had been neatly tied together, leaving him, neither happy nor sad just complete, as though that too were a chapter finished.

His musings were interrupted by the deep resonant voice of E'Alam standing behind them. "Well, Sir Galan, you and our young prince Fallon have concluded your task admirably."

"Aye, friend Wizard, and now I feel the need to return to my own lands and see how things fare there."

The Wizard smiled, "All is well with your holdings my friend. In this bag is the reward I promised you, enough I would imagine to secure your holdings indefinitely, and guarantee you a properly comfortable retirement."

Sir Galan opened the bag and the glitter of the jewels within could be seen even in the fading light. With a grin he said, "Aye and then some." Then turning to Leon he said, "Thou hast been a goodly student and companion at arms. Thy skills be as good as any in the land and better than most. Thy sacred honor will hold thee true to whatever challenge arises in thy future. Fear no man, but use thy skill as a tool to help thy fellow men. Do good and thou shalt find contentment in life, if not happiness, for a warrior's life is seldom a happy one. I told thee that one day I would tell thee who hast sent me. E'Alam be thy benefactor for it was he who saw in thee the special spark that makes a true warrior. We bid thee good-by and wish thee well, for we leave at first light." With that rather long speech, for him, he took Leon into a back slapping embrace and turned away leading his great charger down the path to the village. None could see the dampness that gathered in his eyes.

Leon turned to Fallon, "You have truly been a good friend and a comrade to me. I only wish that I could always count on having you at my side. Please accept this bag that was my father's. Use the contents to purchase all of the armament that a young knight must have, and may your path bring you the security that you seek."

Fallon stammered in confusion, "B … but that is all you have of your father."

"A father I surely have no desire to remember," smiled Leon. "Go. Take it and remember our time together."

Fallon stared into Leon's eyes for a long moment, "Of all the men I know including my own brothers, it is you I would call brother." Then, after a long, eye searching handclasp, he turned, gathered up the reins of his horse, mounted and rode slowly down into the village.

E'Alam placed a strong hand on Leon's shoulder, "Now young warrior, if you will, I would like you to come live with me in the Keep so that I may yet further your education."

Leon forced his damp eyes from the dim figure of his friend's retreating back and turned to face the wizard. "So, it was you who provided me with the opportunity to train at arms."

E'Alam's nod was barely visible in the deepening darkness.

"It would seem, then, that I owe you my gratitude, and perhaps even more."

"No, you owe me nothing. You have been chosen and I but do my duty."

Leon's brow wrinkled in confusion, unseen in the night, "What do you mean, 'chosen' and by whom, and for what?"

E'Alam's deep voice held mirth in it as he said, "You wear the pendant. It has chosen you."

"The pendant?" gasped Leon, pulling it from beneath his shirt and cupping it in his hand. A soft blue glow slowly formed around the two. "How did you know of the pendant?"

"Come," soothed E'Alam, "We will speak of this in great detail over some dinner and I shall attempt to answer all your questions. I have already notified Larkin and his good wife that you might stay with me for awhile, and you may visit them tomorrow if you wish."

Leon nodded as he slipped the pendant once more beneath his shirt. There were questions that needed answering. Turning, they started up the path toward The Keep.

> *When heart is true and arm is strong.*
> *And evil comes by those gone wrong*
> *He'll rise above the battle tide,*
> *To find his strength, when he is tried.*

Excerpt from the prophesies of Orn

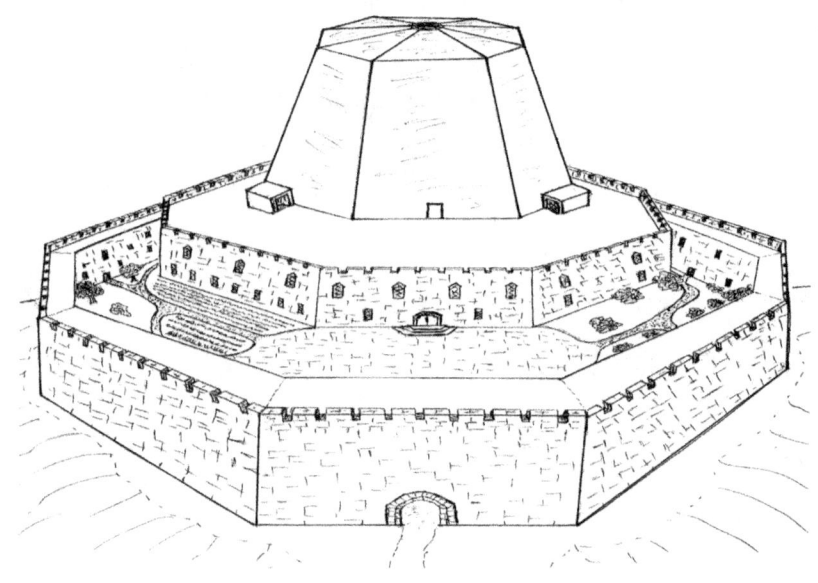

CHAPTER FIVE

The Blue Keep

5522 AS

It was stumbling dark as they approached The Keep. Leon found himself constantly groping for footing, while at the same time E'Alam strolled along quite unconcerned, never missing a step. They entered through the thick outer walls of The Keep by a tunnel. It was high and wide enough for two mounted men riding abreast to pass through in comfort. As they entered this passage a sphere of soft blue light appeared before them and led the way to large doors made of a strange metal that shimmered in the light of the sphere. The doors had obviously been designed to keep out intruders no matter how determined.

E'Alam spoke to Leon, "Place your pendant here on this design." It was a spot that appeared to be in the exact center of the door. He moved forward and did as he had been instructed; the door split silently down the center and swung open. As they passed through it shut again, just as silently as it had opened leaving Leon oscillating between a feeling of being trapped and a feeling of great security. As he often did when confused he placed his hand on the pendant beneath his shirt and a surge of confidence flowed through him, buoyed him up and left him feeling that everything was as it should be.

The remainder of the tunnel was lit by softly glowing globes that hung about the walls, seeming to brighten as they were approached and fade again as they passed. The cobble stoned courtyard was small. It was not designed to hold an especially large number of people, perhaps no more than thirty on mounts. On the left side a stable had been built into the outer wall. On the right appeared to be unused rooms for they had no window or door coverings. They might have been used as barracks in a different age. On both sides of the courtyard were gardens containing shadowy foliage which Leon couldn't identify in the strange light that emanated from globes on either side of the doorway into The Keep.

He followed E'Alam up three broad steps and through large intricately carved doors into the entry room. The exceptionally well crafted marble walls inside were decoratively covered with dark woods. Warm colored tapestries hung here and there providing a feeling of age and splendor. The floors were highly polished marble like the walls both of which had blue vein tracing throughout. More of the strange globes emitted light wherever they went. E'Alam walked straight through another big double door into a large comfortable sitting room filled with warmth and the pleasant smell of a wood fire burning in the enormous fireplace on the opposite wall. Finely woven carpets with strange designs lay upon the highly polished floors and tapestries decorated the beautifully carved and fitted wood and stone walls.

An old man entered from a side door on the left. He was thin with hawkish features, well dressed, about the height of the average villager and quite at ease with E'Alam. "Well, my Lord E'Alam, it appears we will have a guest for dinner. How did things go today in the village?"

"Ah Tidus, this is Leon the bearer I have mentioned. He will be staying with us for a while, if he chooses to accept our offer. In any case, please prepare the east chambers for his use and ask your good wife to set us out some food. It has been a very long, hungry, all-be-it successful day."

Tidus gave a slight bow to Leon, "Greetings Master Leon, and welcome". He then hurried out the door he had entered.

E'Alam followed more leisurely with Leon keeping pace slightly behind. They entered a large comfortable dining room where Leon stood looking at the elegant furnishings. He turned to E'Alam and said, "I can't sit on these chairs I'm still filthy from battle".

Tidus hurried over and placed a large towel over the chair, after which Leon sat down next to E'Alam in one of the comfortably cushioned and intricately carved armchairs at one end of the highly polished table that could easily seat twenty people. A large pleasant looking woman entered with a shallow bowl of warm water and a rough cloth to get some of the grime off of his hands and face. Then she brought a plate of small cakes, steaming mugs and a great warm smile. "Ah," she grinned, "So this is the young Master Leon. Tidus told me he was a handsome sort and 'tis true for sure. I'll have you something to fill your bellies soon." She nodded to E'Alam, smiled, and returned the way she had come.

Leon sat studying both the rich beauty of the room and also the Wizard without seeming to, as he sipped the strangely delightful brew in his cup. E'Alam, with his hood thrown back, was a man of undeterminable age, with gray eyes that seemed to be bottomless pools of mystery as he studied the mug he held before him in fine strong hands. A neatly trimmed, slightly graying, brown beard about two inches long gave his face a regal appearance and exactly matched his shoulder length hair. There was strength in the features set off by a strongly chiseled nose and high cheekbones. It was a face that could demand obedience but would instead garner respect and undying fealty. Surrounding him like a nearly visible aura was an unexplainable mystery, a nearly alien strangeness.

Almost hesitantly, not wanting to interfere with E'Alam's musings Leon said, "I see there are others here besides you."

Looking up from the mug E'Alam said, "Her name is Mia, and now you have met the whole staff. In times past this house enjoyed the presence of many but now we are few, now we keep it all going in a sort of waiting and holding fashion. Tidus and his good wife have been with me for a number of years. They do most of what needs to be done to keep this ancient house comfortable, leaving me free to come and go as I must."

Mia entered again, this time with steaming bowls of thick savory stew, small loaves of fresh bread, butter and more of the rich mead for their now empty mugs. The meal was simple but excellent and Leon, hungry from the day's exertions, fell to with gusto, just barely escaping embarrassment over his table manners by the excellent tutoring Fallon had given him.

Finally satisfied, Leon pushed back from the table. "You promised me some answers, but first, tell me why you chose not to use your wizardly powers to drive away the raiders. It is obvious to me that was a departure from what you have done in the past."

"The pendant is the key, as it is the key to all that we do here in the Keep. In regard to your question, there are four answers. The first is that I simply was not here. Though I have the power to keep watch and communicate while I am away, I have to be here to use the powers necessary to drive a boat full of determined ruffians away from the fjord. In the past when raiders have landed it was for the same reason, and though I am able to return fairly swiftly, at times it is not fast enough, or even possible. When I am here I drive them away long before they find their way up the fjord to our beach, and this happens nearly every year.

"The second, and I feel, more important is, you and your training had to be tested in the fires of actual combat so, should the time come when I cannot help you, you would know the strength of the metal within you.

"Third, the village people needed to know that they can drive away the barbarians if they have a plan and the will to do it. The day may come when they must fend for themselves while we are otherwise occupied.

"And finally, this group seems to have chosen your village for their personal supply station and as such, they had to be eliminated as a threat in order for us to be free to pursue our work with the knowledge that the villagers will be reasonably safe."

Standing, E'Alam said, "Come, let us adjourn into the sitting room to continue our discussion."

Seated in large comfortable, leather upholstered chairs, before the fire E'Alam continued, "As I said, the pendant is the key. For hundreds of years it has lain in the grotto in which you found it. It has powers to summon and has not done so in all of these years, but a few years back, it chose to lead you into the cavern. Remember, the cavern has always been there but none before you had noticed it. You saw what happened when others tried to lay hand on the pendant. They met with resistance or force equal to their attempt."

Leon stared in disbelief, "Are you saying that you saw what happened in the cave?"

"Oh yes! You see I also am a friend of the stone and a bearer." So saying, he pulled a pendant identical to Leon's from beneath his robe where it had hung on its gold chain. "Though I wasn't there in person until you were gone, I did witness the stone choosing you. The stone is the heart of the earth, or perhaps a more descriptive word would be sentinel, or guardian, for in truth it is all of these things and more. And I, and now you if you choose to follow its promptings, are the Stone's foot soldiers; its hands and ears, and eyes. You see, there is a balance between darkness and light, or evil and good in the world, and the Stone is here to help ensure that the balance doesn't shift too far to the dark or evil. When this happens, chaos reigns and mankind can be destroyed; whole worlds can be lost. Yes I said worlds. This is not the only world. My own home world, Sithia, was lost some three hundred years ago; to a demon invasion, but hopefully it will never happen here. I'm not speaking of the wars of man against man. For some reason I shall never understand, these things seem to go on forever. What I speak of is more pure and more deadly. It is the growth of unbridled evil."

Leon sat stunned. No amount of imaginings could have prepared him for this.

E'Alam continued, "In the days to come I shall show you much that will amaze you about the workings of the Guardian and the Keep if you choose to stay, and I have never known such a one, as yourself, to refuse once he has accepted the pendant. But now I believe your mind has had quite enough for one day. Tidus will show you to your chambers."

Tidus appeared as if he had been summoned and led a very tired, very confused Leon off and up a wide stairway to a huge suite with a very large bed unto which—after washing in a large basin of warmed water and being helped out of his clothes and into a sleeping garment, —he fell, not even noticing the magnificence of the room in which he lay.

Heavy drapes being drawn back from the window brought the late morning sunlight streaming into the room and roused Leon from a deep dreamless sleep. Tidus smiled and said, "Good morning Master Leon. Come, here is a robe for you to wear to the baths."

"The baths?"

"Aye, you'll find them quite refreshing."

Under the Keep was a marvelous room, a natural appearing cave with an extremely warm pool of water, which was filled continually from a source that bubbled out of the rock wall onto a ledge just above the pool and then fell gently into the pool. An overflow was on the opposite side. Just two paces away was another pool. This one had cool water and was the perfect antidote to the warm lazy feeling that developed when a body sat too long in the warm pool.

First Leon washed thoroughly with water from a bucket and sweet smelling soap. Then, after rinsing all of the soap from his body he stepped up over the edge of the pool, and slid down into the hot water where he soaked until most of the aches and pains of the previous day's exertions were gone. At Tidus' urging he removed himself from the pool and entered the cool one. After being completely relaxed, and nearly cooked, this pool brought him swiftly back to reality and left him wondering if it weren't, after all, some ancient form of self torture. Upon stepping from the water, Tidus gave him large, soft towels to dry with. Then it was back up the steps to his chambers where his robe was traded for clothes finer than any Leon had ever worn, let alone seen. By now Leon was famished and more than happy to follow Tidus down to the kitchen where Mia filled him up with a delightful assortment of eggs, meats, sweet breads and jellies. To Leon this was an unbelievable feast!

Tidus then led him up to E'Alam's chambers which were across the hall from Leon's. Tidus knocked and then left Leon standing in front of the door. The door swung open, apparently by itself, and Leon could see E'Alam standing, peering intently into a strange foggy mirror on the other side of the room from the door.

"Leon, please come in," invited the Wizard. "If you are rested we should finish our discussion. Have you considered staying with us?"

Leon entered the strange room, where tables were covered with unusual implements, and even stuffed animals and birds, butterflies and beetles, bowls and beakers, flowers and cacti, bats and frogs. It was a truly strange and wonderful room. Leon jerked his attention back to E'Alam. In reality he had thought of little else since he had been roused by Tidus earlier that morning, and though he had oscillated between the excitement of all of this newness, and the settled familiarity of his life at the smithy he had been unable to make up his mind until this moment. But now, as if a voice were speaking to him from within he knew he would stay. "The Smith and his wife are very dear to me," he stated, "I would need time to see them and assure them I will be all right."

"That is as it should be. You will be able to see them as often as you wish, and there are suitable mounts in the stable at your disposal. You must understand that you are not here as a prisoner, a hired hand or even a student, though I believe there is much you will learn. You are here as a part of the web that is the workings of the Stone. You are here because the Stone has chosen you. You are here because the Stone has need of you and whatever skill you will bring to our common battle. You must choose whether or not you will accept its calling."

"Of course I will," replied Leon. "Nothing could please me more or satisfy my seemingly insatiable curiosity."

"So be it my friend. Now, for a few of the answers you requested. Come. Sit." He indicated chairs near the center of the back wall by an open hearth which held a small warming fire. "In the days to come I shall show you much of the workings of the Lodestone, but to begin with, the Stone guards a device we call a portal. The portal is like a gate into a series of parallel worlds, sister worlds to this one. And though the basic topography is similar on each, all are different in their own unique ways, and if you wish to, it is possible to travel to them through the use of the crystal pendant you wear. Also, I will show you or tell you many of the Stone's current projects. Whether the Lodestone and the portal are the controllers and the pendants work through them or the other way around I'm not sure, even though I've studied it for nearly three hundred years." At Leon's raised eyebrows he continued, "Oh, yes! I'm quite old in your eyes, but then as wizards go, I am quite young."

5522 AS, Ganor, fifth Sister World

And so the days in the Keep began. E'Alam introduced Leon to many interesting things, one of which was the large library, filled floor to ceiling with books of every description. There were tables and chairs, strange lighting and a constant temperature and humidity that insured the longevity of the books. As far as he could find, the writings contained no record of a time that the Keep had not existed, nor any record of who had built it. There was a timelessness about it that made it both ancient and freshly new all at the same time. The Keep had been built of finely cut stone the likes of which Leon had never seen, and the mortar that had been used was harder and more resistant to the elements than he could have imagined. Inside, marble walls were overlaid with richly aromatic woods that never seemed to lose their fresh mysterious fragrances. In many of the rooms the walls held fine tapestries depicting strange scenes of people and places that Leon could only wonder at. The ground floor consisted of the rooms Leon had seen that first night plus the large, well-stocked library, a large kitchen and the quarters allocated to Tidus and his wife Mia. There was more living space in other rooms within the great walls but they were all closed off for lack of need. Fully half of the second floor was dedicated to E'Alam and the usual wizardly assortment of books, globes, tubes and other indescribable paraphernalia, all of which was neat and orderly with each device in its appointed place.

The other half of the floor held several, long unused, guest chambers and Leon's rooms.

The most interesting room of all, to Leon, was the Portal Room. It sat on the back of the roof of the second floor of the Keep and was accessed by walking across the roof of the second floor. The roof was approached by way of stairs, one set built within the massive walls to the ramparts through doors that led from the gardens on either side of the Keep, the other by stairways from within the Keep that led up from the second floor to the roof and opened onto the roof along the walls of the Portal Room on either side of its large door. The portal room covered a large section of the roof of the second floor and though its outside diameter was quite a bit smaller than the roof, it easily had a footprint of half of the second floor's total roof space. It was octagonal, reflecting the shape of the Keep. The door was made of the same strange metal that Leon had seen in the tunnel that first night. The back outside walls of the Portal Room dropped straight down the outside and then continued without interruption down the cliff walls and into the fjord hundreds of feet below. Once inside, the walls of the Portal Room held large tapestries on the top half of the each wall depicting, according to E'Alam, scenes from the sister worlds. Hanging beside the tapestries were samples of armor and weapons pictured within the tapestries. The bottom half of the wall held crystal panes that seemed blank until viewed from straight on. The ceiling was as high as the combined bottom two stories of the Keep and seemed to be made of opaque crystal. From the exact center floated a multifaceted blue jewel, the size of a man's head. It radiated soft pulses of blue light directly down onto an eight-sided central pedestal. The side of the pedestal that faced the door was blank, and according to E'Alam represented the world they now lived in. Each of the other seven sides was decorated with a different symbol that represented the world depicted in the slightly opaque windows inset in the walls beneath the tapestries. E'Alam explained that in each of the sister worlds was a fortress identical to the one they now stood in, but of course in those worlds the door to the outside and accompanying blank side of the pedestal represented the world in which it stood. Leon found it all very intriguing and exciting. One of the opaque panels showed, in near darkness, a desert like landscape where hideous creatures groped about attacking each other with fangs and claws and crude weapons. Centered in the distance in that landscape was a dark castle where winged creatures soared in the gloom. The feeling of evil was undeniable. As Leon had paused to look at it E'Alam remarked. "That is the land of Zxantor. Such is the evil that I spoke of the other day. It was once called Sithia, and was a peaceful world of great beauty, and my home world. That destruction is what we hope to avoid in the other seven worlds at any cost."

Much time was spent in the library where E'Alam hoped to broaden Leon's knowledge. Like a great sponge Leon soaked up whatever was laid before him. Books were very rare in the village, and before coming to the tower Leon had never seen a whole book. He had been taught the basics of reading, painstakingly by Mae, the smith's wife, using loose pages of assorted script which were passed around the village for that purpose, and then prodded into a deeper understanding by Fallon during his efforts to improve his courtly knowledge. Now, surrounded by the writings of the ages he felt an insatiable thirst for understanding and E'Alam was delighted to assist him. Interestingly, when he found something within the books that puzzled him he seemed to hear the answer from somewhere within his being as though some inner voice had spoken to him.

From the first, E'Alam began trying to teach him the basics of magic and the art of wizardry, none of which came easily to Leon. For weeks he couldn't accomplish the simplest spell. Then E'Alam suggested that he try to work through the pendant using the pendant as a guide or channel. The pendant seemed to be waiting for him to turn his thoughts to it, to invite it to help. When he did a blue glow pulsed into his body, filling him with the essence of life … magic. Like turning a key it opened previously sealed doors into new compartments within his mind. Images flashed through his entire being and he began to sense a singleness, a oneness with all around him, air, water, fire and earth. Meditation became as important a part of his daily exercising as work with the sword or battleaxe. In his meditations he felt as though he floated free of his body, and then, encased in an aura of pulsing blue light he visited strange places and saw strange beings. He called it dreaming in the pendant, but when he mentioned it to E'Alam he was told that the pendant was teaching him. Whether it actually took him there or merely showed him the places, he could not say. He was reminded of the night in the smithy when he had thought he dreamed, for these experiences were much the same. Once, feeling somewhat lonely he meditated on Fallon and soon imagined that he saw his friend riding a great white charger. He was attired in fine armor accompanying what appeared to be a Prince of the Southland's. Leon called out to him….and, as though he was heard, Fallon turned and looked directly at Leon, smiled and nodded.

The days passed quickly for Leon, and except for a trip or two a week into the village to visit the smith and his wife he stayed at the

Keep. He trained, he studied, and he meditated, then he did it all again. In spite of the feeling of being in touch with everything around him and his new association with the pendant he still progressed slowly in things wizardly. He could cause a glowing sphere to appear in the dark although he suspected that the pendant actually did it. He felt frustration when his attempts at the wizardly art failed. When that happened he would drive himself in his practice routines with weapons until he was so physically drained he would fall into bed exhausted and sleep almost without moving throughout the night.

It was on an evening such as this that Tidus came hurrying to the exercise room to inform him that a strange knight approached the Tower. Quickly Leon threw on his cloak and ran to the tunnel still armed with the sword he had been exercising with. Leon opened the gate and hurried to the mouth of the tunnel. There sat the knight astride a huge white, and in some way familiar, war-horse.

"Well, nave, are you going to invite me in or do I ride through you," boomed a deep voice from within the helm.

"Try to ride through me and your blood will stain the cobbles," returned Leon.

"Time hasn't dulled your tongue any," said Fallon in his own voice as he removed his helm.

Leon could only stand awkwardly apprising his friend, his mouth seeming to flap in the slight evening breeze. Then, suddenly filled with a happy excitement he shouted, "Fallon! Come, enter and welcome, I'll gladly invite you in." With that he turned and led his friend into the courtyard, feeling childlike in his joy.

It had been a wonderful evening. After removing Fallon's armor, treating him to a session in the baths, and filling his belly with Mia's excellent food, the two friends talked far into the night, catching up on the events that occurred during the months that they had been apart. It turned out that Fallon had indeed seen Leon sitting in his position of meditation suspended in a blue sphere, and he had felt a strong and undeniable summoning. So, upon completion of his task for the wealthy desert prince-ling, he gathered his belongings and his squire and rode north. The squire would arrive a day later with their equipment and supplies, but Fallon, feeling a sudden unexplainable urgency that morning, had pushed on ahead to get to the tower as soon as possible. Confused about the urgency that he had felt but happy just the same to renew their friendship, they finally consented to Tidus' promptings and went to bed.

5523 AS, VaLor'

Xzuron sat on his black obsidian throne. It glittered, like cut glass. He leaned forward staring into space.

Above him, floating in the air, the head of the demon sorcerer Kortox grinned with obvious satisfaction, "Go forth and take that which must be ours. Destroy the armies of VaLor' and you shall rule as king."

Xzuron beamed at the thought. He stood and looked around his throne room. Encircling the throne, rich blood red carpets cascaded down the stairs. At the bottom stood his sixteen satros, eight captains inside and eight lieutenants outside in a semicircle, their heads bowed in submission and their hands tucked into their sleeves. "You are to start the invasion at dawn tomorrow," he hissed at his satro officers. "We have assembled the greatest force ever to be assembled, and now it is time to take what should be mine. Soon we will rule the whole of VaLor' and the fools that now live there will be our slaves and fodder for our army. Blood will flow in the streets of the cities of VaLor' like water down the Catch River and the poor idiots who sought to believe in the old prophecies will offer up their entrails to feed my morags. You, my cadre, will direct the warriors we have created to the utter destruction of my enemies. Now go!"

5523 AS, Ganor

After their rather full night and little sleep, just as the sky to the east was beginning to lighten, Leon was startled awake. He felt an urgent humming surging through his body. *"Wake, you are being summoned. Hurry!"* He fumbled between deep sleep and wakefulness. Fighting the sleep, then straining even more, with great effort he brought himself awake and opened his eyes. The humming seemed to be all around him, and it pulsed in strength like a heartbeat in sync with a blue light, emanating from beneath his nightshirt. He pulled the pendant out, and holding it he could feel it vibrate. It was compelling him to go to the Portal Room. He didn't know how he knew, but he knew. He stumbled into the hall and ran into E'Alam just as Fallon emerged from the next suite.

"Quickly!" the wizard said, "Dress for travel and meet me at the door to the Portal Room! I have something to attend to quickly first." Then turning to Fallon, "We leave on a possibly long and dangerous mission. It seems that the Stone has gone to some trouble to have you included. Unfortunately there is no time to explain. You must decide. Come, or stay, it must be your decision. If you would join us be with Leon when he comes up to the Hall of the Stone."

"What?" started Leon, but he was speaking to the retreating back of the wizard.

Tidus appeared coming up the stairway, with an armload of garments. "Here are traveling clothes Master Fallon, should you decide to go, and trust me, your squire will be taken care of." He handed the clothes to Fallon and hurried back down the stairs.

"I don't know about you but I have to dress," said Leon turning toward his room.

"And I don't know what's going on but I'm not getting left behind," shouted Fallon as he charged into his own quarters.

A time shall come when King is naught,
And all VaLor' with fear is caught.
For from the north with ill intend,
The hearts from man their wish to rend.

Shall come the hoards of dark and night,
With sorcerer's will the land to blight.
This plague of doom to sweep the land,
Less laid to rest by stranger's hand.

Excerpts from the prophesies of Orn the Seer

PART TWO

CHAPTER SIX

The Portal

5523 AS

Excitement began to build in Leon as he ran back into his room. Fully awake now he dressed quickly but carefully, concealing his throwing knives as Fallon had taught him. The pulsing light of the pendant seemed to insist that he hurry, and so he did. Now, attired in a loose but warm long sleeved shirt, soft leather traveling trousers, knee high soft leather boots and a traveling cloak with hood he charged out his door and nearly collided with Fallon. Together, cloaks flying out behind them they ran to the steps that led up to the roof, and finally to the door of the Hall of the Stone, the Portal Room. There E'Alam and Tidus stood waiting.

Tidus was handing E'Alam a small pack which the Wizard quickly slipped inside his cloak where it disappeared. Then he handed Leon and Fallon similar packs, "Farewell, my friends. I hope to see you return soon." He then turned and walked to the stairs and down into the Keep.

E'Alam faced his companions, "Well, my young warriors. It is time. This is your last opportunity to change your minds for soon there will be no turning back. Leon, we have tried to prepare you, but it just isn't possible to do so adequately. You, Fallon, you have no idea what lies ahead."

"I have long since decided," replied Leon, "and the pendant knew I would; lead on."

"You lead and I shall follow," assured Fallon.

"So be it." E'Alam turned to the door, swung it open and stepped inside. Leon and Fallon followed quickly.

Blue rays of light shot up into the brightening dawn as they entered the hall. In the center of the ceiling the huge multifaceted jewel pulsed with blue light. The room was extremely bright, but it didn't seem to hurt the eyes while a slight aroma of ozone excited the nostrils. In the flat top of the pedestal Leon could see indents the size and shape of his pendant directly centered above each of the eight sides. The indent on the side with no markings shimmered like the sun shining on ripples in a pond.

The humming increased.

Leon's pendant seemed to resonate with the stone as a visible beam leapt from it to the huge jewel, where it met with a similar beam from E'Alam's pendant.

E'Alam took Fallon's hand saying, "Fallon will come through with me after you. Notice that the indent on the side that represents VaLor' is glowing. We are being called to that portal. Place your pendant in that indent a friend will meet you on the other side. We will soon follow, so step out of the way when you arrive."

Leon slipped the chain from around his neck and placed his pendant into the slight indent. The humming increased. Leon could feel heat emanating from the pendant as the blue light grew until it seemed to equal the brightness of the sun. Then a roaring sound began as though a wild wind were blowing through a tunnel, it seemed to fill Leon and the room. Sparkles surrounded him and grew in intensity until his world seemed to be consumed by them. With a sharp popping in his ears the light turned deep blue and receded leaving Leon a little dizzy. He realized he must be through and quickly stepped back a few steps. As his eyes began to focus, it seemed as though he were still in the Hall of the Stone. Then he noticed the man standing on the other side of the pedestal, and the pedestal itself had changed. Now there were no markings on his side. Almost immediately the humming again increased and then with a popping sound E'Alam and Fallon appeared.

E'Alam moved smoothly around the pedestal as he replaced his pendant around his neck, and put forth his hand, "Lea'Oen, my young friend, how fare you? Leon, Prince Fallon, allow me to introduce you to Lea'Oen, Prince of the High Elves. Lea'Oen is a bearer in this, the land of VaLor'."

Leon noticed the blue crystal pendant hanging around the Elf's neck as he replaced his own.

Leon and Fallon bowed, using the courtly manor that Fallon had taught. Leon said, "Your highness, we are honored to meet you."

The Prince moved over to Leon and Fallon with hand extended, "Please, no formalities between us, for I see that you too bear the pendant and Fallon here is a Prince in his own stead, so let us just be comrades and friends." He clasped Leon's hand warmly then turned to Fallon with equal warmth.

Lea'Oen stood nearly as tall as Leon. He was slight, almost thin but Leon could see that he was quick and agile, athletic and strong as a fine blade. He had a long thin face, large wide gray eyes and pointed ears that nearly reached the top of his head. His hair was deep black with a tinge of green about it, and it was tied back in a shoulder length pony tail that had been clasped tight against the back of his head with a flat tube studded with jewels. He was dressed in soft leather shirt, breeches and knee high boots. Clipped around his shoulders hung a cape, its outer material multicolored much like the leaves of a forest. The inside seemed to be of a fine black material that reflected not a trace of light and moved as though it were soft and very pliable. Strapped to his belt on the left he wore a sword, the scabbard decorated with floral designs in jewels, gold and silver, and on his right, a long slender dagger. His handclasp was firm and friendly and his eyes sparkled with youth.

Fallon stood in some confusion, never having heard of portals, elves or other worlds. Leon clasped Fallon's shoulder, "This must really seem strange to you. It is to me, and I've heard of it all before. Just hold on and as soon as we can stop I'll try to fill you in."

Lea'Oen had turned back toward E'Alam, "Welcome honored one. There is some need for haste. A storm is gathering in the north." And then in a quieter voice, as if meant for E'Alam's ears only, "Is one of these off-world-ers, the one?"

"Time will tell. Are the horses and supplies ready?" The Wizard responded.

"Yes, all is ready." replied the Elf.

"What One?" interrupted Leon.

"All in good time," smiled the wizard. "Come, we must be on our way." E'Alam turned and led the way out of the Hall of the Stone, then sealed the door.

The sun was breaking over the distant eastern hills and Leon could see down into what had been the fjord back in his world. Here it was a deep canyon, barren and stark. All around the Keep he could see rock, sand and stunted brush, desolate and unfriendly. In the court yard, however, bloomed strange exotic plants and flowers. This small area truly seemed an oasis of beauty and life in a dead world. They descended into the court yard on the outer stairs nearly identical to those he had seen back home on Ganor. Finally, they came down into the courtyard. The air seemed fresher, thicker, and more alive. A myriad of pleasant fragrances filled his nostrils and a rainbow of color pleased his eyes as he inspected the growth in the gardens. Quickly they walked toward the stables built in the wall of the keep, just as at home.

The main door into the bottom story opened and a small round man no taller than Leon's waist appeared. "Master E'Alam, will you be staying for awhile? All is ready for you and your guests?"

"No, not this time my friend. We must travel at once," replied E'Alam as he went over to take the small hand in his own. "Soon, perhaps I may spend some time here with you, and once again enjoy the comforts of your hearth."

With disappointment on his round hairless face, the small man said, "Prince Lea'Oen said, 'he feared you would not be able to stay,' but I had hoped. If it must be, then go with speed, safety and in the grace of the Stone."

"Thank you for your concern, my small friend. Rest assured I shall return as soon as it is possible," E'Alam smiled, resting his hand gently on the little man's shoulder. "Would you please take our two guests to the armory and allow them to select weapons of their choice suitable for the trail?"

The small man, bobbing his head and gesturing, led Leon and Fallon into a room in the outer walls, which was obviously an armory. There they chose swords and belt knives from among a selection finer than any they had ever seen. The blades were lightweight but appeared to be very strong. Along their length were strange etchings and letters, though the scabbards were plain and free of decoration. The gnome nearly jumping with excitement said, "You pick well, these are fine blades, from the forges of the southern dwarves. Now, come. We must hurry."

Lea'Oen had gone on to the stables and had just returned riding a tall black horse while leading another equally tall chestnut gelding. A leggy gray stallion followed un-tethered.

The tall gray gelding nickered in recognition as E'Alam approached. The wizard produced an apple for him from somewhere in his robe and quickly mounted. "Windwalker, we ride again," he whispered as he turned him toward the gate with no more than thought.

Leon said, "Ah E'Alam, we are one horse short."

"Oh yes, I nearly forgot," he pulled a foggy sphere, about the size of a grapefruit, out of his robe and tossed it casually to the ground. In a flash a large blob of mist appeared. It slowly dissolved and there stood Fallon's great white warhorse held by his squire, Jerome, who was mounted on his own chestnut gelding with his hand firmly clutching the lead to both Snowball and their leggy pack mule. Jerome, slightly overweight, was tall for his age, taller than Fallon, nearly as tall as Leon. He was neatly dressed in green shirt, matching flat topped cap and cape, then brown trousers tucked into knee high boots. Just above his soft blue eyes, his hair was dark blond and trimmed square just above his collar. Though his beard was slight it was obvious that he was trying to grow a mustache, probably hoping to give his features a more mature look. Although he had packed all of Fallon's armor plus some supplies, on the mule, he carried only a belt knife of his own. He scrambled down from his horse clumsily holding all three animals.

E'Alam smiled at Fallon's surprise and said, "Jerome insisted on coming to look after your equipment, and incidentally, you"

Smiling broadly, Fallon walked over and clasped Jerome's right hand with his own and placed his left hand on Jerome's right shoulder, "You my friend have no more idea what you have gotten yourself into than I do, but you are very welcome."

Jerome smiled, looking pleased with himself and watched as Fallon mounted his huge white war horse which was equally as tall as the horses Lea'Oen had provided, though much broader and more heavily muscled. It had a long luxurious mane and a forelock that hung far down below its eyes, and long hair at the fetlocks that reminded one of feathers. It was a truly powerful animal trained to fight as well as carry its owner. Snowball may be his name, but he was as hard as quartz, not at all soft like snow.

Fallon reached forward and lovingly patted the big stallion's right shoulder, "I am happy to see you Snowball." The nearly pure white horse danced a bit in anticipation and whickered softly, obviously surprised at finding itself in a totally different place than he was, what seemed like just moments before.

Once everyone was mounted E'Alam led them out through the tunnel into a barren, desolate country where very little grew, and nothing at all that was green.

The rising sun cast long shadows to the west as the small group headed south toward a range of mountains clearly visible in the distance. The path descended into a wide valley and Leon turned in his saddle to look back toward the Keep. All he could see was a large mound of broken rock. Without really thinking about it he reached up and put his hand on his pendant, instantly he could see the Keep through its disguise. Smiling he turned back toward the unknown that lay ahead.

Xzuron looked down on his army as it began to file out into the morning light, and smiled. Soon … Soon… A strange, chill, sensation ran down his back. He sensed something important had happened. Turning he stared toward the west, confusion touching his mind. He gestured to one of his ever-present satros and commanded, "Take a tordaq and scout west. Something has happened."

"What am I to look for Master?"

"Look for something unusual," he screamed. "Look for what has happened, then return fool. Must I do it myself?"

Between the worlds the portal door,
Will pass the bearers, yes, and more,
As long as light survives the dark,
And Lodestone blue provides the spark.

Excerpt from the prophesies of Orn the Seer

CHAPTER SEVEN

Mero Wood

Leon suddenly became aware of the unnatural stillness. They had been traveling several hours and had stopped to rest the horses and eat. He sat munching on dark bread and cheese from his pack when it struck him. "There is no life, no sound, no movement, not even the wind. Even the dust that we stir up settles right straight back to the ground. What a strange place this is." He turned to E'Alam, "Was it always this way?"

E'Alam paused mid-bite and slowly lowered the bread he had been about to bite into. "No. Once this land was much like any other. All of the vegetation you saw at the Keep came from these hills and valleys, but that was before even my memory. Just over three hundred years ago there was a great battle between the peoples of VaLor' and the armies of an evil sorcerer named Xzuron. He had spent years building his army beneath the peak of Mount Orag, a dormant volcano north and east of here. He had gathered companies of wild men from the east, trolls from the north, and a few thousand men from the realms of the south. Add to this mix, creatures called morags, which he created himself from the elements and spirit of the land. It was a formidable army. When he came out to do battle he had nearly ten thousand warriors. The much smaller army of VaLor' met his force with skill and determination and nearly turned the battle against him. Then he brought sorcery into play and the wizards of VaLor' responded with power of their own. Such a vast amount of power was brought to bear that Xzuron's army was destroyed, along with most of that of the VaLor'ians, including their king and both heirs to the throne. The land still bears the scars of that battle. Xzuron retreated back into his volcano swearing vengeance, and the united peoples of Valor' set about to devise a plan to stop him should he ever again bring war to their land."

"Why didn't they just follow him and eliminate him, right then, when he was weakened," asked Leon.

"The simple answer is that they also were weakened, their wizards either dead or their power greatly reduced. Their armies were in a shambles, and the loss of a rightful royal heir devastated and disheartened them. They had no other course of action than to retreat, heal their wounds and try to prepare for the future. That was in the time of my father, and he, being one of the few remaining wizards of the time, assembled a counsel of all the nations and peoples in an effort to prepare for Xzuron's return." He paused and ate the rest of his bread, then continued. "With the combined efforts in spells and talents of the ancient dwarves, elves and wizards they produced a solution, hoping that their plan would meet the needs of their progeny in the future, and still fulfill the even more ancient prophecies. As to that, only time will tell. Come, we must keep moving if we are to reach North Fort before it is too dark."

On the flat valley they set the horses into an easy canter that ate up the distance without tiring their mounts. Unlike the horses that Leon had ridden, which were much smaller and with a movement that jarred the very teeth in a rider's head (not to mention the damage it did to one's backside), these long legged mounts were as smooth and easy to ride as Aunt Mae's rocking chair. Leon found great pleasure in the ride, even though it was long.

Late that afternoon, as they neared the far side of the valley E'Alam suddenly raised his hand to halt, and, standing in his stirrups he turned to stare into the east. Then with a wave yelled, "Ride for the rocks! Stay together!"

In an instant they were in a race to reach some large rocks in the distance. Leon had never ridden so fast. Even then he could see that E'Alam was holding Windwalker back to keep him from running away from the rest of them. In bare minutes they reached the rocks and pulled up in the shadow of a large boulder, their horse's sides heaving as they dismounted. They held their mounts' proud heads close into their chests to keep them still, and waited. As the dust settled, a feeling of revulsion came over Leon. He sensed something and then following E'Alam's example, looked high to the north where a great bat-like creature slowly floated high overhead from the northeast. There appeared to be a being riding upon its back. It soared slowly on down the valley until nearly out of sight, then with powerful lifting strokes it rose, banked, and headed back the way it had come. Silently, effortlessly, it flew east until lost from sight.

No one moved or spoke for several minutes. Finally E'Alam said with obvious disgust, "A tordaq and its satro master. Tordaqs have not been seen here for more than a thousand years. Truly we must make haste now. I fear that even with our haste we may have been seen."

As the great bat-like creature had soured past, the horses had shown alarm and fear. Their nostrils flared, eyes rolled and they sweat profusely, but they neither moved nor made a sound. Now, in contrast, they were anxious to get back on the trail and showed it, dancing eagerly in their anticipation.

The road climbed southward toward a pass that Leon could vaguely see now and then as the terrain permitted. The sun had long since disappeared behind the mountains and the light was fading as they reached the top of the trail. They had dismounted and walked intermittently to spare their horses. It had been a long climb and they were glad to see the massive walls of North Fort before them. The fort had been built to completely span the pass, totally blocking undesirable travelers. It was constructed of huge granite blocks reaching easily eighty feet high, topped with crenellations and towers that bulged out from the walls to allow the defenders to send arrows and fire on the outer walls. The walls were fully fifty feet thick at the base and the gate was built of massive timbers covered on the outside with plate steel; it was a formidable edifice.

After the very cautious guards at the gate had verified their identities, a small door—just large enough to allow one horse and its dismounted rider to enter at a time—opened and they were allowed in. The tunnel through the walls was lit by torches and kill holes lined the walls to allow archers to fire into an enemy as they tried to force their way through the passage. This fort was not made for beauty but strength. It stood dark and un-breach-able in the only pass leading into the lands south.

The captain of the fort came hurrying down to personally greet E'Alam and Lea'Oen. The men at arms showed obvious awe and respect for both. Leon, Fallon and Jerome were made welcome and quarters were soon arranged. Later, as they ate a hardy meal at the captain's table, E'Alam and Lea'Oen conversed quietly between themselves, paying little attention to their food.

Abruptly, E'Alam stood and turned to Leon and Fallon. "The appearance of the tordaq has cast a new degree of urgency to our quest. I must therefore leave you. Please continue to travel with Prince Lea'Oen while I go in a different direction. Hopefully, I shall catch up with you by the time you reach the city of Val. Leon, would you come with me? I would speak with you for a moment, alone, before I go."

"Of course," Leon exclaimed as he stood and followed.

They moved quickly into the hall where E'Alam stepped close to Leon. "Leon, my young charge, I would that I did not have to leave you so soon," he whispered, "but we must have more information and I can travel much faster by myself. Remember, you are a chosen of The Stone. Through it, by way of your pendant, you can accomplish much, especially here on VaLor' where magic is indeed more prevalent. Much that you could not have done in the land of your birth will be possible here. Trust the pendant. Through it you can reach out to me as you did to Fallon. Have faith in it, seek to use it, call on it instead of just wearing it. The pendent has saved your life twice now, and you can learn to work together, but keep it to yourself for yet awhile. Trust Lea'Oen. He will always lead you on the right path. Though I call him young, he is nearly two hundred years old, young for an Elf, but old enough to know the ways of this world. Goodbye for now. May The Stone grant you an easy voyage and good speed." With that he turned and disappeared down the hall toward the outer walls.

Leon stood stunned. Questions clamoring for answers assailed his brain, yet there was nothing but the mammoth, cold stone walls to talk to. Slowly he returned to the captain's table.

Unseen in the dark, the shape of a large blue-gray falcon dipped slightly as it leapt from a turret at the topmost tower in North Fort, and then, with powerful strokes of its great wings, lifted high into the night sky and banked east.

Xzuron rubbed his chin with his right hand, "So, that fool E'Alam is back. Are you sure they didn't suspect you had seen them?"

"Master, I flew on down the valley well past them and then circled back slowly so as not to alert them. I'm sure they did not suspect."

"Good. You will be my eyes and ears with this special group of travelers." With a slow wave of his hand down the full length of the satro that stood cowering before him, and a flick of his wrist, the satro disappeared. There in his place stood a large black crow with a bright red spot on its breast. Squawking, it hopped from one foot to the other in obvious discomfort. "Be quiet, or I shall leave you in this shape. Actually it quite becomes you. Now you are to follow our friends and keep me informed of their movements. Between the two of us, I'm sure we can provide a few surprises for them."

Before dawn the captain of the guard roused the travelers. By sunup they were fed, mounted and heading out through the big gates that led south down the well traveled road toward Mero Wood and beyond. Lea'Oen led, followed by Leon and then Fallon, Jerome and the mule. Windwalker brought up the rear, with empty saddle and no lead rope, seeming perfectly content with the arrangement.

The trail down the mountain was more a road, wide and well kept. The farther down the road they went, the more undergrowth and trees inhabited both sides of the way, until the trees were tall and stately. Sometime after midday they paused in a camping area Lea'Oen said was a wagon camp. Wagon trains were common on the roads of VaLor' and they had passed several. They watered the horses at the small stream and snacked on dark heavy bread, cheese, dried fruit and water from their water bottles, then pressed on down the road into the woods. Although the sun was high, the deeper into the woods they went the more like twilight it became. Soon the ancient tree trunks led up into a nearly solid canopy of leaves high overhead. They rode in silent admiration, not wanting to talk for fear of breaking the spell of wonder that seemed to surround them. The air was heavy with the rich smell of the woods. The grasses of the hills outside the forest had given way to mosses, ivies and dark loamy soil.

As evening approached Lea'Oen said, "We will be spending the night with my people. It is not far and I am sure you will find it more comfortable than sleeping on the ground."

They left the road on a narrow path that led twisting deeper into the woods toward the west. A short time later Leon could hear the sound of strange music. It was a happy sound, and soon he could distinguish that many instruments were playing in a sort of informal concert. Lea'Oen picked up the pace. Leon kept thinking that he saw movement in the trees, but each time he turned toward it he could see nothing. Light tinkling laughter teased his ears, and he sensed that young elves were playing with him. He smiled, and placing his hand over the crystal pendant, instantly he saw happy young Elf faces in nearly every direction. He released the pendant and enjoyed the mirth that he had sensed.

It was nearly dark when they rode into the Elven village, and Leon could scarcely believe his eyes. The village was built around an ancient tree with a trunk at least forty paces through. As it rose into the canopy above living bridges arched from it to other huge trees on all sides. Strange glowing spheres, similar to those that Leon had seen in the Keep at home, lit the pathways both on the ground and up in the air. All about him he saw well-tended gardens, one leading to another. Streamlets flowed in every direction, and fountains pulsed in differing hues as the light around them changed in color. Vines and ivies of all description hung or climbed in perfect harmony with the flowers and grasses along the paths and bridges. He thought that this truly had to be humanity living in total harmony with nature.

Walking toward them came two distinguished looking Elves dressed in beautiful pale green silken clothing laced with sparkling small dots of light. One was a tall, quite thin and very handsome, Elf man with long, loose, dark hair that hung below his shoulders with a slight graying at the temples. He looked much like Lea'Oen. Beside him walked the most fragile looking, beautiful, woman Leon had ever seen yet very much an Elf. Her jet black hair fell in a cascade down her back nearly to the ground and she seemed to have small stars nestled over her forehead to form a tiara. Her eyes were wide and a deep gray that seemed to be able to penetrate into the depths of his soul. She walked with the grace of a dancer, and smiled a smile that spoke of warmth, humor and a great deal of knowledge as well as a love for all things.

Not realizing when it happened Leon found himself kneeling on one knee on the grass, his head bowed in respect for the couple. Fallon next to him and Jerome behind had done the same.

"Please rise, sons of a sister world," her voice was like music to his being. "We have known of your coming for ages, and perhaps it is we who should be kneeling to you. Come, stay with us this night. Rest, relax and renew yourselves, for early on the marrow you must hasten on your way." So saying she offered her hand to Leon, who kissed it lightly and stood. Fallon followed suit. Jerome slowly stood behind Fallon.

A large number of Elves had assembled to see the strangers. They were a strikingly beautiful people, bright, happy and full of life.

Lea'Oen laughed, "I see that you are as captivated by my honored mother as are the rest of us. Allow me to introduce to you my mother, Queen Lea'Ah, and my father, King Nelmar. Come, we would have you feast in the hall of the High Elves. Your mounts will be well taken care of as we dine." He turned, and with his guests surrounding him, followed the King and Queen with Jerome bringing up the rear as they walked toward the base of the colossal tree.

As they approached Leon could see a wide stairwell leading down under the very center of the tree. Beneath the tree he was surprised to find a large cavern-like hall. The roof was the living bole of the tree and the walls were the roots. Across the hall and directly opposite the entrance a raised platform held table and chairs for the royal family and their guests. All about the rest of the room were tables and benches enough to hold the sizeable crowd of Elves that had gathered.

The tables were already set and piled with a wondrous assortment of tantalizing dishes, the fragrance a kaleidoscope of delightful aromas. They were seated so that Leon sat to the right of the Queen with Jerome on his right. Fallon sat to the left of the King with Lea'Oen next to Fallon. Musicians came into the hall from side entrances and soon the hall was filled with soft, sweet strains of music from harp and flute and reed. As the music faded into the background magicians appeared and performed exotic feats of sleight of hand, and tumblers exhibited great skills. There were jugglers and singers and storytellers. Leon was enthralled by the Elves and grew to love and respect them in a few short hours. All too soon the Queen raised her hand and signaled that it was time to end the festivities. Lea'Oen escorted Leon, Fallon and Jerome up living stairs on the outside of the trunk of the massive tree to a sleeping room in its branches. The room was completely formed of living wood, floor, walls, roof and even the cots and chairs.

For moments, Leon stood stunned, transfixed, looking at the room in total amazement. But his questioning nature called him back to the question that continued to nag at his mind. He turned to Lea'Oen with a puzzled expression, "What did your mother mean when she spoke of knowing of our coming and of kneeling to us?"

Lea'Oen paused for a moment, then replied, "Our people are an ancient race, and we remember and keep alive many of the prophecies of the old world. Amongst them are suggestions that we would be visited by humans, other than the wizards, from a parallel world. So you see, that makes you kind of special, and as much a curiosity among us as I am sure we are to you. You must rest now. Morning will come all too soon." He turned and disappeared out into the night without fully answering the question. Soft, relaxing music lulled the weary travelers, and in spite of their curiosity, they went quickly to their beds and soon were hard asleep.

Completely rested, Leon, Fallon and Jerome were urged awake before dawn. As their horses were being led to them Queen Lea'Ah appeared from the direction of the central tree. "I would give you a small bit of Elven magic to take with you." She turned to Leon. "For you a pouch of dust that will make you invisible one time, but take care, for it hides not your shadow." Then turning to Fallon, "And for you young Prince, a pouch of dust, the essence of which brings truth to he who would not see it. Use it wisely for its power could save a world. Go swiftly now my young friends, and though you will surely come across difficulties and hardships, may you also find happiness and fulfillment in your journey."

They mounted and rode out at the first indication of light in the sky. All too soon, it seemed, the travelers were back on the main road and headed south. A strange emptiness settled into a small corner of Leon's heart, and he knew that it would not be filled until he once again visited the kingdom of the High Elves.

After a couple of hours riding on the main highway, the canopy overhead started to thin, allowing more sunlight to penetrate. They had been moving at their league-eating canter when they came to a clearing—a wagon camp where they stopped to rest their horses. Lea'Oen looked up sharply and then relaxed, saying, "We are about to have company. They are friends."

Soon, seeming to materialize out of the forest around them, appeared six Elven figures dressed in clothing similar to Lea'Oen's. One of them stepped forward. Then with a slight bow, "My Prince, we have been sent to escort you to Val. Your father the King has been warned of strange happenings along the roads these past few days and would have us ensure your safety."

"Na'Arak my friend, come, tell me what it is that you have heard."

"A communication came this morning, from our cousins in the Dark Woods of Maldor. They say that a blight is spreading out of the north, and they have fears that they may be forced to leave their ancient homes. Our brothers from the North Woods have already been driven from their ancient homes and have joined the Dark Woods elves. They also report that the dwarves of the Catch Mountains will probably come under siege. Word of strange happenings on the road to Val has also been received. There seems to be a shift in the One Power, and our Queen sees danger for the bearer from beyond. All of this has happened during the past two days, and our Queen Mother feels that the reason might be the arrival of our off-world visitors. Lastly, the Council is scheduled to convene at Val in three days. She urges all speed, but with caution."

"Then we must leave at once," agreed Lea'Oen. He turned to the others, "Come, we must be on our way."

"Wait!" barked Leon, "Why is it so important that Fallon and I are escorted? What is happening? What are we being made the center of, and why?"

"Come, let us ride and I'll try to explain as we go," Lea'Oen urged.

"All right," agreed Leon feeling a little sheepish for his outburst, "but we expect some sort of explanation. We came here expecting to use our skills in battle, but there seems to be more here than we anticipated. Everyone seems to know something that we don't, but should."

The six Elves had secured their horses a short distance away in the woods and soon were mounted and ready to travel. Leon wondered how they had been able to catch up with them so fast, but then thought that they surely knew paths through their own woods that might shorten the distance. But that made little sense since he and his comrades were supposed to be making haste as it was.

Once more they headed south. But now, there were two guards riding a stone's throw in advance, another pair just slightly ahead of Leon, Lea'Oen and Fallon who were riding abreast of each other with Jerome and the mule directly behind them, and two more Elves riding a stone's throw in back of them. The road was well traveled and previously there had been very little trouble, but the Elf squad was taking no chances; they were constantly on the lookout. Occasionally one of the riders directly in front of the three would ride out, up a small hill, or over a ridge to check the road ahead, only to return and report to Lea'Oen that all was clear. Now and then they passed a freight wagon, either coming or going. They gave a casual wave and hurried on toward the city of Val.

Lea'Oen proceeded to try to explain the situation to Leon and Fallon. "For as long as we have had the written word, and I suspect long before that, our people have known through prophecy that someone from a sister world would, in a time of great need, come among us and aid us in battle against an evil that would arise out of the north. Naturally, there are those among us who hope that person is one of you, but we just don't know and neither will you until whatever it is happens. Prophecies as you might guess are a bit ambiguous. They never point an exact course in history. They just hint. Perhaps after we get to Val you would like to read them for yourselves. Those who make prophecies seem to know that if they make it too clear, we might be inclined to hurry things along or perhaps change that which they have predicted. To further complicate things, in our world where all of the races have some degree of the magic of our ancient fathers the knowledge of your arrival has spread much faster than we can travel on horseback, and so you are in danger simply because you are here, and we don't even know if you are the one, or ones spoken of, though according to E'Alam you both are well trained in the art of warfare. I hope this bit of information gives you something to hold on to rather than distressing you. I understand your consternation. Be sure that we will do our best to support you."

Leon looked at Lea'Oen. "Yes, I believe you will, but I for one feel terribly unprepared for the type of task that you seem to imply. I'm sure you have military leaders at least as prepared as we are." He paused looking at Fallon who nodded his agreement, "Does the magic you spoke of help to explain how these other Elves were able to catch up with us, or as it seems, to be waiting for us when we arrived at the wagon camp?"

Lea'Oen nodded, "They were, in fact, waiting for us when we arrived. You see, they are a regular patrol that watches that section of the forest. The whole forest is patrolled by squads of Elves and each of the squads carry a scrying stone that has been enchanted by my mother the Queen. When it is necessary it can be used to transmit very detailed messages, and that is how we know the movements of our cousins in the Dark Wood. At the same time, you and I could communicate through our pendants, as I'm sure you know."

Fallon said, "I know that I just sort of came along for the ride, but this gets more strange as the hours pass. Mind you, I wouldn't have missed the experience, but it seems as though all of the legends of my youth, the fairy tales, are becoming real."

Lea'Oen reached over and gripped Fallon's shoulder, "Have patience Fallon, there will still be plenty of work for your sword arm if my guess is right, and as for what you call fairy tales, there may be more truth in them than you might think since there has been travel between our worlds since time began."

Small talk between the two princes continued as they moved at their steady, ground covering pace down the road toward the village of Deepton.

Hand on his pendant, Leon rode in silence concentrating on his inner thoughts. Seemingly without effort the leagues continued to roll by under the hooves of their splendid mounts, and the day wore on. They hurried past rolling hills and small valleys scarcely noticing the beauty of the land around them, the small white fluffy clouds that dotted the distant horizon, or the bird that might sing out in the distance or flutter up at their approach.

Like an unidentifiable smell, a sense of danger fell over Leon and a humming began to surge up from deep within his being. *"Danger!"* The small whisper seemed urgent.

At the same time the horses began to act nervous. Windwalker stopped in his tracks and began slowly backing up. The troop, suddenly alert, splashed through a murky puddle at the bottom of a narrow draw that had high steep walls on either side, and moved steadily up toward the top of the rise ahead. The lead riders had just passed through another shallow puddle in a dip near the top when the puddle suddenly vaporized, lifted up and formed a dense, sulfur smelling, cloud directly behind them. Growling, moaning and screams could be heard faintly from within the fog. The troop stopped. Fear compelled the horses to run but training and the sure hands of their riders held them fast. They spun their horses just in time to see the murky pond behind them lift up forming another brownish, menacing, evil, fog blocking their retreat.

They turned again facing up the draw. Then almost as one, the two elves directly in front of Leon, Lea'Oen and Fallon, drew their swords and charged into the thick churning fog before them. Lea'Oen tried to call them back but it had happened too fast and they disappeared in an instant. He yelled, "Only fire can stop this."

Leon started to curse his lack of magical skill, then, *"Use the fire spell, and the pendant."* He cupped his pendant in his left hand. Calm settled over him, a knowing. The echo of E'Alam's assurance gave him strength. Standing in his stirrups he reached deep within himself, the words of the spell for fire flooded into his memory. Stretching forth his right hand with the spell sharp in his mind, he commanded, "Burn!" A rush of power left his body. He felt as though he were throwing his own life force at the evil before him. Instantly the vile smelling fog was enveloped in flame. Turning in the stirrups he reached within himself again, feeling deeply nauseous, he again pointed and issued the command at the dark mass approaching from behind. He felt dizzy, sick and extremely tired, as though he had drained every ounce of strength from his inner being. Then he toppled forward, unconscious on the neck of his mount and started to slide toward the ground.

Before he hit the ground Lea'Oen and Fallon were there to catch him and ease him down. There they stood as steam boiled off the aberrations before and behind them. A heavy sulfurous stench filled the air, and the hideous screeching and moaning slowly dwindled until there was silence. The site looked like the remnant of a small, very ancient, battlefield. Scattered about were the bones of many men and animals, bits of wood and weapons dating to wars of the past, all ancient except for the bodies of the two elves and their horses. Selflessly they had charged into the deadly apparition, and selflessly they had died.

Lea'Oen turned to Fallon, "This ancient evil hasn't been seen since the last great war. Surely Xzuron is aware of our journey. Only he or possibly one of his satros channeling through him, could posses the power to call forth such evil."

With the help of the others, they carried the two warriors up to the ridge and laid them together. Using their horses and some rope, they pulled the dead horses from the middle of the road and removed some of the more obstructive, ancient refuse.

Lea'Oen then came back and dug a small clear stone out of his saddlebags and sat down beside the road, cross-legged. He held the stone in his hands and stared into it for some minutes then he stood up. "The Queen will send an honor guard to retrieve the bodies and bury the horses, they too should be treated with honor."

They were very near the village of Deepton and so the band rode on, Lea'Oen riding double with Leon held before him on the saddle. As they topped the last low hill above Deepton, a huge blue-gray falcon slid down the air currents and came to land just in front of the troop. The falcon looked at them for a moment cocking its head, first to one side and then to the other. Then it shimmered, raised its wings and changed shape as they watched. There before them stood E'Alam with his arms raised overhead. Windwalker nickered and moved over to stand by him, softly nuzzling his arm. From somewhere within his robes he pulled out a nice red apple and gave it to this special mount.

Turning back toward the riders he said, "It appears that you have not fared too well. What has happened to my apprentice?"

Quickly Lea'Oen filled him in on the events as they had occurred from the rest stop in Mero Wood, then he said, "I was hoping to find lodgings at the inn in Deepton, and a healer to assist Leon."

"The inn is a good idea, but I think that I may be able to help Leon." He quickly mounted and led the small company down into the village.

To the east a large crow with a large red spot on its breast silently circled south toward Val, dipping and rising on the air currents as it went.

The Lands VaLor' he'll travel through,
And see the peoples old and new.
He'll visit village large and small,
But none so fair as Elven Hall.

For there he'll meet the Mother Queen,
The likes of whom he'd never seen.
He'll battle death and test his skills,
Against the ancient fog that kills

Excerpt from the prophesies of Orn the Seer

CHAPTER EIGHT

Of Dwarves and Bones

"Come my young charge. You have rested enough." E'Alam's warm and friendly voice penetrated the deep shroud of sleep that still enveloped Leon.

He stirred, fighting his way up out of the blackness of his troubled sleep. "Wha … What … Where … E'Alam?" Leon's eyes popped open.

"Yes my young hero. You accomplished a worthy spell but I must speak to you about your methods," laughed the Wizard. "You see, you are supposed to draw on the power of the pendant, guiding it through you, rather than drawing the power from yourself and using the pendant as a guide. Now that there is no question you can use the power, all we have to do is refine your methods a little. Our art is the using of one's will to make things happen, but there is always a price. We must draw the power from somewhere, or we must pay the price. The stone provides us with a source of power that is unlimited, and it will gladly pay the price, but you drew the power from within, thus draining yourself so completely that you collapsed. Imagine that you are funneling the energy that you need through the pendant that you wear. Trust me, it will be much easier on your body. Now come. It is nearly dawn and we must move quickly if we are to reach Val by the time the council convenes."

"What happened?" Leon asked, still in confusion. "Where are we? How did I get here? Where are the others?"

"Have patience my inquisitive one, all in good time. Hurry, get dressed, we must leave as soon as possible. Food is on the table downstairs and the others are already up and preparing to leave. By the way, I would never have dreamed that there were so many ways to conceal a knife. If I can only get you as comfortable with the use of the power as you are with your knives, you will be a worthy Wizard." He turned and left Leon scrambling to get dressed, including his knives, and then to quickly follow.

Leon hurriedly ate, while the others prepared their gear and packed the horses. As he came out of the inn they were mounting up and he rushed to follow their lead. He still didn't have all of the answers he sought, but then he wasn't sure he knew the right questions to ask in order to get those answers.

The sun was beginning to lighten the sky over the distant silhouette of the Divide Mountains as the small group crossed the Deep River Bridge at the edge of the village, and rode up the rise to the south.

As soon as they were out of sight of the village E'Alam called a halt. He dismounted and walked up to each horse in turn, fed it a handful of grain and spoke softly into its ear. When he had finished he turned to Leon and Fallon, "That small handful of a rather unique ration combined with a few specially chosen words of power, should speed us along our way much faster than you have been moving."

The horses went into an easy gallop, seemingly with no more strain than they had felt at the much slower canter of the day before. It was a glorious ride, but the pace left little time for the answers Leon had sought. The terrain had flattened and the ride was smooth and easy on both man and beast. Well before the noon hour they thundered past the road to New Home, a kingdom of the Dwarves. Halfway between that road and the village of Falls was a wagon camp where the small band intended to stop, rest the horses and have a quick meal. As they slowed to approach the camp, a great clamor of arms could be heard, but it was hidden from view by a bend in the road. Rounding the bend they drew to a halt. There, down in a slight draw at the center of the clearing, shoulder-to-shoulder fought a double ring of Dwarves, their helms and armor shining and glittering in the sun as they chanted and swung their weapons. All around them a small army of skeletons, wearing ancient armor, fought. A skeletal warrior would be smashed or cut down and another would take its place, then slowly the pieces of the first would come together again. The Dwarves acted in flawless unison. At the sounding of a horn the outer ring would swing in and the inner ring would slide out and take up the fight. In this way they could rest a few minutes before they had to go back on the line.

Between the travelers and the line of battle sat two skeletons upon skeletal mounts. One of them carried a ragged banner, the other sat dressed in beautifully ornate armor studded with jewels. Patiently they watched the battle through empty eye sockets.

E'Alam rode forward, and in a voice that trumpeted over the noise of the battle commanded, "Halt this foolishness!" Quiet fell over the scene as empty eye sockets and those of the Dwarfs turned to stare up the small rise at E'Alam. "Antar, great warrior Prince, what brings you and your sons, from your rest to do battle against your former allies?"

A ragged hollow sounding voice that had to consist more of bones vibrating than vocal cords responded, "How do you know me, and who are you to interrupt my just battle?"

"I am E'Alam, son of E'Ralam, son of E'Talam son of E'Malam who you knew well, and who spoke fondly of your bravery, and the VaLor of your sons. I interrupt you because I respect your honored memory."

"Well spoken, Wizard, son of wizards. We were called forth to stop those who would bring harm to the coming King."

E'Alam sat for a moment in thought, then, "Who called you good Prince?"

"We know not, but it was foreordained that we return on the day of his arrival, to do battle with those who would travel south to destroy him and the kingdom of Val. Three mornings past we rose and were told to attack all that traveled this road south."

"Your presence is welcomed, Prince Antar, but you have been guided to the wrong road, the road you seek is on the other side of the Divide Mountains, and the enemies you seek are the minions of the sorcerer Xzuron, who even now stirs from his stronghold beneath Mount Orag. He has prepared a hoard of morags, for the long prophesied assault on VaLor'." E'Alam walked his horse toward the skeletal prince. "Did you not expect that your dedication to the crown of your fathers would return you to some semblance of your past glory? Your present condition is hardly that. It is my belief that it was the sorcerer who spoke to you as you came forth from your rest, and he did so in an attempt to delude you into bringing harm to the very forces that, he knew, you would wish to aid. You have my word that the King is not yet crowned, and that the forces of Xzuron are mobilizing to attack your homeland. How say you? Will you go to the aid of the King in defense of the Catch River Basin? For it is there that the battle will be fought."

E'Alam had moved very close to the skeletal prince by this time, and his voice had lowered. He continued to speak for a moment gesturing toward the mountains to the east and the road behind them. When he stopped the elegantly armed Prince looked up at the mounted troop, or perhaps it was the road, for a long minute, then with a wave called off his army and led slowly up the road back toward New Home and the trail over the Divides. As the gruesome line flowed past, Leon could feel as though it were a tangible thing, loyalty and honor so strong he could almost reach out and grasp it. The feeling touched his heart as he viewed these evil appearing warriors. He knew their vow could be depended on. He only hoped that he could accomplish his own task, whatever it was to be, with such nobleness.

E'Alam returned to the group, "We must send a rider ahead of them, to assure the Dwarves of New Home that the prince is no threat, and merely wishes to use the trail over the Divides."

Lea'Oen nodded to one of the Elven riders, who spun his mount and galloped up the road past the slow moving line of skeletal warriors.

E'Alam turned to the Dwarves most of whom now sat or lay on the grass in fatigue. "Well, my friends, it seems as though you have had a considerable workout this morning."

"Why couldn't you have arranged to show up a couple of hours earlier Wizard?" responded a smiling Dwarf with a great yellow beard. He was dressed in more gold and jewels than Leon could have imagined one man could carry. His armor shown like the sun, gold and red at the same time, and though he had taken several sound hits no dents or even scratches could be seen. He stood about as tall as the middle of Leon's chest, but he was broad of shoulder far in excess of Leon and stocky all the way down to his feet. He had an air about him that spoke of royalty and age at the same time. He stood with dignity, sure of himself and his abilities. Leon liked him at once, even before being introduced.

E'Alam turned first to the Dwarf and then to his companions, "King Dygor, may I present our guests from a land afar: my apprentice, Leon, and his dear friend, Prince Fallon, and Fallon's squire, all of the same land. They have come back with me to help us in our battle against Xzuron, which brings me to our need for haste. The hoards are moving in the north, and we must hurry to Val to meet with the council. You should be with us."

The Dwarf King turned toward his company, "As you can see, we are in no condition to travel, but we shall hurry on as soon as we are rested."

The malicious grin on E'Alam's face could be seen even under his hood. "You could ride with us."

"Not on your life," spouted the king. "I do not ride! I like my feet firmly planted on the ground, where I can stand and swing my ax as a Dwarf was intended!"

E'Alam walked over to the king, speaking as he went, "I suppose I could change you into a horse. Then you could keep up with us with four feet on the ground, but I doubt that would suit your dignity." He stopped in front of the shorter being and laid his hands on either shoulder as he continued to speak in softer tones. Soon he turned to Windwalker and said, "You could ride with me. Windwalker can easily carry us both, and I could hold you secure so that you need not fear falling."

"Fear?" stormed the Dwarf, "I fear nothing!"

Then before the dwarf could think about it E'Alam smiled, "Good, then it is settled."

Dygor frowned in realization of what had happened. "Wizard, I should know better than to bandy words with you. You have been tangling me in my own tongue for two hundred years now, but I never seem to learn." Then he smiled, "So be it. My company will catch up with us in Val."

"May I suggest that you send a messenger back to New Home to mobilize your forces and hold them ready for word to march. Our time grows short."

They stayed long enough for E'Alam to assist the Dwarf healer as he attended to the few small wounds that they had sustained. Once again the Wizard spent a few moments feeding his special mix of grain to the horses and speaking softly into their ears. They all mounted and were soon thundering down the road toward the village of Falls.

A very large black crow, with an unusual red spot on its chest, lifted out of a small grove of scrubby trees nearby and beat up into the clear blue sky on powerful wings. Catching an updraft it circled higher and higher, then it slid north and soon disappeared out of sight. It probably wouldn't have been noticed even if someone had been watching.

The village of Falls sat close to a very grand display of waterfalls that cascaded in giant steps down from the Plains of Planor; then quickly formed a rushing river that fed eventually into the Lake of Life. As the river passed the village named Falls it became very narrow, swift and deep. At this spot the ancients had built a marvelous bridge that arched across the river seemingly without joints or seams. The villagers suspected it was magic that kept it standing, but since it had spanned the gorge since before man could remember no one seemed too concerned about its dependability. The mounted party slowed as it passed through the picturesque little village and over the bridge. Then, as soon as the village was lost from sight they resumed their rapid pace down the road.

Halfway between the village of Falls and the capital city of Val was a spacious, well used wagon camp and there amidst wagons of every description they stopped to rest the horses and riders. E'Alam had led them to one side where they could be more or less alone. They munched on trail cakes and water from the clear mountain stream that flowed past out of the high plains above. As well as being a wagon camp, the trail from the plains above joined the main road here, but no wagons traveled this trail. It was far too steep and narrow.

As the companions sat or stood about involved in idle chatter, a distant tinkling of bells disturbed the otherwise quiet afternoon. The wagoners quickly gathered up their horses reins and led them—pulling their carts and wagons—to the side of the clearing. The sound of bells increased, accompanied now by the rumbling of many hooves rapidly approaching down the trail from the plains above. The clamor continued to build until nearly a hundred horsemen raced into the clearing, neatly avoiding collisions while filling the large clearing with beautifully accoutered horses flying over the ground in circles within circles, until no more riders came down the trail. Then, as if by a single unspoken word all stopped and stood, un-moving. The horses sides heaved with exertion, but other than that not a muscle twitched. Then, as one they turned to face E'Alam and the companions.

Leon, Fallon and Jerome stood mesmerized by the sight before them. The elegance of the horses was beyond anything they had ever seen. Aside from their pure athletic, beauty they wore wide bands of velveteen material fastened to their harness, and trimmed with colored fringe and fancy bells. Small packs were secured behind each saddle. The riders wore finely tanned leather pants and vests decorated with colorfully painted floral designs, soft leather boots with pointed toes, and brightly colored silken shirts with open collars and billowing sleeves. Very little jewelry was worn except earrings. Around their heads they wore material matching their shirts wrapped into a turban, a trailing cascade of fabric hanging down to their waists. Across their backs were slung gently curved swords in brightly decorated scabbards, and each had a short powerful looking bow and a quiver of arrows strapped to the right side of their saddles. They were a fine boned, proud looking people as fair to look upon as the animals they rode.

At the sound of a bell they began to circle again at a fast trot. Then with great precision, stopped in seven groups, each one wearing different colors and led by a single rider whose apparel, while similar, was also decorated with fine stitching of golden thread, and who held himself with even more dignity than the rest.

In the center, stood a horseshoe shaped formation of riders wearing white shirts and turbans. Leading that group was a distinguished looking man with a short, jet-black goatee. He was dressed completely in white, even to the leather of his vest, pants and boots. He sat astride a great white stallion which he now urged forward toward E'Alam. His strong features and clear blue eyes exhibited pleasure as his rich voice reached out to the companions, "E'Alam, it has been long since you have visited the lodges of my people. Good it is to see you and Windwalker once again."

E'Alam strode forward followed closely by Windwalker, "The pleasure is mine old friend. How has the foaling gone lately?"

"Three days past, each of the seven Clans, had seven mares that foaled twins, and all lived. As you know twins are rare and seldom live for even an hour. As you also know this was to be our special sign of the coming of the King. We are anxious to get to Val to see if it is true. Our scouts spotted you on the road to Val, and since that is also our destination we hurried to join you. But what is this. You travel with strangers. Would we be intruding?"

"Nay friend, we would more than welcome your company. The three young men you speak of are visitors from a distant land. I will introduce them to you."

"One moment," the rider responded as he turned in his saddle and called, "D'Nee, come and meet the visitors E'Alam has brought." Then turning back, "She would be very upset if I didn't include her. She has grown into such a willful child."

As the rider approached Leon and Fallon both were glad that she had been included. Jet-black hair coiled gently in one loosely gathered wave down over her right shoulder nearly to the roundness that hinted at her full figure. High cheekbones set off her clear, pale blue-gray eyes. They were lighted with a definite touch of the mischievous, and looked over her proud nose with deep intelligence. Full lips smiled a little wickedly. She was strikingly beautiful, while at the same time appearing ready to enjoy some joke at their expense.

E'Alam turned first toward his youthful companions, "I take pleasure in introducing," he gestured toward Fallon, "Sir Fallon, a Knight and Prince in his own land, and his squire Jerome. And this brawny blond fellow is Leon, my apprentice, and an accomplished warrior. They travel with us in a quest for adventure and what better reason than to lend their rather excellent fighting skills to our cause." He then gestured toward the mounted man, "Over Chieftain of the Clans of Planor, Krantor and his daughter, D'Nee. I can see by your expressions that it is too late to warn you of the charms of the women of Planor."

Krantor responded, "Welcome to you, for our soothsayers predict a great battle is coming soon." This he said as he dismounted and offered Fallon and Leon, strong wrist gripping warrior handshakes, and a nod to Jerome.

E'Alam laid his hand on Krantor's shoulder, "Come, tell me the rest of the news of your family and the affairs of Planor while your men rest for a short while. Then we shall hurry on to Val and they can follow at a more leisurely pace."

Krantor turned to the riders and called, "Dismount and rest!" Then to his daughter he said, "Speak with our young guests while I visit with E'Alam." Turning, the two men walked slowly toward a nearby stream chatting pleasantly, leaving Leon and Fallon in the mesmerizing care of D'Nee, while Jerome tended the mounts.

It would normally have taken two days to travel the distance that they traveled that day, but here they sat spread out along the crest of the road looking down on the city of Val. Leon and Fallon sat on either side of D'Nee with the rest of their band on either side of them, and Jerome slightly behind Fallon. They were gazing down into a wide valley dotted with farms and orchards, and there, an hour's ride ahead, lay Val, the capitol city of VaLor'. Leon was amazed at the sheer size of it. Then, as the setting sun reflected off the inland sea—the Lake of Life—all of the towers sparkled as though they were diamonds. It was like the sun reflecting off the facets of a pile of broken glass. Leon was speechless. At the last instant, just before the sun dipped out of sight into the lake, a tight beam of brilliant blue light shot from the top of the highest tower in the city to rest on Leon, D'Nee, Fallon and the mounted riders on either side. Then it disappeared. It had lasted a mere instant, and after it was gone Leon couldn't be sure that it wasn't a figment of his imagination, or a trick of the eye. That would have been the end of it had he not heard the intake of breath from all of those around him. Turning toward them he saw smiling faces, but as he started to ask a question E'Alam urged Windwalker into a fast gallop down the road and the whole party dutifully fell in behind. Curiosity rode like a cloud over him as they raced on toward Val.

And when he comes to Val the fair,
The Ray of Kings shall greet him there

Excerpt from the prophesies of Orn the Seer

CHAPTER NINE

Val

It was dark as they approached the huge gates of the city which were closed for the night, but a small door large enough for a man to enter stood open in the center of the right side of the main gate. Two uniformed sentries guarded the door.

As the riders approached, E'Alam shouted, "Hello the gate!"

"Who goes, and what is your business? The gate is closed for the night."

"Then I suggest that you get the Captain of the guard, and tell him that E'Alam and royalty from across the land have come to attend the council meeting, which I assume is in progress at this very moment."

Both guards jumped inside the door, shutting it as they went. Sounds of scurrying feet, shouting, sliding of latches on the man door and opening of heavy bars and chains on the huge gate could be heard. When the big gates began to swing open, light from within pierced the night. Inside, a well dressed officer and a large platoon of guards stood at attention as if they had been waiting for their arrival.

The officer cleared his throat, "E'Alam, welcome back to Val," he said respectfully. "Who are the guests you have brought with you?"

E'Alam led the troop forward into the light, "Some you know and some you don't. As you can see, this is King Dygor of New Home, and to my left, Over Chieftain Krantor, his daughter and their escort, Prince Lea'Oen of the High Elves and a few of his brother elves and these three are friends from a distant land, Prince Fallon, his squire and my apprentice, Leon. I would appreciate it if you could send someone ahead to inform the Lord Chancellor of our arrival and arrange rooms and food for your guests."

The officer turned and pointed to another who appeared to be a lesser officer and motioned him toward the heart of the city. The man spun, mounted a waiting horse and sped off into the night. "Please allow me to escort you to the palace," the officer suggested, "It would be an honor for my men and myself."

"Thank you," E'Alam said. "We would appreciate your company."

The officer and his men quickly mounted their horses. With the officer leading and his men riding along each side of E'Alam and his party, they moved forward on the wide, cobbled, lantern lit roadway into the heart of the city.

Leon was in total awe at the size of the city around him. The largest number of buildings he had ever seen had been in the home of the High Elves, and here there had to be hundreds, perhaps thousands of times that number. It wasn't very late, so there were a large number of citizens going from one place to another. Most of the shops were closed but the inns were doing a boisterous business. The people were dressed in garments that were generally of better quality than those of Leon's home, though not as nice as those worn by he,

Fallon and the rest of their party. There were people walking, riding on horses and even a few small wagons, but all quickly pushed to the side of the wide road to allow the guard and their visitors to pass.

Fallon laughed quietly, "Big isn't it. This city rivals any I have ever seen, and I have traveled quite a bit."

By the time they reached the palace grounds Leon was completely lost. They went through a high wrought iron gate and into an expansive yard where lanterns lighted hedges and pathways that lead off in various directions. A double arrow's cast up a wide cobbled pathway stood a palace the likes of which Leon could not have even imagined. Strange glowing globes and lanterns lit it up with a sort of fairy light that caused him to stare with eyes wide and mouth open. As they approached the highly ornate main door it was opened wide and a small group of dignitaries came out to welcome the travelers.

"E'Alam, honored Wizard and friend of the land, it is so good to see you again." The speaker was a tall thin man of some age, with silver touched hair and goatee. His face and large, honest, hazel colored eyes easily expressed the sincerity of his words. He was immaculately dressed and his clothing somehow gave the appearance of being a uniform, even though they obviously were not. He moved with an easy grace, his long limbs flowing like a dancer while at the same time displaying strength and suppleness. He was definitely a man in charge of events around him.

"My Lord Chancellor, it is good to be back even though I fear that the times are wrought with danger." As he was speaking, E'Alam and his companions were dismounting. Grooms appeared to take the horses off for a well-deserved rest. Jerome followed them leading Snowball himself; it was his honor and privilege to care for Fallon's white horse, which could be difficult with grooms that it did not know. And he wanted to check all of Fallon's armor to be sure it was all ready for use. After all, that was his primary duty.

E'Alam turned again to the Chancellor, "Come, I would introduce you to my guests. You know King Dygor, Over Chieftain Krantor, his daughter D'Nee and Prince Lea'Oen."

The Chancellor made a fluid bow, "Welcome once again to the Halls of the King. I pray that you will find all to your satisfaction during your stay."

The three gave a return bow and the Dwarf responded, "I'm sure all will be as perfect as it has been in the past. But you still have not come to visit my humble kingdom in New Home and you assured me you would."

"I'm afraid that the duties of Chancellor leave me with very little time of my own. However, rest assured should the King return during my tenure that would be one of the first things I would do." The Chancellor smiled and then returned his attention to E'Alam, "And these others?"

"From a different land indeed, my apprentice Leon and his close friend Prince Fallon. And the young man that you see leading the princes war horse is Jerome, the Prince's squire." E'Alam gestured toward each in turn as he introduced them, then back toward the tall slender man, "Lord Leando, Chancellor of Val, Protector of The Crown and Defender of The Land." Bows of respect were exchanged. "My Lord Chancellor, perhaps you might be so good, as to have Princess D'Nee, our outlander guests and our escorts fed and shown to their rooms so that they might begin recuperating from their rather arduous journey. King Dygor, Over Chieftain Krantor, Prince

Lea'Oen and I shall accompany you to the council meeting where we shall endeavor to fill you in on, that which we know of, the events taking place in the north."

"So it shall be," said the Chancellor. Then he turned to Leon and Fallon, "I would enjoy a further opportunity to speak with you both in the morning," and looking at Fallon, "I'll see to it that your man is properly cared for." He then placed a hand on the shoulder of a close-by young servant all dressed in white trimmed in red, and nodded to him. The servant turned and led the travelers into the wondrous building and through numerous halls until Leon was totally lost. But eventually they found food. After eating they were led to their rather magnificent apartments, baths and beds where sleep took them almost immediately followed by dreams of strange new lands and people.

E'Alam quickly led The Lord Chancellor and the rest of his party into the great council hall where sat the heads of state of all of the free peoples of VaLor'. He went straight to a chair just to the right of an intricately carved, empty head chair and sat down. Leando took the chair directly to the left of the head chair and brought his fist down hard on the table. The buzzing of voices stopped and all attention turned to the chancellor.

"We would hear from E'Alam. Is one of these that you have brought with you, The One? Are we once again to have a King to rule these lands?"

E'Alam stood, "All I know for sure is that the Stone chose them. We must give the prophecies time to work, while at the same time giving our visitors time to choose to aid us. You know that we cannot force them, or put undue pressure on them without breaking the chain of the prophecy."

"We don't have time for games!" came a sharp voice from the other end of the table. "Besides, we know it is one of them. The finger of light leapt out to you as you came over the ridge this afternoon. This is clearly spoken of, not to mention that it has not occurred since the death of the last king three hundred years ago."

Another voice added, "We must send them after the sword. It is our only hope against the power of the sorcerer."

Mutterings of agreement could be heard around the table.

E'Alam held up his hands. "Patience my friends. The Stone works in its own time. Would that it were not so, but it is. Both of these young men are special in their own way. Both are accomplished warriors, whose abilities are seldom matched in their own world, and I suspect it might be so here as well. Either would make VaLor' an excellent warrior king. But the prophecies do not seem to speak of two. We must allow them to choose, lest we pick the wrong one."

Lord Leando spoke up, "Tell us what you know of the north. Our information is sketchy at best."

E'Alam's face grew grim, "I witnessed a horde pouring out of the bowels of Mount Orag the likes of which this land has never seen before. I saw morags by the hundreds of thousands with satros prodding them on. In the skies above, tordaqs with satro riders keep track of the hoards progress. This is truly a plague the likes of which we have never even dreamt. It will take all of our skill to battle these odds, and without the Sword and the King, we may not have a chance. Even so, we must prepare as though we expected to do it ourselves, and pray that this is the time for the return of your King. Only the quest for the Sword will assure us of that. I feel that all we need say here tonight has been said, and I suggest that we find our beds and return here in the morning to plan for war. I will ask our young friends to join us for that planning. They might have an idea or two that we could use. But remember, we must allow them to choose for themselves or our chances of success will be greatly reduced."

High up in the walls of the council chamber perched on an outside window ledge, a large black crow with a red spot on its breast bobbed from side to side as it stared down into the council room. It seemed to be listening to the discussion below. As the council began to leave the hall the crow leapt off the ledge, and with strong thrusts of its wings, soared up into the black of the night and headed north. It flew fast and straight, gaining altitude as it went.

Val He will find as from a dream,
A Fairy City it will seem.

Excerpt from the prophesies of Orn the Seer

CHAPTER TEN

Allece

Leon woke to the sound of birds. Early morning sunlight filtered through the high, curtained windows. He washed quickly, dressed in a hurry in his last clean clothing; strapped on his concealed knives and sword, and went to a large glass door that led outside. Stepping out, he found himself in a garden of great beauty full of trimmed and manicured hedges lining pleasant pathways. Lush flowering vines and trees could be seen in all directions, their aromatic perfumes tantalizing his senses with each breath. Ponds with strangely exotic fish dotted the grounds while stone statuary and benches lined the paths. He began walking slowly, enveloped by the rich fragrances and strange beauty that surrounded him. Amidst the sound of water splashing softly over small decorative, waterfalls, and a soft breeze rustling lightly through the trees, he heard faint, soft, strains of humming. He moved slowly toward the sound. Then he saw her. She was sitting on a stone bench next to a small pond, humming softly as she dropped small pieces of bread into the water and watching as multicolored fish lazily rose to the surface to feed. After standing silently for a short time, he started toward her, not wishing to disturb her but intrigued and curious. He deliberately scraped his boot as he walked.

She turned with a start, but then smiled, "Good morning. I didn't hear you approaching. I don't believe we've met. My name is Allece. Lord Leando is my father, and you must be one of the strangers that arrived last night."

Leon felt suddenly weak and unsure, nearly stammering as he replied. "Yes, I am called Leon. I am apprentice to the Wizard E'Alam, though I fear I lack much skill as yet."

She stood and glided toward him with easy steps, smiling as she came. She was about as tall as his eyes, tall for most men in this land, and definitely tall for his native land. Her slender grace brought to mind her father's fluid movement of the night before. Her hair shown like spun gold in the early morning sun and appeared like a gossamer frame for the picture of pure loveliness that was her face. She had high cheekbones, striking light blue eyes and a mouth that bespoke of strength and tenderness at the same time. She had an elegant, long neck and graceful limbs. She wore a deep blue gown that nearly touched the ground, with short sleeves that reached almost to her elbows and a modestly cut bodice that still managed, somehow, to accentuate the fullness of her youthful figure. A white sash tied around her waist and white slippers completed her attire. She looked, to him, like a vision of all that a woman should be and left him feeling so clumsy that he was afraid to speak.

"Have you eaten yet this morning?" she inquired.

"No. I heard the birds and felt drawn into the garden, forgetting, at least for the moment, all about food."

"Then come." Slipping her arm into the crook of his she guided him toward another part of the garden. "We shall go together." They walked easily, quite naturally side by side as they wound their way through the garden to tall glass doors that opened into a rather raucous assembly of diners enjoying their morning feast.

Leon was impressed by the number of people. At the head of the hall could be seen the usual raised table, but with an elaborate, unoccupied chair in the center. E'Alam sat to its right and the Lord Chancellor to its left. D'Nee and Fallon sat on the side of Lord Leando, and King Dygor, Lea'Oen and two other noble looking men sat beside E'Alam. There were several unoccupied places on either side for other guests and it was to these places next to Fallon and D'Nee that Allece led Leon.

Fallon looked up, "I might have known you would have an excellent reason to be late for morning feast," he teased, winking at D'Nee.

Leon looked a bit sheepish and responded, "Allece, may I present my closest friend, Prince Fallon, of my own land. I'm sure you already know the Over Chieftain's daughter, D'Nee. Prince Fallon, the Lady Allece, daughter of the Lord Chancellor."

By this time Fallon had risen, "I am honored my Lady," he responded.

"Please," she said, "just Allece. There is quite enough formality around here without our engaging in it for no practical reason. I'll not call you Prince Fallon if you refrain from calling me Lady Allece. Please sit. Let's eat and you can tell me about your home and what brought you to the Hall of the King."

She sat between them and they spent the meal talking of their homes, being careful not to mention that it was a different World. They had agreed with E'Alam that it would be easier to explain if people merely thought of it as a different land in this world, for in truth there were many such.

Leon finally managed to ask Allece a question that had been patiently waiting at the back of his mind, "Why is there an empty chair in the middle of the table?"

"It is the chair of the King," she responded. "You see, my father is like a caretaker who watches after the kingdom for the absent King. About three hundred years ago the last king and both of his heirs died in the great battle at Comark Plains leaving no heir to the throne, just as had been prophesied. Since then, my father's family has presided as chancellors and so they have ruled in his stead, waiting for the coming of a new King. There is much prophesy about that event and all VaLor'ians look forward to his coming"

As she finished speaking, a tall, quite handsome, young officer entered the main doors of the hall and strode purposefully to the head table. He stopped before Lord Leando and spoke, "Greetings Father. I bring word from East Fort. We have ridden through the night so that the council might have the latest news from the north."

"Excellent, Gaelnn. Have a quick bite and meet us in the council chamber. We are anxious to hear your report, but I'm sure it can wait while you eat. Sit over here with your sister. I'm sure she would be happy to introduce you to our guests."

The five young people quickly developed a bond that would find them happily entertaining each other whenever possible throughout the days to come. They attended the council meetings, ate, played and exercised together. Leon was completely captivated by Allece. She had a quick wit and a wonderful sense of humor, while at the same time seeming to understand all that was being said in the council meetings. She was athletic and when not in the palace she dressed in soft leather breeches and loose-sleeved shirts, like the men, for their play and when they were riding or in other ways entertaining themselves. She soon demonstrated that swordsmanship was not reserved for the men of Val. Indeed, at practice he soon learned to watch her closely or she would best even him in fencing or light swordplay. While Gaelnn and Allece were quite skilled at arms they were impressed by the strength and abilities of both Fallon and Leon, and totally amazed at their talents with throwing knives. When it came to horsemanship, however, D'Nee far outshone the rest, and Leon was an easy last.

The report that Gaelnn brought had been delivered to North Fort by Elves of the Dark Wood, and spoke of an army of morags driving everything before it as it swarmed over the foothills of Mount Orag. Morag was the name the VaLor'ians had given to the creatures that were created from the essence of the earth, beneath the slopes of Mount Orag. They were soulless, mindless, savage warriors with only one objective, to do their Master's will. Since they felt no pain, remorse, or any other normal feeling, the only way to stop them was to dismember them or confuse them by killing the satro that mentally guided them. They did die, fortunately, but there were so many.

For three days the council had argued the pros and cons of various tactics, never coming to agreement on the proper course of action. Then, in the evening of that third day the representative from

Harbor Town sighed aloud, "What we need is the Sword of Valor', then we might stand a chance."

Leon turned to Gaelnn who sat next to him, "What is the 'Sword of VaLor'?"

Gaelnn sat for a moment then began, "After the last Great War, when VaLor' was nearly defeated, the remaining heads of the peoples combined, forming a council. They summoned the wizards and magic wielders of all of the races together, and hatched a plan that they hoped would save us when the evil again came out of the north, for ancient prophecies had foretold its return. The plan included a Magic Sword made by the best spells of the Dwarves, the Elves and the Wizards, and it would save VaLor' when properly called to use by a stranger, a warrior presumably from another land. For three hundred years worthy men have sought the sword, they came from many different lands, but none has been successful. None have even returned from the attempt."

And when he mentioned that, it could only be retrieved by the hand of a stranger, Leon glanced sharply at Fallon who was already looking at him intently. The look that passed between them was not lost on Allece, though she quickly concealed that she had noticed.

Leon turned back to Gaelnn, "What did they mean by the 'a stranger' part?"

Gaelnn shrugged, "Some say it means a different time, and many a brave warrior has taken up the quest for just that reason, never to be seen again. Others claim that it refers to travelers from lands far removed from here, and more men have sought it who fit that description. Those who might be considered lore masters say it refers to someone from a different World, but this seems less likely to me than either of the others. Every time there is an uprising, or a skirmish between cities, a few well-intentioned, brave warriors are lost in the search. The Sword is supposed to bring unmatched power to its wielder. Unlike others, I have little interest in old tales. Of this much I am sure, none have ever returned from their quest for the Sword."

Leon's body was beginning to hum. And with that humming, an undeniably strong attraction was building in him. The same he had felt as a boy when he was drawn into the grotto so he might find the pendant. He felt as though the others must surely feel or hear the humming, but looking at them he could see that was not so. Almost in a panic he looked at E'Alam. The Wizard's eyes were glued on him. Slowly E'Alam nodded and stood, turned and left by a side door. Leon rose to follow, remembering his friends he sat again. Slightly down the table sat Lea'Oen. He too was watching Leon intently. Leon smiled weakly and looked back to his friends. He didn't hear much more of what was said that evening, nor did he say anything until the four friends were nearly to their rooms.

"Please join me, I would like to speak with all of you in the privacy of my room."

When they had settled in chairs surrounding a small table he turned to Gaelnn, "I must try to find the Sword. Will you help me? Something draws me, as though I have been searching all my life for this moment, as though it was for this purpose that I was born. I can't explain it but I must try to find the sword."

Gaelnn sat with a stunned expression on his face.

Allece laid her hand on Leon's arm slowly shaking her head.

Fallon smiled a smile that only adventurers know, and touched his friend on the shoulder. "My friend, this may be either the greatest folly or the greatest quest we shall ever attempt, but I am with you."

D'Nee sat silently watching Fallon with deep concern in her eyes.

Allece was still shaking her head, "This is pure madness. Didn't you hear Gaelnn? No one has ever returned. How can you be so silly?"

Leon removed the pendant from beneath his shirt, and then preceded to explain how it came to him, its unfathomable attraction, how it had saved his life, how he had grown up in the shadow of the Blue Keep, and finally, how the pendant had brought him to their world. He paused for a second, "I have long since decided to follow wherever it led, and now the prompting is stronger than it has ever been." He concluded by stating, "My only thought is to help the people of VaLor'. If it would cost me my life for the chance of stopping your enemies it is an acceptable trade. My success might mean victory and that's worth the gamble. I'm sure others have said this, or something similar, but I feel sure that I can find the Sword. Something undeniable, while at the same time unexplainable, draws me to it. I came seeking my destiny and the Lode Stone is my guide."

They sat surrounded by silence for some time, then Gaelnn cleared his throat and said, "I have heard of the pendant bearers, but classed the tales as folk lore, but now it seems that more of the old tales are true than I had expected. I will be your guide. We leave at first light. It is normally a three-day journey, two if we push the horses. I shall go immediately and arrange for our supplies. Sleep well for you will need the rest."

After Gaelnn had gone, the four sat for a few minutes in silence. Then each went to their quarters. No sooner was Leon alone than

E'Alam entered as silently as a shadow by way of the garden door. Leon was not particularly surprised. In fact, he had expected him.

E'Alam hesitated, looked at Leon for a moment, then, "I wish I could give you the assurance that you want, but it is just not possible. I can help you some, though. A long time past when I was only a couple of hundred years old I went in search of the Sword, not to possess it, but to know if it was real, and whether it could be found. It is, and it can be found. But only a being from another world may retrieve it. And, only a bearer of the pendant may use it to its full potential. That explains why Fallon is not the one. Take no one with you beyond the caverns of the dead or they may not come back." He stopped as if he were listening, "You have a visitor. I will see you off in the morning." He left by way of the hall just as a soft knock sounded on the garden door.

Allece stood, framed by the fairy light of the lanterns from the garden. Her dress was pale blue, and white ribbons were plaited with great care in her hair and a white sash was tied at her waist. She looked beautiful to him. "Would you walk with me?" she asked reaching out her hand toward his.

Stepping into the garden he eagerly took her hand saying, "There is nothing I would rather do."

They started walking hand in hand, each feeling the warmth of the other as they quietly strolled along the garden paths. Then each had an arm around the other's back, and still they walked along in silence reveling in the touch of the other as their bodies brushed gently with the motion of their walking. Finally, they stopped, turned toward each other and stepped forward each wanting to hold the other, their arms drawing the other close. The smell of her hair filled him with desire, then slowly she turned her lips up to his and he tasted the joy of her love, and felt her responding to the wild beating of his heart. Never had he imagined an experience such as this; so this was love, he couldn't have dreamed it would be so sweet.

With an almost superhuman effort he gently pushed her back. Then, taking her face between his two hands, he kissed her eyes, then the tip of her nose and finally her lips again. "Now I will never feel complete until we are one. After this is all over I will go to your father to ask his blessing, if you agree."

"Oh yes," she whispered, "If only we did not have to wait."

Gently he turned her and led her to her door, kissed her again and returned to his room, not to sleep, but to toss and turn far into the night as visions of Allece passed before his eyes. With some surprise he realized that his "life without purpose" now had two definite purposes, and sadly, they pulled in different directions.

> *He'll find in Val the better part,*
> *Of all it takes to fill his heart.*
> *But love must wait on higher call,*
> *When Lodestone summons one and all.*

Excerpt from the prophesies of Orn the Seer

CHAPTER ELEVEN

Old Home

The sky was just beginning to lighten as Leon, Fallon and Gaelnn arrived at the stables. True to Gaelnn's word all was ready for them. Their horses carried light saddle packs, barely more than bed roll and trail food. Weaponry was limited to the swords at their sides and, of course, their knives. It was to be a fast trip and wisdom demanded that they travel light. Snowball and Jerome were left behind. They wore hooded travel cloaks and the typical soft leather clothing that Leon was becoming used to.

E'Alam appeared just as they were mounting. "Since haste is needed I felt your mounts might be able to use a little of my special trail rations." He walked from horse to horse, fed them a little grain and spoke to each as he had done before. When he finished he gave Leon the small bag of feed saying, "Stop and rest for an hour about midday, then feed them the rest of this and they will be ready to hurry on their way." Then he paused and looked long at Leon. "I have seen the path you follow. I cannot tell you what you will find there for time will have changed it, but I can advise you to wrap the power of the pendant around you. See through it, become one with it and you shall succeed. You will find the way if you have faith in the pendant. Don't be afraid to use its power." E'Alam moved back into the shadows and vanished.

As they approached the great wrought iron gates of the palace grounds, Allece stepped out in front of them. "May the one power be your guide, would that I could ride with you." She paused, looked at Leon and whispered, "Please come back safely." Then she turned and was gone.

They left the city by the river gate near the Stead River, which they crossed on a barge pulled back and forth by heavy ropes wrapped around a large capstan and turned by four draft horses. It took some time to reach the other side, but once there they quickly urged their horses into a mile-eating gallop along the road that led through the grassy plains to the south. About midday they stopped at a wagon camp near the foothills that were the beginning of Mount Stead. The horses grazed and rested as the three ate from their trail supplies. Leon gave each of the horses a share of the feed that E'Alam had provided and once more they mounted and continued up into the hills. Now they must move slower. In spite of the special feed it was a long, uphill ride alternating between a walk and a trot. Leaving the grasslands behind they moved steadily into the foothills. Trees began to dot the slopes becoming thicker as they ascended. The terrain grew steeper, then rockier, but the well-engineered road maintained its steady incline. The beginnings of a forest surrounded them, each stunted tree somehow managing to find enough soil to eke out the nourishment it needed to survive.

As the day progressed the forest grew heavier, the trees taller and denser. Abruptly the road led out of the trees onto an ancient lava flow looking like shining, dark reddish brown syrup that had been poured down the slope of the mountain. It was about an arrow's cast across and the road appeared to have been chiseled through it many generations before. They were half way across when the horses suddenly started to fidget and snort with fright. Out of the trees behind them bounded a number of extremely large wolves with red eyes and ragged, blotchy coats, looking as though they were all hide and bones with little or no fat on their bodies. Their tongues lolled out of the side of their mouths. Froth foamed from their jaws, jaws filled with vicious looking teeth and fangs. The wolves paused, and then howled what could only be taken for a victory statement. The three riders started to bring their horses around for flight on up the road when an answering howl came from the woods in front of them. Soon, more wolves broke into view setting up a clamor in response to that which the first group had started.

Leon became aware that his pendant had humming, *"Danger!"*

The road was now blocked in both directions. The horses were nearly beside themselves with fear. Soon it would be a fight just to stay mounted.

Fallon yelled, "Tie the reins up so that they won't drag on the ground and turn them loose."

As soon as this was done the horses charged up the lava flow and out of sight over a rise. Surprisingly, not one of the wolves followed. Instead, they grew suddenly quiet and closed in to circle the three. Low growling and a sort of anticipatory whining could be heard issuing from the throats of the huge beasts. They stood at least twice as tall as any similar animal that Leon had ever seen. Where once their eyes might have held a sort of natural intelligence now they glowed red and there was only an obvious unrelenting urge to kill, and they paused only long enough to catch their breath.

"Comark wolves," muttered Gaelnn, "I have never heard of them being this side of the Divide Mountains, and they seem obsessed with us or a few at least would have followed the horses."

Leon had his sword in his right hand and had wrapped his cloak around his left forearm. "It is me they seek. Watch their eyes." He moved a little to the side and all of the wolves followed his movement by shifting their bodies as if to follow.

With a great bound a huge gray wolf came at Leon. Moving instinctively, Leon transferred his sword to his left hand and launched a throwing knife at the throat of the huge beast. It crumpled into a heap at his feet, its spinal cord severed; it lay snapping until it stilled. Suddenly all of the pack was in motion. Leon quickly exhausted his knives and started swinging his sword, wishing for the first time that it were heavier and longer. They were soon surrounded by a mound of dying and dead wolves, but the pack was still numerous and still determined. Leon knew that eventually they must succumb to the rending of those hateful, slavering jaws. Then, as E'Alam had told him, he turned his thought to the pendant. The voice nearly shouted, *"Trust in our help!"* A spell of fire again came to his mind, though altered to burn in a ring. He grabbed the pendant and held it high, calling up a ring of fire around them through the pendant. Instantly a ring of blue fire erupted. Howls of disappointment and hate rose from the throats of the enraged wolves. Several tried to jump through the fire and turned instantly to ash. Slowly the fire spread out, gaining in intensity and pushing back the pack. Suddenly arrows flew out of the woods into the wolves with deadly, killing accuracy. Within minutes only dead wolves remained.

"Rangers!" yelled Gaelnn, happily.

Leon extinguished the fire, put the pendant away and turned to see a small group of tall rugged looking men clothed in forest colors emerge from the woods.

"Ho, Gaelnn," greeted the man leading the group, "What brings you to this part of the realm?"

"Flek, glad we are to see you. We were on our way to Old Home, and it was beginning to look like we might not get there," Gaelnn responded.

"From what I could see, it looked like your young mage here just about had everything under control." Flek was a large man, dressed all in forest colors, he was nearly as tall as the Elves, but much broader of shoulder, wore a close cut beard and had an ever so slight aura of the rogue about him. Leon liked him instantly.

Gaelnn turned to his companions, "Flek, this is Leon, apprentice to E'Alam, and his traveling companion and good friend, Prince Fallon. They have journeyed here from … ," here he paused for just an instant, "a far land to aid us in our fight against Xzuron. How is it that you happened to be here just when we needed you?"

Flek grasped the wrist of Fallon and then Leon with a warm clasp, "Welcome to the land of Val. Fighters such as you are more than welcome." Then, as if an afterthought, before letting go of Leon's wrist he said, "But you, Leon, you seek the Sword. May the one power grant that you find it for we sorely need it now." Then letting loose, he smiled at Leon's look of surprise and continued. "This pack of Comark wolves crossed over the Divides about seven days ago and we have been trying to corner them ever since, gathering men as we came, but they kept just ahead of us until this morning when they split up and took up a waiting stance on either side of this lava flow. They are an intelligent species, but this was more than we could fathom. We didn't dare attack just one half of the group out of fear of losing the other. They obviously had a mission because they passed many an opportunity to feed and kill which they usually do just for fun. Your arrival provided the answer, but it all happened so fast we nearly lost our chance to help. It would appear that Xzuron would rather see you dead than successful in your quest, and that alone is a good enough reason for us to help you all we can."

"How did you know?" asked Leon.

"It all seems pretty obvious to me. Xzuron is preparing to attack in the north, visitors from a distant land arrive and seek the Halls of Old Home. All of the pieces of the prophecies are falling into place. But come, we will accompany you the rest of the way. We have horses back in the woods and the three men whose horses you'll ride will go and find yours."

While the Rangers were getting their horses Leon and Fallon searched through the bodies of the wolves for their knives, cleaned them and secured them back in their hiding places. Finally, at an urging from the pendant, Leon raised the pendant and directed a flare of extreme fire at the dead wolves slowly turning to cover them all. Soon, all that remained of the wolves was ash. Quickly they mounted and headed on up the trail toward Old Home.

A large black crow with a red spot on its chest lifted into the approaching night, banked and with purposeful strokes flew north.

The last half league of the road was carved out of the steep, rock walls of a deep canyon. The Stead River flowed below them at the bottom of the canyon. A few scrubby pine trees clung to the sides of the rock walls. Various colored lichens and mosses brightened the otherwise drab world of gray rock and crevice. Leon began to hear the sound of cascading water, and as they rounded a bend in the trail he saw a waterfall that tumbled nearly two thousand feet into the bottom of the canyon. Mist made everything wet and the roar of the water was deafening. Around another bend and all signs of the waterfall were gone—no sound, no mist, nothing. The awesome power and beauty of the falls lingered in his mind as they rode on up the road.

As the light of day was fading into the black of night, the road led into a large open glen, and then disappeared into a huge cavern through a high wall built of cut stones each as high as three men. The wall was five stones high and in the center was a large metal door that stood open, but was guarded by several armed Dwarves.

As the mounted party neared the gate a gruff voice called out, "Who would enter the Halls of Old Home?"

Gaelnn responded, "I am Gaelnn, son of the Lord Chancellor of Val, and I bring with me friends from a distant land."

Only then did Leon notice that the rangers were no longer with them. Spinning around he just caught a glimpse of them as they disappeared back down the trail into the coming night. He turned to Gaelnn; "I would like to have thanked them for their help."

Gaelnn smiled, "It is not their way to wait for, or even expect thanks, and they are extremely uncomfortable in the confines of the underground halls of the Dwarves."

A distinguished looking elder Dwarf greeted them just inside the gate, "Greetings Gaelnn, you have been expected. He turned toward Leon and Fallon. I am Gathro, first advisor to Doranon, King of the Dwarves of Old Home. Please dismount and I will take you to meet with the king. He is looking forward to meeting you. Our people will care for your mounts." He bowed slightly and led them off as though it were perfectly normal for outsiders to visit these halls. He led them down wide, smokeless, torch-lit, corridors, deep into the heart of the mountain, where they entered a large chamber seemingly carved out of solid quartz which glimmered and shown with reflections from the many glowing spheres, that hung high on the walls. The walls reached nearly fifty paces high and were easily fifty paces from one side to the other. Columns that would take three men clasping hands to reach around lined the way straight through the center of the hall every twenty paces. The hall was easily a hundred paces long. The walls beyond the columns were decorated with ancient banners and shields such as the Dwarves use, and large tapestries depicting valiant exploits of their ancient heroes. The floors were polished to a near mirror finish and decorated, here and there, with colorful, thick woven rugs and furs. A single musical pipe could be heard in the background. At the end of their walk through the hall they found sitting amidst numerous pillows on a large, jewel encrusted throne the most ancient looking being Leon had ever seen. His skin was nearly transparent and the wrinkles of age gave his face the impression of immortality and a sense of great wisdom.

The three and their guide stopped about three steps in front of the King and dropped to one knee in respect.

"Stand, please stand," his gentle voice pleaded barely above a whisper, "for if your quest succeeds then I might be required to bend a knee to you and I am much too old. Come Gaelnn. You and your friends sit and tell me of your needs." The old King indicated stools covered with furs that were arranged in front of his throne.

Gaelnn responded, "Your Highness, this is Prince Fallon and Leon, E'Alam's apprentice. They come from a land far from here and seek to help us in the battle that is brewing in the north."

The old man smiled, "My friend, they come from a different world all-together. I have read the signs, and now it would appear to be the time of the prophecies. My guess is that it is you, Leon, who would seek the Sword. Am I correct?"

"Yes, your majesty. I little understand the whole picture, but I have been told that its power would help us to defeat the hoards from the north. And I have also been told that many have disappeared trying to recover it. I am willing to take that chance if it might enable me to help the people of VaLor', many of whom I have come to care for deeply."

"Are there no other reasons?"

"Well," Leon replied, his face turning slightly red, "I have become very much attracted to Gaelnn's sister Allece, something I believe he was unaware of until this minute, and I would do anything to keep her from harm."

"Both are worthy reasons. Are you aware that there are great responsibilities attached to the Sword?"

"I know only that it will bring some sort of power that could allow us to defeat the invading armies," said Leon.

The old King motioned Leon closer. After Leon had slid his stool over close to the King, the King took both of Leon's young hands in his ancient ones and stared long and hard into the young man's eyes. "Yes," he sighed, "the path will be thorny, but I can see that if you can retrieve the Sword, you have the metal within you to complete the task. I can tell you nothing of the path except where it begins since none but E'Alam have walked it and returned to tell the tale. And of course, E'Alam being a Wizard, tends to keep what he learns to himself. But I give you my blessing to make the attempt; and I hope that this truly is the time for bringing forth the Sword." He turned to Gathro, "Gathro, have my son Prince Doran see to it that our young warrior is led to the gate, that he may begin his quest." Turning back to Leon he said in his hoarse whisper, "May the power of the Stone guide your steps," and then he closed his eyes and drifted off to sleep.

Leon and Fallon were led to an adjacent chamber where they met Prince Doran, first son of Doranon. He was tall for a Dwarf, with a wealth of red hair and a beard that reached to the neck of his open shirt. He was muscular, as it seemed all Dwarves were, and tended to always have a smile on his round face. Down into the bowels of the mountain they went for what seemed like a league, through winding tunnels with low roofs and great halls with vaulted ceilings that were lost in the darkness beyond the light of their torches. Finally, after what seemed like a very long time, they entered a narrow cavern where, as far as the eye could see, lightly glowing crystals lit engraved stones set into the high walls above the lighting spheres. "The caverns of the dead," explained their guide. "Here it is that we lay our dead, families one above the other high above the light of the spheres. Each is entombed in a cubical behind their personally engraved stone. The engravings tell of the life of the one who rests within, thus ensuring a line of remembrance for our fathers that will remain unbroken as long as the mountain stands. This is only the first of many such chambers."

The Dwarf Prince led them nearly the full length of the chamber before he stopped in front of an apparently blank wall. He reached out and gently pushed on the wall. It swung open easily without any noise except the exchange of air. The air that came from within smelled stale, though not bad, rather as though it had not been disturbed for a very long time.

Leon turned to the Dwarf, "Thank you for your help." Then to Fallon, "Well friend, we part again."

Fallon took him by the shoulders, "I'll be here when you return. Go and do what you must."

Doran handed him a package and some torches in a bundle, "Here is some food and a water bottle for your pack. Our custom is to wait four days, and then assume that the quest has failed. Someone will be here to receive you should you succeed during that time."

Leon turned and entered the hallway; the door slid shut as silently as it had opened. He stood holding the torches that the Dwarf had given him. Already he felt lonely. He was surprised to find that the short hallway led to a flight of stairs, stairs that seemed to be molded out of the rock, for not a scratch or mark of a chisel could be seen anywhere. The walls were equally smooth and flush as the inside of a pipe. The stairs climbed at a steep angle, seeming to go straight up without an end in sight, their assent soon lost in the gloom of darkness beyond the glow of the torch. The torch flickered giving off a soft yet smokeless light. There were enough torches to last him for four days. But as efficient as they seemed to be, they were still a cumbersome bundle to carry. Leon pulled the pendant from beneath his shirt and its clean blue light lit up the stairs before him. He could just as easily have conjured light, but he preferred the pendant for it also gave him reassurance and comfort. He doused the torch and continued the climb, leaving the torches behind. The stairs were shallow and wide so they were not hard to climb, but they went on and on until he thought his legs would turn to mush. Higher and higher he climbed, stopping now and then to rest and eat some of the supplies from his pack. Time became a blur and no longer mattered. Exhaustion enveloped him. It seemed like days since he had slept but still he pushed on. When he began to think that he could go no further the stairs abruptly stopped and he found himself in a narrow level hallway. He sat down to rest, and slept even before he was fully down.

Beneath the mountain he will go,
In quest of secrets he must know.
Through perils great and perils small,
To seek the treasure sought by all.

Excerpts from the prophesies of Orn the Seer

CHAPTER TWELVE

The Watchers

E'Alam entered the council room and walked over to his accustomed chair. The council had gathered early that morning, as was their custom and now, as before, they were busily engaged in discussion of the coming war. He stood silently, looking at the assembled leaders and their advisors. Soon the noise level subsided and all looked at him.

"Leon has gone in search of the Sword. He left this morning. Now we must be ready to act when he returns. All of the leaders of the land must be at the gates of Old Home when he returns. I say when, instead of if, because I feel that he is The One. We should leave our generals and advisors here to plan mobilization, because it needs to be done whether he is The One or not. Providing all goes well we will have sufficient time to make the trip and be ready to greet him when he emerges from the mountain."

The council erupted in many voices all trying to talk at once.

E'Alam held up his hands, "Patience my friends, I only suspect he is the Chosen of the Stone. It would appear to me that all of the signs are met. You must decide if you accept the signs and are ready to follow me to Old Home, or reject those signs and stay. I leave within the hour and I have taken the freedom of advising your staffs to be ready should you decide to accompany me." Having said this he turned and walked from the room.

Doran strode purposefully back toward Fallon. He had left hours earlier to get them some food since Fallon refused to leave the wall. Now he returned with one arm carrying a pile of furs and the other a large reed basket. "Fallon, since you choose to remain here perhaps you should eat and then sleep. It could be some time before your friend returns. When E'Alam went in it took him four days to make the trip, and it should take Leon at least as long." He laid the furs on the stone floor and opened the basket, which contained delightful pastries, wedges of cheese and slices of meat still warm from the ovens. Suddenly Fallon was famished and gratefully dug into the feast set before him, nearly forgetting to express his heartfelt thanks to his host.

After his meal and a long drink of the excellent mead the Dwarves preferred as a national drink, he turned to Doran and asked, "Can you tell me anything more about my friend's quest, what it all means?"

Doran looked down the long chamber in silence for a moment. "Your friend searches for the Sword for the purpose of helping the peoples of VaLor'. Is this not so?"

"Aye, and of course there is the adventure that also drives him as it does me. We were trained in the arts of war in a land, at least temporarily at peace. And we wanted to reach out and apply our skills to a good cause. E'Alam seemed to offer us just that sort of challenge."

"Do you not know what being the bearer of the Sword means to the people of VaLor'?"

"Yes, that it will bring with it a great power, power sufficient to battle the hordes of Xzuron." responded Fallon.

"You have not read the prophecies then?" Doran asked quietly.

"We have been told that they existed, and given some understanding of them when we asked questions. But no, we have not seen them."

Doran paced a few steps away and back, then repeated the pacing, stopped and stared hard at Fallon. "The returning of the Sword, can only be done by the true and rightful High King, King of all VaLor'."

Fallon sat stunned, staring at the Dwarf Prince. Then he started to chuckle, and finally laugh out loud, a sound that these halls had not heard in many a generation. Then remembering where he sat, he regained control of himself and jumped to his feet. He laid a hand on the Dwarf's broad shoulder, "My friend, please excuse the affront to your dead. Now it all begins to make sense, the training, and the instruction in courtly etiquette and fashion. E'Alam knew all along, but wouldn't or couldn't say anything."

Doran's face beamed, "He truly went after the Sword not knowing?"

"Not only not knowing, but had he known he most likely would not have gone. The very thought of ruling a kingdom would have scared him off. He would be uncomfortable ruling a village, not that he couldn't do it if he had to. It's just that he would not seek to do it by choice."

"This but strengthens the probability that he is The One, for it is implied that the King would be of such a mind. The probabilities strengthen. I must go and report this to prepare my people. I shall be back. But you, Prince Fallon, should try to rest." So saying the dwarf hurried out of the long chamber leaving Fallon to his thoughts, which eventually shifted to the image of D'Nee.

Her striking beauty had haunted him from the first day he had seen her. Now, just closing his eyes brought her image to him, laughing and teasing in her easy way. They had often slipped away from the others on some pretext or other, usually to visit the stables and brush and curry her favorite mount. These little escapes had brought him closer to her, and to his great surprise she had shown equal pleasure in being with him. There was no pretense in her. She was open and free with her feelings, not hiding or holding back as might have been the case with the women from his home world. She was also shrewd when it came to the art of mounted warfare. But then, that was to be expected of the daughter of the Over Chieftain of the Planorian clans, and since it was the custom as youths, girls were trained as warriors right alongside the young men.

Fallon mulled over his part in this adventure, once again quietly chuckling at his friend's predicament. How would Leon take the idea of suddenly being crowned King over all of VaLor'? The Stone had played a fine joke on him. Still, others who had gone for the Sword had not returned. He hoped his friend was all right. Worried in spite of what he now knew, he drifted off to sleep.

A loud humming aroused Leon from his deep, recuperating sleep, *"Wake, be wary."* He sat up suddenly, searching for possible danger. Everything seemed to be as he had remembered it. Cautiously he stood up and peered into the gloom ahead. He had no idea how long he had slept, and except for slightly cramped and aching muscles in his legs, he felt quite refreshed. The intensity of the humming reduced once Leon was fully awake. Still, he felt the presence of danger.

Slowly he adjusted his pack and sword and started moving along the passageway. He had gone about a hundred paces when it opened into a large cavern. Light filtered in through large rents in the ceiling. The air was foul with the smell of carrion. His hand had gone automatically to his pendant, closing off its light. He tucked it back inside his shirt and crouched down just inside the passage until his eyes adjusted to the light in the cavern. The chamber was quite large, a seaming natural cavern. However, it was laced by a huge spider web, the strands varying from the thickness of his finger to the thickness of his wrist, and his path went right through the middle, under the web, to the other side where he could just make out the shape of another tunnel opening. High up at one of the rents in the ceiling a large bird, apparently attracted by the smell of carrion, had flown into one of the many web traps where it began thrashing in fear. Instantly a huge black spider launched itself on the prey from out of the shadows near the opening. In a minute the bird was encased in a cocoon of death to await the pleasure of its captor. Leon crouched, wondering how he would get through. He noticed bits of bone and armor that could only have been human remains lying casually in piles, along the side of the path.

He watched as the huge hairy spider returned to its hiding place. He was sure that spiders of normal size had very poor eyesight, but he wasn't sure of this monster. He studied the path for some time. Then slowly, quietly, he crept in and picked up a fallen helmet that lay just a few feet inside of the cavern, and quickly returned to his hiding place in the passage. Carefully picking a spot that was clear of webbing, he pitched the helmet to the side of the cavern. It rang loud when it hit the stone floor. Immediately the spider was out of its concealment staring at the helmet, then turned and stared at the spot where it had lain. With unbelievable speed it came to a web just over the spot where the helmet had been. Suddenly the web started bouncing violently as the spider sensed an intruder. Leon slipped silently back into the passage, cold sweat beading on flesh as fear quickly enshrouded his body. He crouched at the ready, sword out, his left hand reaching for the pendant under his shirt. When he touched it the fear eased and calmness returned. He slid his sword back into its scabbard and removed the small bag of Elven dust from his belt pouch, poured the contents into his hand and cast it over his head. The dust was very light and settled slowly onto his body. As he watched, his body seemed to blend into the rock that surrounded him. Next, he removed the pendant from his shirt, carefully keeping it covered with his hand until he had moved to the opening of the cavern. He then called on the pendant for bright light and stepped out. With a great screech the spider fumbled its way back up the web a short way. Promptly Leon covered up the pendant and started moving across the floor being careful to avoid the web while staying off the path. Leon moved as silently as he could. The huge spider followed, watching the path as it regained its confidence. It seemed to be following the sound, as slight as it was, of Leon walking. Suddenly it lurched forward and dropped to the ground directly in front of the passage Leon was headed for. It turned, apparently listening for the intruder.

"So you would force a fight would you?" said Leon out loud.

Surprisingly, a high screeching voice came back to him, "Your trickses won't fool me mortal. I will feeds on your boneses just as I have all the otherses. Come, join the verminses that has dared to enter my lair. My master Xzuron will be pleased that I have stopped one suches ases you."

Leon now stood just a short distance from the great hairy thing. It was getting ready to spring when Leon's first knife found its mark deep in a huge multifaceted eye. Before the shock had completely sunk in, the other eye was hit, and in a heartbeat Leon's sword found its way deep into the huge body. Screeching a hideous cry it tried to reach out and catch its attacker. Leon was barely able to avoid its grasp as he darted first one way and then another. Spreading black body fluids, it surged once more toward him and fell still at his feet. Leon stood back, watching for long moments before retrieving his weapons. Then he turned and looked around him. Little piles of weapons, with a few bones mingled in amongst them, lay scattered around the passageway. Brave warriors had died within a few steps of safety. Silently he entered the passage, shaken but wary now of what might lie ahead.

The passage rose at a slight incline. Soon all light from the rift in the ceiling of the cavern was gone, and Leon wished he had kept the torches burning. Then at least he would have an idea how much time had passed. After what seemed like, at least a league he stopped to eat and rest, then continued on up the ramp-like passage. He came to a fork in the passage. Both branches looked alike and he could not decide which to choose. Finally he walked into the fork on the left. Just a few steps in the pendant began humming, causing him to stop. He started to retrace his steps but curiosity overcame his fear. He called on the pendant to help him and then crept slowly forward. Not many paces into the passage he noticed two lines in the thin layer of dust that covered the stone floor. The lines ran across the passage before him. He took out his sword and pressed down on the ground the other side of the line, then watched, amazed, as the floor pivoted down exposing a hole that appeared to have no bottom it was so deep. When he removed the sword the block swung back up into position. Now it was visible due to the lack of dust that had slid off into the hole. Thanking the guidance of the pendant he retraced his steps to the fork. Once there he removed a knife from his sleeve and scratched a rough drawing of the trap door on the wall with an arrow pointing into the tunnel.

Then he turned into the right-hand branch and continued up the slight slope until it led into a small room. Standing here and there about the room were seven life-like statues all frozen in mid stride. They appeared to be ancient warriors all captured by some great sculptor in a most life like manner. On either side of the room exactly in the center stood two large manlike statues, their heads nearly touching the ceiling. They had no face with the exception of a single eye that seemed to look straight across the room into the eye of the other, yet at the same time seeming to see the whole room. In the wall opposite Leon was a metal bound door, apparently the only other way out. As Leon started toward the door a beam of light suddenly emitted from both of the statues at the same moment. They converged on him spreading out to encompass his whole body. Leon could feel his flesh tingling. Then, as suddenly as it had begun it stopped and the light drew back into the statues. Feeling no real reason to fear, and lacking an alarm from the pendant, he walked slowly to the door. There was no handle. He pushed and tried to pry with his fingers and then one of his knives, all without success. Exasperated he stood back and studied the door for several minutes. Finally, about shoulder high he saw a slight indentation, matching the shape of his pendant. Could it be so simple? Slowly he placed his pendant up against the indent. The door slid silently open.

The passage beyond was short, no more than a healthy stone's throw. As Leon entered he could see an orange light at the end. Slowly he crept toward the light noting that as he went forward the temperature increased until it was like standing out in the sunlight on a very hot summer day. He crept slowly forward until he could see in. Below him was a large chamber that appeared to be a chimney for the long dormant volcano that had made these mountains sometime in the lost ages of the past. Directly in the center was a hole glowing red with the heat from the heart of the earth, and above it a flue rose out of the top of the chamber carrying most of the heat with it. The walls of the chamber were smooth as glass and probably were formed when the mountain was molten.

The room had been a bubble in the molten lava and was formed when the mountain was being born. The floor was flat and halfway between Leon and the fiery hole slept a very large dragon, its body completely encircling a stone table. Directly in the center of the table lay a sword and an ornate scabbard. The distance was so great that he couldn't make out any details, but he knew this was the sword he sought. The body of the dragon was a nearly transparent, red in color and it rippled with the movement of its breathing, its claws sheathing and unsheathing in its sleep like a cat. Fangs, the size of a man's arm, gleamed in the yellowish orange light. Every so often the tip of its tail would flip and then settle down once more as it slumbered.

> *From Hall of Death he now must go.*
> *Through test and trial he will grow.*
> *Until at last in Stead's deep heart*
> *He'll grasp the mission and his part.*
> *And know, at last, why he must stay*
> *And what the role is he must play.*

Excerpt from the prophesies of Orn the Seer

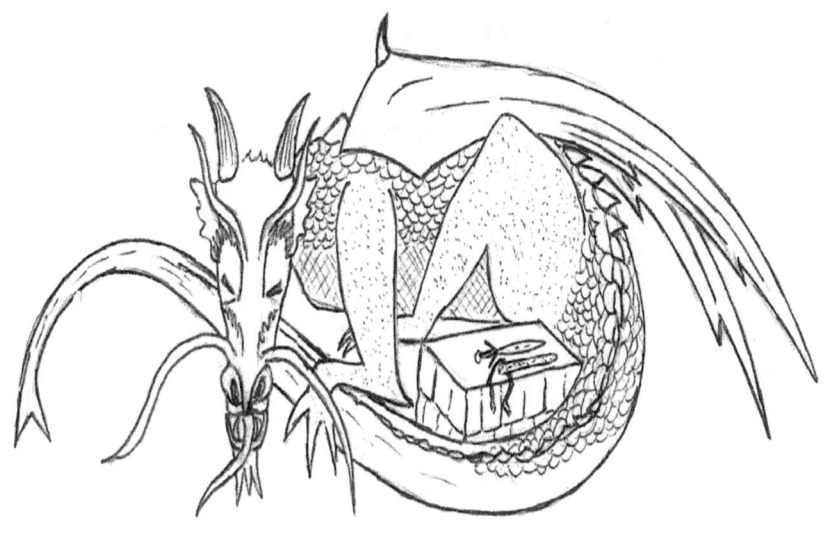

CHAPTER THIRTEEN

The Wyrm and the Sword

Leon stood for some time staring at the beauty and power of this thing that kept him from his goal. Then he sat quietly down against the wall just inside of the passage where he could still see the table, determined to watch until a way to approach the table might come to him.

A sudden wash of hot air brought Leon abruptly awake. Panicking, he realized that he had fallen asleep. Opening his eyes he saw the great head of the Dragon, poised not an arm length in front of him.

A deep rumbling voice, said, **"SO, IT IS A HUMAN UNDER ALL OF THAT ELVEN INVISIBILITY DUST."**

Leon scrambled to his feet and drew his sword, but he neither attacked nor fled. For some reason he felt no fear, only surprise. His pendant was quiet, and had there been any real danger surely the pendant would have been humming its warning. "Greetings," he said, "you are another of the little surprises that they neglected to tell me about."

"AH, THE OFF WORLDER HAS COME AT LAST, A LITTLE SHORT OF MANNERS PERHAPS, BUT DEFINITELY NOT OF THIS WORLD. DO YOU INTEND TO STICK ME WITH THAT PUNY LITTLE STICKER OF YOURS? I CAN WARN YOU NOW THAT IT WON'T EVEN SCRATCH MY HIDE."

Leon fumbled his sword back into its scabbard and grinned in embarrassment. "I didn't mean to cause you affront. I was merely surprised, and since I have come on this little foray, a sword in hand was often of more value than one in its scabbard. How did you know I wasn't of this world?" And then in after thought, "I am Leon, and yes I am from a different world, Ganor to be precise."

"WELL, LEON OF GANOR, NICE TO MEET YOU. I AM GORATH, SOMETIMES KNOWN AS THE DRAGON OR WYRM OF MOUNT STEAD. AND AS TO YOUR QUESTION, WERE YOU OF THIS WORLD YOU WOULD NOT HAVE MADE IT PAST THE GUARDIANS. YOU WOULD RESIDE NOW IN THE OUTER CHAMBER AS A HIGHLY LIFELIKE STATUE UNTIL THE OFF WORLDER CAME TO SET YOU FREE."

"How is it that you know so much about me?"

"I HAVE BEEN AWAITING YOUR ARRIVAL SINCE THE SWORD WAS CAST. I AM YOUR MOUNT IN THE WAR THAT COMES. THE OPENING OF THE DOOR TO MY CHAMBER BROUGHT ME OUT OF THE MAGICAL SLEEP THAT I HAVE ENDURED FOR ALL THESE AGES. I HAVE BEEN AWARE OF WHAT WAS TAKING PLACE, BUT AT THE SAME TIME USUALLY, BUT NOT ALWAYS, ASLEEP—IN A TRANCE, MUCH LIKE DREAMING."

"So much has happened that I can't understand," Leon said, not sure why he was talking so freely to this ... Dragon.

"YES, I SEE. IT WAS NECESSARY TO KEEP YOU IN THE DARK, AS IT WERE, TO ASSURE THAT YOU CAME AFTER THE SWORD FOR THE PROPER REASONS, AND NOT FOR THE POWER IT WOULD BRING YOU."

"I want no power except that which will help the people of VaLor' to fight against their enemy."

"WANT IT OR NOT, YOU ARE STUCK WITH IT THE MINUTE YOU PICK UP THAT SWORD. BUT DON'T WORRY, YOU WILL BE ABLE TO HANDLE IT. NOW GO AHEAD AND PICK IT UP SO WE CAN BE ABOUT OUR TASK. I AM ANXIOUS TO GET OUT OF THIS CAVE AGAIN, AND PLEASE BRUSH OFF THAT DUST. I GUARANTEE YOU, FROM NOW ON YOU WILL WANT TO BE SEEN, AT LEAST FOR A TIME."

Leon walked down a flight of stairs to the floor level as he brushed himself off, then slowly, haltingly, moved toward the stone table and the sword that lay upon it. Both scabbard and sword were etched with intricate designs that he could not begin to read, and the pommel was topped with a large blue jewel the same color as his pendant. Almost reverently he reached out for the sword and it leapt into his hand. Then, as though he had known the ancient language all of his life, the inscriptions became perfectly clear to him. His body tingled and felt suddenly full of life and he knew. Yes! This was the purpose for which he had been born. He held the Sword out and felt its balance. He marveled at its craftsmanship, and honored the smiths who had molded it from simple materials of the earth, to the thing of perfection that he held in his hand.

"WELL, ARE YOU GOING TO STAND THERE ALL DAY LOOKING AT IT, OR ARE YOU GOING TO GET ABOUT THE BUSINESS OF USING IT?"

Leon nearly jumped as he came back to himself. Grinning foolishly he replied, "It really is a very special Sword, but it seems that I do have certain duties to perform, starting with the freeing of those poor souls in the outer chamber. Then I must try to tell Fallon of my change in plans, for I'm sure he waits for me still in the hall of the dead. I'll be back in a few minutes." He turned and climbed back up to the passage, through the door and into the chamber of the guardians. As before, a sudden light came from the eyes of the guardians, but this time Leon held up the Sword, somehow knowing exactly what to do. The light from the eyes of the guardians hit the jewel on the pommel of the Sword and changed into a rainbow of color, and in an instant those who had stood as statues for generations shook themselves as though they were waking up, looked at Leon, the Sword and one another. Then they dropped to their knees before him. "Quickly now," he said. "It is time for you to return to the land of the living. VaLor' has need of you. Come. For today we ride a Dragon." He continued to hold the Sword up as each of the seven—four men an Elf and two dwarfs—who had appeared to be stone but moments before, went through the door into the hall of the Dragon. Leon followed.

As Leon entered the dragon's hall he noticed the seven warriors talking in a group to the left of the passage, while Gorath looked on in what seemed to be amusement.

He brought the pendant up before his eyes and thought hard of Fallon. Soon, in his mind, he saw his friend sitting, waiting for his return. He thought *"Fallon, I return by another way. I shall soon be at the gates,"* Leon spoke the words in his mind. His friend's head snapped up and looked directly at him. Then he nodded, stood up, gathered his things and hurried away. Leon returned his concentration to the hall of the Dragon.

He strode purposefully toward the seven warriors saying, "I am called Leon. How may I address you?"

Of the seven, two were Dwarves, one was an Elf, three appeared to be VaLor'ians and the last was a tall man of obvious great physical strength and very dark skin. He wore strange armor decorated with feathers and carved bones. As one man the seven dropped to one knee and dipped their heads. Then the dark man spoke. "Though we were all of high station in our home lands, our names have been forgotten for many generations, and so it will remain. You may call me Shadow, for it is such that I would be. We have stood in a state of dreaming, somehow aware of the tides of time and events that have flowed through VaLor', living, but not aging, asleep, but not waking for all these many years. Each of us came here in different ages of the past three hundred years to seek the Sword, to aid our peoples in battles that have long since been forgotten. Now, if you would have us, we would serve you as your personal bodyguard in the war that approaches from the north. We seek but the chance to die with honor among other warriors of VaLor'."

Leon turned and walked slowly toward the stone table. He stopped, removed his old sword and its scabbard, fastened on the new scabbard and slid home the Sword of VaLor'. He stood in deep thought for some moments thinking of the dedication of these men. He turned and said, "So be it. You shall be my shadows until this war is over. I only pray that it will not cost you your lives, but I must call you something, so you shall be Shadow Number One, and the others shall have numbers as well." Turning toward the dragon he said, "This magnificent creature is Gorath, and he wishes us to hurry and get on with our task. It seems that, for the most part, he too has lain here in a state of semi-sleep and would once again experience the feeling of wind against his wings." He tossed his old sword to Number One and turned to mount the Dragon, the others quickly following.

The bumps on the dragon's back made perfect saddles, and by gripping its scales with their hands they felt at least somewhat secure. **"HOLD YOUR BREATH AS WE GO UP THE BLOW HOLE. THE AIR WILL BE HOT, AND THERE MIGHT BE GASSES THAT WOULD HARM YOU. IT SHOULD ONLY TAKE A MOMENT TO REACH THE TOP."** Then with a great flapping jump Gorath lifted them up and flew toward the hole in the roof.

The test He'll pass of ancient lore,
And take to hand the sword VaLor'.

Then free from stone the warriors' might,
And lead them from the guardian's sight.

From all the land they witness when,
He'll ride the wyrm, that flies again.

Excerpts from the Prophesies of Orn the Seer

CHAPTER FOURTEEN

Coming Of The King

E'Alam and the assembled leaders of free VaLor' stood at the gates of Old Home waiting for something to happen. It was evening, and though the sun had long since hid behind the tops of the surrounding peaks, there remained plenty of defused light. So it would be for several more hours. The two day trip to Old Home had been quickly organized and quickly taken; now a certain look of impatience could be seen in the faces of all who waited. They stared at the huge open gateway, as if by their will alone something might be happen.

The sound of the wind made them turn their faces upward, and then, torn between fear and wonder, they stood gaping at the sight.

As Gorath flew closer the horses grew agitated. Seeing this he settled down some distance from the gates where Leon and his guard climbed down. E'Alam on Windwalker approached at a gallop, coming to a halt a few feet away from Leon, Windwalker seeming perfectly at ease in the presence of the Dragon.

Gorath dropped his head close to Leon, **"I MUST GO AND SEE TO THE REQUIREMENTS OF MY STOMACH. IF YOU**

NEED ME JUST CALL AND I WILL RETURN, BUT FOR NOW MY PRESENCE IS MORE A NOISOME DISTRACTION THAN AN AID."

"Aye, so it seems. I hope that appeasing your appetite won't include the demise of too many poor farmers' cows. Happy hunting."

Abruptly, with a great thrust of its massive wings, the huge creature lifted into the sky and turned toward the western peaks, gaining unbelievable speed as he went. He soon disappeared toward the setting sun.

E'Alam stepped to Leon's side and led him at a fast walk toward the assembled council, "Now comes the most difficult part for you. Come, I would introduce you to your subjects."

Leon stopped dead in his tracks, "My what?"

With mirth in his voice, E'Alam responded, "Come. Don't stand there with your mouth open. You are the Sword Bearer." A slight pressure on Leon's elbow had him moving forward again, though haltingly. They were nearly to the waiting assembly when E'Alam urged. "Remove the Sword and hold it point up before you." They stopped and Leon did as he was instructed. E'Alam raised his voice trumpeting, "Leaders of VaLor', I give you, the Sword Bearer. I give you the High King of VaLor', King Leon." In the next breath the only one left standing on the field was Leon, Sword outstretched.

Stunned, he stood before the assembled VaLor'ian leaders and the steadily increasing number of Dwarfs. Then lowering the Sword, which suddenly seemed to weigh as much as an anvil, his knees suddenly so weak he nearly collapsed, he said, "Please stand." As they stood they began cheering and continued to cheer until the crescendo of their many voices filled the valley, echoing off the steep walls and reverberating down the canyons. Leon's knees felt weaker still. He grabbed for E'Alam to steady himself and in a small voice said, "What have you done? You know I have no desire for this sort of thing."

The wizard smiled and spoke softly, "That is the very reason the Stone chose you for the job. Smile. Want it or not, these people and their fathers before them have been waiting for you for many generations. Relax, you'll be all right. I have trained you as well as I could in the short time we had. If you rely on the Stone, your good sense, your training and your heart, you will do fine. Good advisers like Prince Fallon and Gaelnn will be a great help."

Leon held up his hands for quiet as a litter, born by stout Dwarves approached from the gates of Old Home. Seated upon it was the aging King of the Dwarves. The assembly parted to allow the litter through and soon it halted before the still stunned, new, High King. The bearers set the litter down and Leon stepped over to be closer to the ancient King.

"Your Majesty," said Leon, "you need not have come out. I would gladly have come to you."

"Please excuse me for not kneeling my Liege. I warned you it might happen that my turn to kneel would come, and it would be difficult for me to do." The old king chuckled. He then reached down, with difficulty, and picked up a large roll of sealed, finely tanned hides and handed it to Leon. "This is for you. It has been passed down through the ages of my line to be placed in the hand of the High King."

Leon took the package and gently broke the seal on one end and slid out the contents. With near reverence and the help of E'Alam he unrolled a bright yellow banner. It was half as wide as Leon was tall, and twice as long as he was tall. Across the field of bright yellow stretched a red Dragon, and diagonally across the dragon was a semblance of the Sword of VaLor'. One of the old King's attendants quickly produced a stout standard which he had brought, and helped to fasten the banner to it.

Shadow Number One stepped forward, "With your permission Sire." At Leon's nod he gripped the pole and raised the banner high into the air. Once again a tumultuous cheer rose from the throats of the assembled leaders and the many hundreds of Dwarves that had gathered to watch.

Out through the gathered throng burst Fallon and Doran, barley stopping short of colliding with the assembled dignitaries of the counsel. Gathering what decorum they could under the circumstances, and still breathing hard from the exertions of their trip up from the caverns of the dead, they walked over to Leon.

"Would someone mind filling us in on just exactly what all the cheering is about?" asked Fallon.

E'Alam grinning, responded, "Prince Fallon and Prince Doran, allow me to present the Sword Bearer, Leon, High King of VaLor'."

Fallon and Doran quickly dropped to one knee, "I knew you couldn't stay out of trouble," whispered Fallon.

Laughing Leon said, "Up you two!" Then turning to the rapidly growing crowd he raised his voice, "Hence forth the custom of kneeling will not be required, encouraged or expected. It would please me if this decree were carried throughout the Land."

"I'm afraid that even threats of the headsman's ax would find that decree hard to enforce," chuckled E'Alam, "They have waited and hoped for far too long. Now they must show their love, for the title if not for you personally. Relax. The awe will soon wear off. I have taken the liberty of arranging for boats to be waiting for us for the trip across the plains. It will save us over a day. We must hurry on. If we ride through the night we should be in Val by this time tomorrow."

"That sounds fine. Where is Lea'Oen? I expected to see him with the council!"

"He has taken it upon himself to go to the Dark Wood for a first hand look at the conditions there. Knowing we could contact him through the pendants, he should be there about the time our army is ready to leave Val."

The trip back down the road to where it branched toward the Stead River was nearly all done in the fading light of evening. Darkness, however, covered them for some time before they reached the river.

The Shadow troop had taken up positions in front, on either side and behind Leon where they vigorously assumed their task of guarding him. Fallon and even E'Alam had to get permission to ride close to their friend. Leon finally stopped the procession and assured Number One that he must have room to breathe, and that these two and Gaelnn were his closest friends and advisors and that the guard was to allow them access whenever it was requested. After that E'Alam and the three young friends were given a little more room, but the Shadow troop still kept a close vigilance.

Torchlight and the sound of music and laughter told them the location of the river landing long before they reached it. Silently Gaelnn and Number One slipped into the night ahead of the procession. Soon a shout went up and a great clamor of people running here and there replaced the laughter and music, and by the time the procession reached the landing, the crews of the barges were in place ready to cast off. Number One had reassumed his place at the head of the procession and unrolled the banner. When they entered the light of the torches, a deep silence greeted them, at first and then a shout erupted as though it were on cue.

E'Alam nudged Leon forward.

Leon moved to the front. Then standing in his stirrups held up his hands for silence, "Peace my friends. I appreciate your welcome, but there is much need for haste. Can we travel the river by night?"

A great, bulky man with as red a beard as Leon had ever seen, wearing a bandanna around his head, large gold earrings and clothes as bright and colorful as a rainbow stepped forward. "I be Vistag, Chief of the Water People, and if it would please ye, I could lead this flotilla down-river blindfolded and barely standing from drink. But as I am now sober, I would be doubly pleased to lead the way. Your wish is my command, my King."

And so the flotilla headed downstream. Men and horses traveling at the speed of the river, each barge maneuvered by long sweeps that answered quickly to the orders of the pilot, who was continually instructed by Vistag. Lanterns at each bow and stern kept the flotilla in line, and even though the night was as dark as tar the barges flew along, swift and sure toward the dawn and Val.

Leon stood shrouded in darkness just outside the glow of the bow lantern. His body was immersed in fatigue but his mind raced along, pursuing the events that had taken place in the last few days. He felt like a leaf adrift on a stream being pushed this way and that with no control over the direction, or the speed. He also felt the weight of the responsibility that had been placed upon him; his mind burned with fear that he would not be up to the task, but his heart, his inner being, felt great excitement and told him that he had to try. And yes, he must succeed. By taking up of the Sword, his life had been tied to this land in a way that he had never imagined. There was no longer any question of duty, only his own doubt in his ability to do what would be asked of him.

"Be assured by the knowledge that the Stone picked you. You but need to ask and we will help when we can."

Out of the darkness stepped E'Alam "Come, even kings must sleep." The Wizard led him to a pile of furs and gently eased him down. Then, placing his hand over Leon's eyes he spoke of sleep, and the young King did so, immediately.

The sun was high in the late morning sky when Leon finally woke. The ever-present Shadow troop had rigged an awning over him and kept the noise down as much as possible. He felt refreshed but terribly hungry. As soon as they saw him stir Number One presented him with a tray heaped with enough to feed the whole Shadow troop. He smiled to himself and promptly attempted to eat it all. He very nearly succeeded.

The boats were nothing like the galleys that plied the coasts of his homeland. These were very wide and flat with a high platform at the stern from which the pilot gave directions. They were brightly colored, with gaily-painted figures and scenes on every imaginable flat surface. There was a mast, not very tall, that held two garishly colored triangular sails which billowed out to either side and pushed the boat downriver even faster than the current, as long as the wind was from the direction of the stern, and they had a centerboard that could be let down or raised as the need arose. With a wizard as skilled as E'Alam along, the wind always seemed to blow from the stern.

The men who manned the sweeps and handled the boats were a vibrantly happy people who laughed easily and often broke out in song as they worked. Their loose fitting clothing was as bright as their leader's with gold chains much in evidence. There were no women on the boats and when Leon inquired about this he was told that the women stayed at their village when their men traveled the rivers.

The river was quite wide as it flowed through the plains. Grasslands spread from the water's edge as far as the eye could see, even when standing on the elevated stern platform. Leon spent about an hour watching the water and the shore speeding by. Then, knowing he was wasting valuable time, he called for a war council of all of those who were aboard his vessel. As the day wore on they discussed the various aspects of the coming war, from assembling manpower to feeding of the gathered troops, both stationary and on the move. They talked of mounted troops and archers, of pike men and swordsmen, and they spoke of supplies and the strength of East Fort. They drew rough maps and spoke of little known trails. Though no actual battle plans were made ideas began to form in the mind of Leon, and, like a sprouting seed, slowly took shape. Fallon proved invaluable as he gave freely of his training in the strategy of making war.

As evening approached Leon and Fallon stood conversing at the bow of the boat where they could be more or less alone for awhile, even though three of the Shadows stood less than two steps away.

They were deeply engaged in evaluating the strengths and weaknesses of the soon to be assembled army of the VaLor'ians when the boat sped around the last bend in the river. There, before them stood beautiful Val sparkling in the rays of the setting sun. Leon felt a sudden surge of joy sweep through him at the very sight of the city and his thoughts quickly jumped to Allece.

Without warning a tight beam of blue light flashed from the crystalline dome of the Hall of the King, touched them for just an instant, then vanished.

"It would truly be hard for you to sneak into that city," laughed Fallon, as a cheer went up from the boatmen. It was clear they had been waiting for this to happen.

"How is it that others always seem to know something that we don't," murmured Leon.

E'Alam and Gaelnn quickly approached, "We will soon be at the landing," said E'Alam. "I suspect there will be a bit of a crowd waiting, so we will mount and ride off the boat with your guard close around us. I have assembled a selection of flashy armor from amongst the councilors to make you look a bit more kingly. After all, now you must make an impression."

Leon groaned aloud and turned to the armor, "How did they know this time?"

Gaelnn responded, "This time they were expecting you. The last time you entered the city, only E'Alam suspected who you were."

As the boats approached the landing a huge throng of people could be seen lining the landings and the road up into the walled city. Leon felt overwhelmed. All he wanted was to hide and perhaps sneak in later. He was embarrassed and unsure of how he would handle the whole affair.

Fallon gripped his elbow, "This is the hardest part. I have seen it often, and as long as you feel this way you will be all right. If you ever start wanting it or expecting it, then you need to examine your motives. Just remember to wave and smile and nod your head. You'll do fine."

Soon they were mounted, off the barge and winding their way up the wide cobblestone road into the city. Leon had never seen so many people. He waved and smiled until he thought he must scream at the pain of smiling.

Neatly uniformed guards, who did an excellent job of holding back the cheering crowd, lined the road through the throng. At last the gates of the palace came into view and behind them, the peace and quiet Leon sought … or so he thought.

Fully armed and mounted, the palace guard blocked the entrance to the palace grounds and, unlike the guards of the streets of Val, refused to give ground to the approaching new King and his retinue. There he sat, surrounded by the leaders of all of VaLor', unable to enter the gates. The Captain of the Guard urged his mount forward and in a loud voice demanded, "Who is this that comes to the palace of the King?"

E'Alam, who had been speaking in low tones with Shadow Number One, now nodded him forward. Number One, banner un-furled, urged his mount to the front of the column, then replied in a loud voice, "The High King of VaLor' comes to claim his throne."

"What proof do you have that would verify this claim?" responded the Captain.

Standing tall in the stirrup, flag held high, the shadow replied in his resounding voice, "I, for one, am one of those who were frozen as in stone for generations and he has set us free. Secondly, I had the honor to ride the wind with him on the great dragon Gorath, wyrm of the Stead Mountains. And lastly and most importantly, he has recovered and now carries the Sword of VaLor'."

E'Alam had leaned close to Leon, "Bring forth the Sword and hold it high," he prompted. Leon did as he was instructed.

The Captain spun his horse around to face the guards and the many occupants of the palace that had come to witness the coming of the King. In a thundering voice announced, "THE KING HAS COME!" As one man the guard dismounted and dropped to one knee, then stepped back leaving a path through to the gate, which swung slowly open. Standing just inside the gates were the Chancellor and all of those who had remained at the palace. As one, they dropped to a knee, and then stood again. The Chancellor walked toward Leon. He stopped, bowed his head and said, "I and my ancestors have kept your house for your coming. May it please you to accept that which we have done."

Leon returned the Sword to its scabbard and responded loudly, "I am sure I will find satisfaction with all that you have done!" Then in a small voice that only the Lord Chancellor could hear, "Can we please get this over with? I hate being the object of so much attention."

The Lord Chancellor smiled knowingly. Then he quietly responded, "I think we can hurry this along a bit," Then he turned and shouted, "MAKE WAY FOR THE KING!" and quickly led the way to the palace.

Once inside, Leon and the whole company were hurried to the council hall where drapes across one end had been drawn aside, revealing an ornate throne to which Leon was escorted. After Leon had gone through a solemn ceremony where he proclaimed his desire to serve VaLor' and uphold its traditions and its people, the Lord Chancellor placed a delicate gold crown on his head. Then all were dismissed to reconvene in the morning.

At last Leon, the Lord Chancellor, Allece, Gaelnn, E'Alam, Fallon and the Shadows were all that remained. Leon quickly jumped off the throne as if it had burned him. He removed the crown and turned to Lord Leando, "Thank you for trying to hurry that along. I really was uncomfortable."

"I could see this was so, my King. How may I be of service to you now that my job is done?" smiled the Lord Chancellor.

With a trace of panic in his voice Leon said, "I see no reason to discontinue the office of Chancellor, and I know of no one better qualified to continue to run this state and act as my chief advisor." He looked at E'Alam and Fallon for reinforcement. They smiled at his discomfort and nodded their approval. He turned to the Lord Chancellor again, "Since it seems I must have Number One and his comrades near me at all times, could you see to it that they are comfortable?" He turned to Number One, "In the palace at least, only one of you need be by me, and then only when I am out of my personal chambers, and alone." The Shadows nodded in unison, and followed the Lord Chancellor out of the hall.

Leon turned to the others, "Now, can we please get back to some form of normalcy?"

"Not likely my friend," Fallon responded grinning from ear to ear. "No, I think things will never again be as simple as they once were, nor as boring either."

"The hour is late," said E'Alam, "and we will need to be rested for the council meeting in the morning, so perhaps we should find our beds. Gaelnn, could you show our new King to his quarters."

E'Alam turned, leading Fallon and a hesitating Allece from the Hall.

"Well," said Gaelnn, "come, you'll enjoy this."

Just a few doors from the throne room, Gaelnn paused before a large door with shadow guards at either side, "This is the Royal bedroom suite." He pushed open the beautifully carved dark wood doors and led Leon in.

Reluctant he'll ascend the throne,
And King he'll be, raised by the Stone.

Excerpt from the Prophesies of Orn

CHAPTER FIFTEEN

Planing and Parting

The King's bedroom suite was beyond Leon's grandest imaginings. It was huge, three times the size of the entire smithy where he had spent so much of his youth. Rich, wood paneled walls, lush tapestries and magnificent gold inlaid furnishings surrounded him. Luxurious carpets were placed in appropriate places on the highly polished hardwood floors. There was a mammoth fireplace on the right wall and on the left, a bed larger than any he had ever seen. Framing the bed on either side hung lush heavy red drapes that reached from the fourteen foot high ceiling to floor. Across the room before him, high windows looked out onto a wide balcony that was suspended out over the gardens he had walked in with Allece so long ago, at least it seemed a long time. He turned to Gaelnn, "Is this real?"

Gaelnn grinned, "I'm afraid so."

Leon stared around in disbelief. "It's quite grand, but it has the feel of a rather beautiful, rather secure, cage. This whole life is so restricting I can hardly breathe. How do they survive, those who live like this?"

"For the most part they get quite used to it, as I'm sure you will."

"But … the lack of privacy, the inability to do anything without someone watching and guarding you from who knows what."

"Even here in the palace, you are not totally safe. There are those who follow the wishes of Xzuron and would kill you in a moment if they could get near you. So be cautious at all times, and your guards will do the same. Hopefully, that will be enough."

A light rap on the door caused them both to turn toward it.

"Enter," called Leon.

A small man entered carrying a rather large bowl of steaming water. With difficulty he made a slight bow, "Perhaps your Majesty would like to wash a bit before you retire." It was more a statement than a question.

Gaelnn turned to Leon, "This is Platen your manservant. It is customary that you have one. He will help you with all of your personal needs from what you should wear on which occasion, to when you eat, sleep or dance. All of this will soon become second nature to you making his job less demanding. In the meantime I will try to be around should you need my services." With that, forcing himself to hold back the grin that was coming, he turned and left a stammering King Leon in the capable hands of Platen.

It was some time later, after much difficulty, Leon managed to convince the determined Platen that he could indeed wash himself, dress himself for bed, and then when he was ready for bed, get in unaided. Also, he really did appreciate the small man's obvious talents as a manservant and, again, he truly was not ready for bed … yet. He finally managed to usher the little man from his chambers.

The slight movement of the heavy ceiling to floor drapes at the right of the bed had caught his attention, but since there was no warning from his pendant he was more curious than alarmed. Quietly he walked to the drape and in a quick movement flung them back. Allece stood there, hand over her mouth to keep from giggling out loud. Now that she was found her merry laughter spilled out, causing him a little embarrassment at the knowledge that she had witnessed his discomfort at the hands of Platen.

"How did you get in here?" he asked in mock anger.

"Oh please, your Royal Highness," she responded feigning fear. "I am but a poor serving girl driven here by my desire to see so great a personage as yourself." Then she stepped forward into his waiting arms. After a long embrace, and just before the fires within them became uncontrollable, she gently pushed herself back and said, "Come, I will show you how the kings of old often frustrated their guards. It's a little secret only a palace brat would have had the time to unravel." She turned and placed her hand on a stone in the wall about shoulder high and pressed, the wall next to it swung silently open revealing a narrow passageway. She slid into the opening pulling him along behind her. Then, uncovering a softly glowing sphere, she turned and slid the door shut. She pointed to the trigger stone, "This is the trip stone to allow you back in." Then she led the way down a narrow flight of stairs. When they reached the bottom she whispered, as she pointed, "This is the trigger stone to this door, and here is an eye hole to check the garden before you step out." She looked through the hole, and then opened the door. They stepped out into the garden. Soft lamplight lit the surrounding area with a gentle glow. She indicated the outer trigger stone, and then led him into a denser part of the garden. "Now, tell me all that happened. I am bursting to hear about it."

They sat on a finely sculpted bench beneath flowering trees. He held her hands in his as he related all that had happened. After concluding the tale he told her how he had missed her and how uncomfortable he felt in his new role, then concluded with his vow to proceed to do whatever he must to preserve the people of VaLor'. They spoke of little things, each captivated by the other to such a degree that what they said mattered little, so long as they were together.

Suddenly Leon became aware of the pendant humming, loudly. *"Beware! There is danger above."* How long the intensity of the humming had been building he could only guess, though he knew that it had been but a very short time. The voice was insistent.

"Quickly," he said, "get behind the bench and keep down."

He looked up through the trees into the dark night. *"Use us, hold up the pendant."* The voice was stronger than it had ever been. Grasping his pendant he projected his desire for better vision and in an instant could see the huge bat-like creature hovering above the trees, its dark passenger searching the lush vegetation with great patience. It spotted Leon and before Leon could react, it cast a bolt of energy at him. The force threw Leon back. His pendant had thrown up its defensive shield, he was jarred but unhurt. Once again a bolt of energy arched down at him. Leon held the pendant out in front of him and called on the pendant to reflect the charge back at the tordaq and its rider. With a scream of pure surprised pain, the bat creature tumbled into the garden and lay thrashing in agony, smoke rising from its charred flesh. The dark rider stood unharmed and turned again to face Leon. With a flick of his gnarled fingers he sent a rain of arrows into flight toward Leon. Again the pendants shield protected him and he responded with the knives he always carried about his body. Contemptuously, the robed figure brushed them aside and prepared to cast another spell at Leon. Suddenly the dark figure was engulfed in white-hot flame. Unharmed, it turned to face the new antagonist as E'Alam entered the now smoking glade of the garden. Not hesitating, Leon drew his sword and charged the dark being. He plunged the Sword of VaLor' into the side of the detestable robed figure. A hideous, shrill scream filled the night, and in a flash nothing remained of the figure but a small film of white ash and the fragments of the red stone it had worn about its neck. The great Sword throbbed in Leon's hand as he stood there for a moment slightly dazed. Then he spun, and raced back to the now scorched bench calling Allece's name. She stood and he gathered her into his arms, waves of relief flooding through him at the touch of her.

E'Alam touched Leon's shoulder, "Quickly my children! You must be gone before the guards arrive if you would prevent unnecessary questions. Leon, I will see you in your chambers as soon as I am finished here." He then turned to the bat creature where it still rolled in agony.

Leon and Allece ran to the door, into her rooms where he took her in his arms. "Even being close to me is dangerous, we must be extremely careful until this whole thing is over … I love you!" he whispered. They kissed and separated, Leon returning by way of the hidden passage to his own room.

From the balcony he could see lights and people running into the garden from every direction. He quickly went back inside, laid the Sword across the foot of the bed and changed into the nightclothes that Platen had laid out for him, promptly kicking the clothes he had worn under the bed. At the sound of banging on the door he hurried to unlatch and open it and found the whole Shadow troop trying to get into his chambers at once.

Affecting a voice of indignation, Leon demanded, "What in the world is going on."

Shadow One pushed past the others into Leon's chambers and said, "Something has happened and we were concerned for your safety."

Leon feigned surprise. "What happened? As you can see I am quite all right." Shouting and running feet could be heard throughout the palace. "Let me get dressed and we can go find out what has happened."

Shadow One took control, "No, your Majesty, I feel we would better serve you by keeping you here until things settle down."

"Then perhaps you would like to come in and wait," Leon, stepped aside to let all of them in.

No sooner had he settled into a chair than there was an urgent knock on the door. Shadow Two went and let Fallon and Gaelnn in. Fallon started to speak, and then looked at Leon in his nightclothes, smiled and said, "Could we speak with you in private your Highness."

Leon turned to Shadow One, "I think that would be all right, don't you?" Shadow One reluctantly agreed and led the troop out.

When the door had closed, Fallon withdrew a couple of Leon's knives from his cloak, "How many of these did you throw at that thing? And how did you get out and back in again?"

"In answer to your first question, I don't have the slightest idea. It happened all too quickly. Five, now that I count. I think Gaelnn could probably answer the second question."

Gaelnn looked as if he were about to say, 'Who, me?' but he didn't. Instead he said, "Young people in a palace have even more time on their hands than those who live in the country and exploring is limited to the palace grounds. Very little escapes their discovery."

The curtain by the bed drew back and E'Alam stepped into the room.

Leon felt that the secret was very well known indeed.

E'Alam motioned them to a table by the windows where he sat and directed them to do the same. When they had seated themselves he spoke quietly, "These, I believe, are yours." He laid three more of Leon's throwing knives on the table. "This is the first time he has ventured to send one of his satros to strike across the Divide Mountains. He is obviously trying to get Leon. It has to be an effort to break our spirit. We must move even faster; we must take an offensive position."

Leon got up and walked to the door and asked one of the shadows to go and bring him a map of VaLor'.

While they waited Leon directed his thoughts at his pendant, *"Are you listening?"*

"We are always here, and happy that you are finally seeking us."

"Stay with me please, I need all of the help you can give me."

"We will be here."

Soon the guard returned. Leon paused, still consulting with the voices of the pendant, then invited the Shadows back in. At the table again, noting the questioning look of the three seated there he proceeded, "It appears that Xzuron has been busy." The rangers swept the ash, which was all that remained of the wolves, from the lava flow leaving it so clean even E'Alam was unaware of the attack that had occurred there. "That makes three other times he has attacked us directly, considering that evil fog and the skeletal army we met on our way here. We need a plan and we need it now." He turned to the Shadow troop. "You could play a large part in this. I suggest a ruse, a decoy. I know I am asking a lot, but I would like one of you to impersonate me with the others protecting him as if he were me while I take the Sword and go in search of Xzuron. I know this will put you all in great danger, but it may leave me free to accomplish my task."

Long moments passed, then a tall blond Shadow stepped forward, "I am Tandor! If it would please you, my King, I would be happy to take the challenge. If my shoes had slight risers and my clothing was padded some, and if I were hooded I might be able to pass the casual glance."

E'Alam nodded thoughtfully, "I could provide a spell that would insure your disguise to all except those who might touch you. Leon, it would help if you start wearing scarlet apparel so that the people associate that color with you. It is the custom anyway and should help the effectiveness of the disguise when it is used."

Leon turned to the Dwarves, "What do you know of the Divide Mountains?"

"They were my home," said one as he stepped forward. "Though it was hundreds of years ago, very little changes in the world of Dwarves."

"Two questions," said Leon. "Is it possible to go through the mountains instead of over them? And would it be faster if we did?"

"Yes, my Lord, to both questions. It would not be possible, however, to bring horses through the paths below."

Leon took in a deep breath and exhaled slowly, "My friends, it might just work. Here is what I propose. We will need a replica of the sword of Valor' and of the war banner. Gaelnn will proceed to East Fort as second in command of the army. His father, Leando, will continue to act as Tandor's advisor. E'Alam, could you see to that?" E'Alam nodded, and Leon continued, "His presence should add even more credence to our ruse. Fallon will come with the Dwarves and me to New Home. We will leave at night and travel until we are far enough away that our presence won't be noticed. Fallon and I will go in disguise until we reach New Home, then Fallon will go over the mountains with horses and supplies, collecting the Rangers, if possible, as he goes. I will go through the mountain so I can arrive there first. I should be able to observe the movements of the enemy, and meet Fallon and his horsemen by the Easting River where it nears the flat lands. Are there any comments or suggestions?"

Fallon nodded saying, "We could enlist Krantor and his people as additional cover. It would be quite natural for them to go back to Planor by that road."

E'Alam cleared his throat, "I knew all of that training at the hand of Sir Galan would prove useful. I will speak with King Dygor, Krantor and Leando and request their discreet aid. Then I believe it would be best if I traveled with Leon as far as New Home. My powers may be helpful in concealing Leon's presence, even in such a large company. Unless there are any other comments or suggestions I think we should adjourn to our beds. One last thing. No one should speak of this to anyone except those directly involved."

After they had left his room Leon sat in silence for a few minutes. Then, pulling his pendant from his shirt he stared into it and focused his thoughts on the Elf Prince Lea'Oen.

Lea'Oen crouched down behind a sharp mound of rock watching the valley beyond. To any other eye, he would have been invisible for he had his cape reversed so the black side was out; he looked like a darker shadow in an already dark night. He turned in recognition, then removed his own pendant and spoke softly to Leon. "How is life as the High King, friend Leon?"

"It's not all that the uninitiated would expect it to be, but how did you know?"

The Elf chuckled, "For one thing, if your quest had not been successful, you would not be speaking with me now. For another, there's that crown on your head."

Leon grinned sheepishly as he reached up to remove the crown, "How is it there?"

Lea'Oen sighed, turning very serious, "I never even imagined the numbers of enemy that I have seen here. They cover the floor of the valley like a death gray plague and destroy everything that gets in their way. They are already nearly to Dark Wood. My cousins there are preparing to allow the morag army to march through the woods unimpeded, hoping to prevent them from trying to burn the forest down. The spells they have invoked should help. After the main body is through, they will fall upon the morags from behind."

Leon stared thoughtfully for a moment and then said, "I hope to be at the Easting River in about three days. I will contact you then. In the mean time, try to keep out of danger. It might be helpful if you could ask the Elves of Dark Wood if they would wait for word from us before they strike. We may be able to combine our efforts to a greater benefit for all. Have you been in touch with the Elves of Mero Wood?"

Lea'Oen nodded. "Yes, they are sending our Elven warriors across the Divides even as we speak. My mother senses that you will need them at the Catch Mountains."

"Her wisdom never ceases to amaze me. Please give her my thanks. I'll see you soon." He smiled and broke the contact.

The council was already in session when Leon entered the hall with Gaelnn, Fallon and a few of the Shadow guard. He was dressed in scarlet, with a scarlet cape and the crown that had been bestowed upon him the day before. The Shadows wore scarlet capes trimmed in gold. They also wore golden breastplates and armlets over short-sleeved crimson shirts and baggy, loose crimson pants. Their black, knee high boots reflected the lights around them.

Leon strode straight to the King's chair at the head of the table. Stopping behind it, he turned to face the members of the council. "The events of last night have convinced me that we must move quickly." Turning toward a distinguished looking man of middle years and an obvious military bearing, Leon said, "Commander, I have asked Gaelnn to act as your second in command, and as liaison between you and me. I have given him instructions for immediate movement of the army. He will convey my wishes to you. I, with my personal guard, will review the assembled troops today. We leave immediately." With that he turned and left the hall with his guard in tow.

Leon spent that whole day being seen by as many people as he could, especially the army. He even made up an excuse to visit the river gate to speak with Vistag. By the end of the day the whole city was abuzz with tales of the handsome King and his faithful personal guard, and how regal they all looked in their bright crimson attire.

At the evening meal with Allece sitting next to him, Leon made it a point to announce that King Dygor and Over Chieftain Krantor and their companies would leave that evening for their homes where they would proceed with the gathering of the Plainsmen and the northern Dwarves, so they might soon be brought to the aid of those who would fight at East Fort.

After the meal Leon and Allece strolled in the garden under the watchful eye of the Shadow guard. She stopped suddenly and turned to him and asked, "What is going on? You're planning something, aren't you!"

He took both of her hands in his and looked long into her eyes, "Yes, I leave tonight for New Home, but no one must know since there is one who will assume my identity. That's why we are walking here now, so that I might say good-by again. We never seem to have enough time for ourselves. Perhaps after this campaign is over I will have time, at last, to tell you how much I love you." They walked on in thoughtful silence not wanting the moment to end, but knowing it must. It was nearly dark, when, with aching hearts, they tenderly kissed and parted at her door.

From palace grand to Dwarven hall,
The King will go to aid them all.
Though day be dark he'll stand the test,
And stone will guide him in his quest.

Excerpt from the prophesies of Orn the Seer

CHAPTER SIXTEEN

Road To Maldor

As darkness settled over the land of VaLor' the participants began to gather in Leon's private chambers. Leon had removed his crimson clothing and crown and packed them in the bottom of a small backpack with a few personal items. He was once more dressed in the traveling clothes and hooded cloak that he so much preferred.

After all were present, Tandor changed into kingly crimson clothing, and then stood quietly while E'Alam worked a spell. When the spell was done even Leon had to use the pendant to see through the disguise. With imitation crown and the replica of the Sword of VaLor' Tandor fit the part nicely.

E'Alam, looking pleased with himself, nodded at Tandor, "Well, your Majesty, this will hold for about four days. Then you will feel the change coming on. When the change starts you had better get out of those clothes and back into the uniform of the guard. Gaelnn will have a story prepared to cover the disappearance of the King, and if you stay close to him, you will surely be with Leon again, before the coming battle."

Shadow One moved over to Leon and knelt. "My Liege, I have vowed to carry your banner into battle. How may this be if I am not with you?"

Leon reached out, "Come, stand my friend. You all shall fight at my side as we have agreed. I will send our special steed for all of you when the battle is imminent. Be ready."

Dygor stepped forward, "King Leon, I have been speaking with, your Dwarf Shadow a lost cousin from the past, and he mentioned passages that we no longer use. Perhaps it would be advisable to take him along to ensure that we can find the proper passage. I can arrange for one of my men to take his place in the guard and I doubt that anyone will notice the change."

"A sound idea," approved Leon. "Well, my friends, it is time we begin. If there are no questions I will meet you at the stables." He looked around the room at the anxious faces, then nodded and turned toward the curtains by the bed. A warning hum from his pendant brought him to a crouching halt, knife in hand. He waved to Fallon to go to the right, and for the others to continue their conversations. Firmly grabbing the curtains both he and Fallon jerked down hard at the same time. As the heavy material crumpled down a startled, muffled, cry came from a figure entangled in its bulk. The Shadow guard, were on the figure in an instant. They removed a dagger from the hand of the struggling form of Platen.

Gaelnn grabbed the little man by the shirt and shook him, "Why! Why would you come here like this?"

Spittle dribbled down the little man's chin as he turned glowing red eyes toward Leon, "He will die, the Master will never allow him to succeed." He grinned and began laughing hysterically … then lapsed into convulsions and fell unconscious to the floor.

E'Alam picked up the assassin's knife and smelled the blade. "It is covered with poison of the most lethal type. We will have to remain alert to the possibility that he shared our little plan before he attempted this assassination."

Platen moved, opening his eyes as if from a deep sleep. Fear filled them, then tears. "Saw … hurt crow … went to … help … balcony … evil crow … in … my mind … sorry … so … sorry." And he fainted again.

E'Alam turned to peer out into the dimly lit gardens just in time to see the form of a large black crow leaving the balcony rail. In an instant he was charging toward the balcony's glass doors. He shouted, "I'll join you on the road!" Without stopping he leapt out over the rail, changing into a large blue-gray falcon as he fell, then he winged rapidly up after the shape of the crow as it flew north.

Leon moved toward the wall where the curtain had hung, "Now more than ever we must move quickly." He touched the hidden lever and disappeared into the dark passage beyond. Silently the wall closed behind him. The others filed out by the main door and hurried to attend to their various tasks.

Leon slipped into the garden, staying in the shadows. He wore his hood up over his head and walked silently but surely toward the stables where preparations were being made to depart. Soon, all were mounted and Leon stepped out of the shadows and climbed on the extra horse that Fallon was leading.

The main body of Dwarves had marched out much earlier in the day. Only a few remained to attend their King, and to these few was added the Dwarf Shadow. As usual, there was consternation from the Dwarves about riding such tall horses, but they rode and did quite well. Krantor and his entire mounted company left with them. Fallon, Leon, several grooms, including Jerome and a score of men at arms who rode heavy draft horses, kept in the middle of the procession. They were developing a heavy mounted corps that were protected with armor copied from that brought for Fallon and Snowball, and though they were as yet un-skilled, they were learning. Soon the twinkling lights of the beautiful city of Val were lost in the distance behind.

The great blue-gray falcon dove like a falling stone, smashing into the smaller bird in a flurry of black feathers, sinking its talons deep into the flesh of the crow and then continuing a more controlled plummet toward the earth below. When they reached the ground a bright flash of light ignited in the darkness, then silence. Gracefully, the falcon lifted once more into the dark sky and banked away toward the road to New Home.

As dawn started to turn the eastern sky yellow and pink, Tandor as King, with Gaelnn on one side and Leando on the other, led the largest army ever assembled by the united kingdoms of VaLor' out onto the road to East Fort. They were repeatedly cheered as they passed the assembled divisions of their army, which stretched for miles along the road. Two days hence they would be joined by the Dwarf forces of Old Home who would be waiting at the camp near the junction of the Rushing and the Catch rivers. The Dwarves would have traveled underground nearly to the Rushing River, and then followed it to the crossing. Two days after that when the forces of VaLor' reached East Fort, the horsemen of Planor would arrive, and the army would be complete.

Moving along the road were countless wagons of food for man and beast, as well as all of the implements of war. It was a slow trip, but all seemed in good cheer. By pacing themselves they managed the eight leagues a day that had been their goal. The mounted officers and leaders could have moved much faster but their presence cheered those on foot, so they stayed, often walking themselves.

Gaelnn and Leando kept themselves between Tandor and the high command to avoid any slip that might give away their ruse, and constantly worried that they might not reach the Fort before the spell wore off.

As planned, Prince Doran and his Dwarf army were waiting at the Rushing River camp adding three thousand tough warriors to their ranks.

Looking about him, Gaelnn marveled at the might represented here. Surely not even Xzuron could stand against such as these. The attitude of the entire army was one of confidence, they knew that they now had a chance to win. After all, they were led by the Sword of VaLor'. Gaelnn began to feel great pride in this—the army of VaLor'.

As they approached the huge, cut stone structure that was East Fort, Gaelnn could see thousands of horsemen collected off to the left, on the plain outside the fort. Flags and banners flapped in the breeze directing the incoming companies to their bivouac areas. Gaelnn led the imitation King into the fort where they were given special quarters in the tallest tower of the Fort. Just before dark Tandor made a tour of the troops in the Fort and the bivouac area and then had to dash to the tower as he could feel the change beginning to take place.

It was with relief that Tandor finally removed the scarlet clothing of the King and dressed himself once again in the colors of the Shadow Guard. At least once a day he would put the scarlet cape back on and walk around the battlements atop the tower, where he could be seen but not identified from below.

In the days that followed, Gaelnn would spend much time in the tower, as if he were in conference with the King. Then he or Leando would direct the movement of scouts, provisioners and troops through the ranking commander. In this way, they kept up the appearance that the King was among them.

It all seemed so easy to Gaelnn. When the hoards of Xzuron reached the middle of the plains of Maldor he began sending mounted troops out in sorties, hit and run encounters allowing the mounted archers to ride within an arrow's cast and fire into the hoard, killing great numbers of them. But it made no difference. The fallen were eaten on the spot and the hoard kept moving as though nothing had happened, This great gray swath of death moved, unchecked, across the plain south toward East Fort.

Gaelnn called for the construction of a defensive parapet to be built on the fort side of the ford across the Catch River, where archers could launch a deadly rain of arrows on the morags when they attempted to cross the ford. He then accompanied the sortie troops as they went against the morags and saw firsthand the ease with which the morags died. As the horsemen would close in for each attack he would feel a surge of pleasure at the howling, contemptuous rage that rose out of the hoard as they charged on foot after the horsemen. The morags were quite fleet of foot in a lumbering sort of way. If a horse fell, they could be on the horse and rider, ripping both apart before any one would be able to form a rescue attempt. Though they couldn't possibly keep up with a fast moving horse or run very far, they could easily outrun a human, and being much larger than any human in the land, they indeed made a formidable foe. They were not clever as they fought. Their advantage was numbers and weight to overwhelm their enemy, but it was clear to Gaelnn that a clever swordsman could easily overcome a morag warrior. So sure was he that he dismounted to attack on foot after the horsemen had lured a small group far enough away from the main body of the hoard. As he had suspected, his swordsmanship easily allowed him to dispatch the morag before him. Several of his command did the same to the rest. The rush of that victory was intoxicating to him, and he rode back to the fort forming new plans. He would take the war to the enemy! He didn't need the Sword of VaLor' to beat this foe, all he needed was a stout heart and the natural speed and VaLor of his men. Thoughts of the inevitable glory filled his mind as he dismounted from his faithful steed and turned the reins over to a groom.

Leon never ceased to be amazed at the workmanship of the Dwarves in their halls and chambers, and New Home was equally beautiful as that which he had seen in Old Home. It had been a day since he had left Fallon and E'Alam, and watched as they wound their way up the trail that led over the Divides.

Krantor's company had turned up to the plains at the wagon camp where they first met Leon, temporarily separating Fallon and D'Nee who had become very attached to each other.

Now Leon followed the Dwarf Shadow and a couple of King Dygor's warriors through seemingly endless passages, caverns and halls. The torches they carried cast shadows on images and scenes carved in the living rock of the walls that had not seen the flicker of light for hundreds of years. He could have used his pendant or even called forth a magic sphere to light their way, but he chose to allow them to use the light the Dwarfs were familiar with. They had, sometime earlier in the day, entered corridors long since lost behind hidden doors, opened now by the Shadow Dwarf to the surprise of the others. A rushing sound faintly touched Leon's ears, and as they walked it grew louder until it was difficult to talk over. Walking cautiously, for the floor had become quite damp, they entered a narrow tunnel carved by water rushing through it and on into the distance.

The Dwarf Shadow turned to Leon, and moving close to him shouted in his ear, "The Life Blood of the Easting River. Our path will parallel it for a while." Then he turned and led off down the tunnel on a path that had been cut out of the wall centuries before. After following the river for some time the path turned aside, branching back into the solid rock of the mountain. A short distance ahead they entered a large natural cavern where they were forced to stop. The path ended in a sharp drop into a deep fracture in the solid stone that surrounded them. Leon could see where a natural bridge of rock had once stood, and where it now lay fragmented at the bottom of the ravine they must now cross. The ravine was not wide, though much wider than anyone could jump.

Leon could see the path continuing on the other side. He turned to the Shadow, "Is there another way?"

The Dwarf shook his head, "I'm sorry my Liege, I did not know. We could return and bring back equipment that would allow us to cross, but we would lose much time."

"I know, my friend. How far is it to the surface after this ravine is crossed?"

"It's just a short distance, perhaps a half league."

Leon stood in silence staring at the ravine for several minutes, his thoughts turning to the admonition of E'Alam—to trust in his abilities and in the Pendant—remembering his lessons from the Blue Keep, he sat down in his meditation position, pulled out his pendant and gazed into it in deep concentration, seeking its aid. His mind filled with the spell and the knowledge he needed. In his hand the pendant began to vibrate, and then his body took up the vibration. *"Now, think yourself across the crevice."* In his mind he lifted himself up and floated across the ravine and then set himself down again. And so it was; he found that he was now seated on the other side of the ravine from the Dwarves. He was nearly as amazed as the Dwarves. He stood enjoying the look on their faces, nearly laughing, then becoming serious he asked, "Would any of you like to join me?"

"It is my duty," called the Shadow. The others slowly backed away from the edge of the ravine wagging their heads from side to side.

Leon held his pendant out before him and concentrated on the Dwarf Shadow, *"Now imagine him across."* He could feel the vibration building within him. A soft blue beam of light reached out and surrounded the Dwarf. With increased confidence he thought of lifting and drawing. The humming increased—slowly the Dwarf lifted and floated across the ravine, gently settling down next to him. He then turned to the remaining Dwarfs, "Please invite King Dygor to bring his warriors after us as soon as he can. You know better than I what you will need to get across this ravine."

"How are you able to do these things?" called a wide-eyed Dwarf from the other side of the crevice.

Shadow stepped forward proudly. "He is a bearer of the stone. He carries the Sword of VaLor'. Before you stands the High King, how else?"

Leon had drawn his cloak aside so that the beautifully decorated scabbard was visible.

The Dwarves dropped to their knees in recognition. They then jumped back up saying at the same time, "As you wish," and "So it shall be." Then they turned and charged back up the passage.

Chuckling, Leon turned and followed the Dwarf Shadow into the passage before them. Since the torches were with their departing friends, he called for a sphere of light and followed his guide, hardly thinking of the new ease with which he had made the light appear.

Fallon called a halt as they crested the final rise of the Divides. It had been an arduous climb, but by rotating horses with the spares, they had made good time. If all were going as planned, Leon should be approaching the Easting River by now, and Gaelnn should be at East Fort. In the fading light, they set up camp in a hollow just over the summit, beneath the granite cliffs that shouldered the path. The hollow provided some protection from the wind that seemed to blow non-stop across the Divides. E'Alam had cautioned them against a fire and so they ate cold trail rations and fed the horses their grain. Finally, the weary travelers settled down in their blankets for the night.

The scream of a panicked horse brought Fallon to his feet in an instant. E'Alam stood in the center of the hollow intently gazing into the night above them. A sliver of moonlight gave everything in the clearing an eerie look, and for the first time Fallon noticed that the wind had stopped. A shaft of pure power shot out of the night sky like a lightning bolt and crashed down on E'Alam. Just as it touched the wizard it was stopped by a blue aura which suddenly flashed into being around him. Untouched, E'Alam pointed and a bolt of energy launched back at the creature above them. Fire lit up the sky as the wings of a great tordaq began to burn, but the fire was instantly extinguished.

Grooms had run to the horses and were striving desperately to calm them when another charge hit the ground at the edge of the clearing. Fallon, surprised, thought he heard a woman scream. The monstrous bat creature descended to a point where even Fallon could see it. Once more a rush of power came from the being on the tordaq, smashing, into the ground next to Fallon. The exploding energy threw him aside like a leaf in the wind. Dazed, he lay at the edge of the clearing watching as E'Alam again discharged a great bolt of energy at the creature above them. He heard a scream from the tordaq when it was hit.

Pulling out his pendant E'Alam pointed it up, sending a thin blue beam shooting into the hated rider. Losing his seating, the satro tumble off the beast and fell toward the rocks below. Just before it hit the ground, the satro regained control, but was immediately hit by another tight blue beam. The satro simply ceased to be. Crying in fright, the huge tordaq surged up into the night and winged north.

E'Alam spun around to inspect the damage. None was serious. Then he strode purposefully toward the edge of the clearing, grasped one of the grooms and brought him forward. Fallon joined him just as he was pulling the hood off of his captive. It was Allece.

Fallon stammered, "H … how, whose, where did you come from?" Then, he looked at her proud face, "That was a stupid question. You have been here all along."

She nodded, and remained silent.

"What are we to do with you?" Fallon asked to no one in particular. "This is a neat turn of events," he murmured. "It's too late to send you back, and now we must move even faster than before. That rider-less tordaq is bound to bring some form of investigation."

She smiled at his words, knowing that she had won. She would go with them. "I'm sorry about the scream. It won't happen again."

"In other circumstances it could have cost us all our lives, and perhaps even ruined the mission," commented Fallon.

She dropped her eyes to look at the ground, "I can't say that I'm sorry for being here though. I must go with you, so I can be near … him."

Fallon reached out and put his arm around her, "I know. He has that affect on people."

"Come," said E'Alam. "We must make haste to find cover before we are spotted again."

In minutes they were mounted and riding down the trail into the unknown. E'Alam led, finding the trail with the help of his pendant.

Lea'Oen smiled as he spotted Leon and his companion cautiously approaching, from upriver. When they were nearly abreast of him he stepped out, startling them and nearly receiving a throwing knife for his cleverness. "Easy!" he said, "We Elves function much better without these little stickers of yours letting air in here and there."

"You Elves have the most irritating habit of popping out of the woods without any warning," was Leon's response, as he reached out for a hearty wrist clasp. "Good to see you Lea'Oen. My companion here is out of the past, one of seven, of which only one has given his name. They asked that I make them my personal guards, my Shadows, and have attached themselves to me as such, so they might die with honor in the coming war. He is Number Five."

"From what I have seen, he shall have plenty of opportunity to do that. Things on this side of the Divides are turning very nasty, very nasty indeed."

"Tell me what you have found," prompted Leon.

"First, let's get under the trees where we are not so easily seen from above. Those demons on their tordaqs are everywhere."

Lea'Oen led them into a densely covered spot, not far from the trail, where it was obvious he had been camping. He offered them food and settled down, comfortably leaning back against a log. "It is like looking at a sea of swarming maggots. They trample, destroy or eat everything in their path, including each other. It makes my stomach turn just to watch them. In my opinion, it is fruitless to attempt to do battle with them. We could wear out all of our troops and they would still keep marching on until we were buried under the weight of their numbers and devoured. According to my mother, a force of morags led by a satro has moved to bottle up the Catch Mountain Dwarves, and that seems to be working. She has sent a large force of our warriors to their aid, but they have no one who is a match for the power of the satro. That satro and his army do not seem to be in any hurry though, and the Dwarves are holding their own, but they can't get out. The Elves of Dark Wood are waiting to attack the main hoard as you have asked, and that is about all I have to report."

Leon sat deep in thought for long minutes; then he removed his pack and dug out a map. He sat staring for quite some time. Finally he said, "Time is our enemy. Is the Catch River navigable?"

Lea'Oen looked puzzled, "Yes, but it runs, toward us. From Mount Orag, it would be of no use to us."

"True, but if the Catch Mountain Dwarves were freed; they could use the river to catch up with us. Then we could all use the river to catch the Hoard. Our numbers would not stop the morags and their masters, but the Sword still has a part to play in all this. I'm not sure what it can do against such numbers, but I know I must confront Xzuron with it."

"It will work!" exclaimed Lea'Oen. "My people are as comfortable on the river as they are in the forests."

"Now," said Leon, "if I can just divert E'Alam to the Catch Mountains instead of here, perhaps he can deal with the satro."

It was rapidly becoming dark, so Leon decided to wait until he felt that E'Alam's group would have settled down for the night before trying to contact the Wizard.

Through battle great and battle small,
With Stone and Sword he'll lead them all.

Excerpt from prophesies of Orn the Seer

CHAPTER SEVENTEEN

Battle of Catch Mountain

E'Alam and the company had just left the hollow and headed down the trail, when Leon appeared floating in the air before him. "I thought you would be settled down for the night by now," said Leon's image.

E'Alam frowned, "We had a little visit from a satro and decided that moving would be the smartest action we could take. How are things at the river?"

Leon's image looked thoughtful. "At this moment all is well, but the hoard has moved onto the Plains of Maldor and, in our opinion, they are so numerous that no amount of manpower can stop them in the open. The Catch Mountain Dwarves are bottled up in their mountain by a number of morags under the command of a satro. Mero Wood Elves are on their way to assist, but they are no match for a satro. I was hoping that I could talk you into switching to the north trail; it leads toward the Catch Mountains pointing you in the right direction to be able to help the Elves. We will need every man of them when we catch up with the morags."

E'Alam stroked his beard a moment. Then, "I could go there very quickly by myself leaving the others to ride on down to you, but first I must find them shelter for the night. I seem to remember a cave of adequate proportions about an hour's ride from here."

Leon's image continued, "My hope is to have the Dark Woods Elves build rafts to carry us all down river when you and the others have joined us. The New Home Dwarves should be along in a day or so, and I still hope to call in the Rangers. By combining our forces we should be able to prepare a bit of a surprise for our friend Xzuron."

"I will do what I can at Catch Mountain. You get your surprise ready. Fallon can lead this party on down the mountain. If he travels by day he should have little enough trouble. Expect him tomorrow evening. I will contact you when I have news." Leon's image disappeared and E'Alam hurried on down the trail in search of the cave he had seen nearly two hundred years earlier.

The plains of Comark were desolate. Little vegetation grew, and what did looked more like sticks standing in the dry wind than the green foliage found on the other side of the Divides. There were no grasses or even mosses. Instead there was sand and rock, and rolling mounds of dirt that once had held vibrant grasslands. Crevices and ravines were sharp contrasts in the landscape, caused by the flash floods, represenying the only form of water that found its way into this unfriendly land.

As forsaken as it was, the Elven warriors had chosen to travel straight across it rather than stay on the much easier to travel roads, because they would be less likely to be seen if they stayed away from the main roadways. Their hope lay in the surprise that would result from their appearance out of the wastelands. The march from Mero

Wood had taken them a week of hard toil with little real rest, and now a thousand Elves grouped, sleeping and resting, in a deep depression just a mile from the stone Gates of the Catch Mountain Dwarves. Kenanton, in spite of his age, had led the Elves quickly and unseen to the very gates of this, the northernmost kingdom of the Dwarves. At dawn they would strike. The sliver of a moon earlier that night had made progress very slow for fear of being seen by a mounted satro. As a result they did not get as much rest as he would have liked, but they were as ready as they could be.

The sky was beginning to lighten slightly when the Elves quietly roused, ate their fill of trail rations and prepared their weapons. Most of them were archers, and each one carried a long, narrow Elven sword with its runes and spells. They were a peaceful people who hated war, but they believed they must do their share to protect the land of their choice. So they had become skilled warriors. Their normal life span, several hundred years long, was of little concern to them weighed against the security of their homes. Like most warriors, they would readily face possible death in battle for the greater need of all VaLor'ians.

In the softly growing light, as night slowly inched toward day, a large blue-gray falcon spiraled down out of the night to land a short way up the slope of the depression. It raised its wings up high, shimmered and transformed into a man. E'Alam walked quickly to where Kenanton stood. He spoke in a low voice, "Kenanton, I thought you had retired to the comfort of your lodge."

The two grabbed wrists in a warrior's greeting and Kenanton replied, "It is good to see you E'Alam. The stone knows we need your aid. Our spells are of little use against the power of a satro. Has the King been crowned?"

"Yes old friend, and even now he waits for us to free these besieged Dwarves and join him by the Dark Woods. I have scouted the enemy from my special vantage point, and feel that if we are careful, we can surround them and do a great deal of damage with your bowmen before we have to get within sword's reach. I have spotted the satro and will try to neutralize him."

As the last streamers of pink and gold gave way to blue sky a hail of Elven arrows filled the morning air and morags began falling in gray swaths. The satro rose up into the air and, standing on a platform of power, turned to throw killing bolts of energy at the attackers. Arrows deflected off his shield of force and he laughed a delightfully scornful laugh at the puny efforts of the archers. Then he stopped in surprise as he was washed with energy from E'Alam. Unhurt, he turned to face the Wizard. Sneering in contempt he threw a ball of fire at E'Alam. Where it struck E'Alam no longer stood. Raw energy hit him from another direction and his platform began to crumble. He could not maintain his concentration while fending off the attack by E'Alam. Settling on a rise of ground, he turned his total efforts to E'Alam.

Fire flew in great intense waves. E'Alam stood on a man high boulder, unfazed, enclosed in his faint blue aura, returning fire for fire. Suddenly a stab of bright red energy smashed into the large rock under him causing it to explode, sending bits of rock in every direction. E'Alam disappeared.

Laughing maniacally the satro turned to deal with the Elven attackers only to be hit by a tight blue beam from E'Alam who now stood behind him holding his pendant before him. The satro could see the beam pulsing from the pendant. He screamed in disbelief as he watched his chest burn away. Then ... he was no more. Only fragments of his shattered red stone remained.

At the first flight of Elven arrows the Dwarves had become aware of the battle going on before their gates. As the morags' attention was turned away from them, they threw open their gates and charged into the mass of gray flesh that was the army of the morags. Now, hand-to-hand battle gave them a way to vent the frustration they had felt at being bottled up behind their own gates.

Without their leader the morags became confused. They fought, but without direction. Still ... they were terrible killing machines, killing just because that had been the last order. Dwarf fighters were some of the finest in the land and their method of fighting in double ranks provided a nearly unbreakable defense, but still some fell to be quickly replaced by other eager Dwarf warriors. Slowly the morags were pushed back from the gates and thousands of fighters swarmed out, forming new ranks, pushing the morags back even harder. Fire and arrows struck the morags from the rear, and Dwarf axes, hammers and swords from the front. Soon E'Alam had to stop assisting for fear of harming the Dwarves. Still the fighting raged on. As the first arrows had flown, Kenanton had sent a unit of his men to block the road so none of the morags could escape, this to ensure word was not carried back to Xzuron. As the sun topped the peaks of the Catch Mountains it was done. Fifty-four Elves had perished, another thirty-two were badly wounded. The Dwarves had lost a hundred and ten, and the severely wounded equaled another hundred and thirty two. It had been a costly battle, but this force of several thousand morags had been completely wiped out.

Standing amid the carnage before the mighty Dwarf gates, E'Alam and Kenanton greeted King Gowen. The Dwarves of the Catch Mountains had nearly been wiped out in the last Great War, but now they were strong and extremely annoyed at having been attacked by the minions of Xzuron again.

King Gowen's golden sandals stamped the ground in anger. He pointed at the injured dwarves around him, "These good men have fought bravely, but I fear that a greater danger awaits us." His round eyes squinted in the morning sun, and his salt and pepper, chest long beard bobbed in agitation. "Unbeknownst to the sorcerer we have watched his power grow. We built tunnels into the very heart of his lair and watched in disbelief as his army grew. Their numbers are uncountable. This is but a handful led by a lesser satro. If his power had been stronger or the spells on our gates a little weaker, they would surely have overrun us long before now, leaving us with no option but to use our escape holes, abandoning our ancient home to these vermin!"

E'Alam nodded, "It would seem the sole purpose here was to keep you at bay until later, when greater power could be brought against your gates, perhaps after he had gained the victory he seeks at East Fort."

Kenanton nodded in agreement, "My Lady, the Queen, suggested that it might be thus."

The Dwarf King suddenly stopped his angry gesturing and turned to E'Alam, "Has the High King arrived?" He spoke quietly seeking hope where there seemed to be none.

E'Alam smiled, "Yes, my friend, and he carries the Sword. He would have you and your armed men hurry down river to join him at the Dark Wood. He wishes to attack the rear of the sorcerer's army. What say you?"

A strangely vicious look of joy entered the features of the Dwarf King. He couldn't have agreed more.

Fallon lead his small band down the mountain path at first light, intent on joining Leon before the day was over. Shortly after leaving the cave the trail wound down into a wide glade. There, line on line of green clad horsemen sat, obviously awaiting his arrival. From his position at the center of the trail a large familiar figure rode up the trail to greet him. It was Fleck, the ranger.

"Prince Fallon, we meet again. I have it on very good authority that you and our new King might need some help." He pointed at several large hawks souring overhead.

"You speak to hawks?" asked Fallon incredulously.

"Oh yes, and so could you if you tried. But come, we must hurry. There is much that must be done." With that he turned and led the way down the path at a brisk trot, his band of rangers quietly falling in behind Fallon's people.

Leon sat in meditation. In his mind he floated over what had been a great grassy plain. Now it was trampled and stripped bare by the uncountable feet of the morags as they moved south, each day closer to East Fort. The mass of surging gray flesh lumbered away into the distance while a number of very large morags disassembled and carried the opulent black and blood red tents and equipment of Xzuron and his lieutenants. Xzuron floated above his army seated in a silver sphere that undulated with red pulses of light. Four of his satro lieutenants drifted on the morning breezes high above, mounted on their huge bat-like tordaqs. The remaining nine were spread out around the mass of morags, directing their movement.

With a flick of his will Leon now floated just south of the morags. In the distance toward East Fort a large army could be seen encamped on the plain, banners waving in the breeze, outriders keeping a vigil on the advancing morags. At their present speed it appeared that the morags would make contact in a matter of hours.

Leon snapped back to his surroundings, fear gripping his heart, a faint cry ringing in his ears. Then he realized that the cry had been his own.

Lea'Oen was watching him, with concern on his face "What is it my friend? What have you seen?"

"I fear that our armies have decided to engage the morags. This must not be! There are just too many of the enemy." He stood and then paced back and forth apprehension covering his features. "I must try to stop them or I sense disaster will be inevitable."

Once again he sat down in meditation, thinking of Shadow One and his personal guard. He saw them still guarding the high tower of East Fort. A worried Leando sat staring out a window as Number One paced back and forth in an extremely agitated manner. Then he thought of Gorath, and in an instant saw him surrounded by large fish bones, sunning himself on a high cliff overlooking the ocean, In his mind he thought, "*Gorath, great steed, I believe I have need of you,*" the huge dragon looked toward him and nodded, uncoiled himself and stepped off the edge of the cliff. He dropped like a stone. Then with a great surge, soured high up into the cloudless sky and banked inland.

"Someone comes, my friend," whispered Lea'Oen, bringing Leon completely back to himself.

Quickly they moved to where they could watch the trail. Soon, a long line of Dwarves came into sight hurrying down the trail.

Leon followed Lea'Oen down onto the trail, surprising King Dygor who strode at the head of the column.

"Blast! You're getting as sneaky as that Wizard," grumbled the King with a grin on his face. Then he solemnly bowed, "Your Highness. What a surprise!"

Leon laughed out loud, then placing his left hand on the short King's shoulder, gripped him by the right wrist. "Welcome Dygor. You've made good time."

King Dygor had come with two thousand well-trained and provisioned warriors, their armor glittering in the early morning sun. Soon they were on their way to the Dark Woods to aid the Elves in building the rafts while Leon and Lea'Oen returned to their campsite to await the arrival of Fallon.

From near and far will come great aid,
To fight the evil blade to blade.

Excerpt from the prophesies of Orn the Seer

CHAPTER EIGHTEEN

Maldor

Gaelnn had found it quite easy to convince the old warrior head of the armies, that it was Leon's wish to take the battle to the morags. And now, resplendent in his armor and Elven sword at his side, he sat astride a pure white armored charger watching the approaching morags. This would be his day! This would be the day that the armies of VaLor' destroyed the minions of Xzuron. The plan of battle was simple. He would lead the charge, driving a wedge into the center of the oncoming morags splitting them open, allowing the foot warriors to move into the center of the wedge and cut down the demoralized morags. Archers would fire deep into the enemy ensuring more confusion, while two thousand mounted warriors of Planor cut into the leading enemy on either side. The warriors of VaLor' would show these brainless morags! They would crush them.

As the sun passed the height of its arc the two armies moved closer together. When they were an arrow's cast apart Gaelnn stood in his stirrups and signaled the charge. In seconds the wedge was flying at the approaching morags. By the weight of their horses and their mighty arms they drove deep into the enemy and the battle was engaged. From atop his charger he could see the morags falling back. Then ... too late! ... his mind suddenly cleared. What was he doing here??? He realized that it had been a trap. He was stopped just as surely as if he had run headlong into the stone walls of East Fort. The battle raged on all sides of him. The realization hit him that for every one of the morags he killed two more moved right in to take its place. How could he have been so foolish! He signaled for retreat but the morags had closed in behind his company. Gratefully he noticed that the trap had sprung before the foot warriors had charged into the wedge. Quickly he called for a circle of defense while the hideous laugh of two satros who had closed the trap behind him rang in his ears. He knew at that moment he would die. He only regretted leading these brave warriors to a sure death—all for his pride. Fire blazed into the ranks of his troops as the satros gave unnecessary aid to the morags. His horse went down under him. He was fighting for his life alongside a couple hundred remaining VaLor'ians. They would die But they would die well, he thought, as a great mass of gray flesh pressed forward. Suddenly something felt very wrong inside him; he looked down to see blood spurting from an open wound near his groin. He gripped the wound with his left hand to stop the bleeding, somehow staying on his feet. He turned his efforts back hard toward the line where they had entered shouting, "VaLor'! VaLor'!" He slowly inched his way toward an opening. He stumbled and went down under the feet of the pressing morags. Looking up he saw the back of a satro. He surged to his knees and thrust his sword up into the robes, into the very center of its being. It had not seen the blow coming and had set no defense against a blow from the ground. It crumpled in a scream of hate and a flash of red light. All around him morags seemed to lose orientation. He stood and yelled for his men to follow and led a limping charge out of the pack of milling morags. Arrows flew into the morags from the reserve forces of VaLor', but the morags seemed to have found sudden direction and began to press hard after Gaelnn's men. He stumbled and fell as a wall of gray death rumbled toward him.

Slightly before midday Gorath swept over the peaks of the Divide Mountains, soaring down the canyons and settling easily in the small glade where Leon and Lea'Oen stood waiting. They hurried to greet him. Leon had clothed himself in his kingly scarlet and quickly mounted the great dragon's back. With a wave to Lea'Oen they lifted on powerful wings into the skies, and banking south they flew off rapidly toward East Fort. Lea'Oen would take Fallon on to where the rafts were being built. Hopefully they would meet Leon again there.

"WELL, WHAT SEEMS TO BE HAPPENING MY YOUNG FRIEND?"

"I believe there is trouble at East Fort. We must hurry to see what has happened, collect the Shadows and determine if we can help."

"HANG ON AND I'LL PUSH A LITTLE HARDER."

The flight to East Fort was swift and they arrived just as the sun was reaching midway in the sky. Much to the general confusion of the guards in the Fort, Gorath set down lightly on the high tower and settled himself to watch the surrounding terrain as Leon leapt clear and ran down the stairs and into the rooms where Leando and the Shadows waited. "What has happened?" He asked, half afraid to hear the answer.

Leando stood, his tall lean frame seeming bent and weary beyond his years. He waved in the general direction of the plains of Maldor and spoke in a shaky voice. "Gaelnn has led the army to face the morags. I tried to stop him, but he was possessed with the idea that power of arms alone could overcome the morags. He ... my son ... is a fool. He knows the prophecies, but it seems he has always doubted them, and now his doubts have led him to certain folly." He groaned softly and sat back down, head in his hands. "I am so sorry, my Liege, so sorry." The once proud frame of this great man shook in silent grief.

Leon laid his hand on the Chancellor's shoulder, "I know this has brought you pain, but pull yourself together. I need you to organize the Fort for the siege. I will go to Maldor to see if anything can be done. If I know Gaelnn, what he has done has been what he thought was best for VaLor', as well as for himself." Turning he called, "Shadows! We ride the Dragon! Come!!!"

As Gorath arrowed down toward the battle they could see a red flash and the sudden breaking away of a number of well-mauled regain their direction and charge after the fleeing VaLor'ians.

Leon yelled to Gorath, "Can you breathe us some fire, my friend?"

"OH YES, AND MUCH MORE. I THINK I'LL JUST SIT ME DOWN BETWEEN THEM AND HAVE A LITTLE MORAG FRY. AS I SEEM TO REMEMBER, THEY DON'T TASTE SO BAD EITHER."

Fire bathed the morags as Gorath settled down, his very size sent them tumbling back into their own ranks. A red flame shot toward Gorath from another satro. It splashed against him with no affect.

Gorath laughed, "PUNY SATRO! YOUR FIRE IS NOT EVEN A DISTRACTION."

The satro paused, then laughing gleefully turned toward Leon and cast a bolt of white energy straight at his chest. In an instant, instinctively, Leon held his medallion up before him, and watched in amazement as the beam was mirrored back at the satro even more intense than it had arrived. The satro looked surprised, then worried, then he screamed as he dissolved into a puff of smoke. At once the morags lost purpose and turned in a full rout, pushing hard back into their own ranks.

The reserve forces moved quickly forward and gathered the VaLor'ians onto horses, urging them to a fast retreat toward camp.

Leon and the Shadows followed at a more leisurely pace, acting as a rear guard. Then they mounted and soared off to the VaLor'ian camp.

As Gorath settled next to the brightly colored main pavilion Gaelnn was being carried into the healers' tent on a stretcher. Leon followed and stood watching as the surgeons worked on his friend. The surgeons were good. They repaired the cut artery, using their unusual craft and dressed the wound with herbs the likes of which Leon had never seen. Then the old surgeon turned to Leon and whispered, "I doubt if he will live through the night; he has lost too much blood. Even if he does survive, the leg will not be much good to him in the days to come. I'm sorry, but there is nothing more we can do."

Leon stared down at his friend. Then he asked the surgeon, "What of the others?"

"For the most part, those who survived retained superficial wounds and other healers have cared for them."

"FRIEND LEON," came the familiar voice of Gorath. "COME, I WOULD SPEAK WITH YOU."

Leon hurried out of the tent to where Gorath sat lazing in the late afternoon sun.

"THERE IS ONE WHO MIGHT HEAL YOUR FRIEND. YOU KNOW HER AS QUEEN MOTHER OF THE HIGH ELVES. IF HE CAN BE SAVED, HER POWERS CAN DO IT, BUT WE MUST HURRY, FOR DARKNESS APPROACHES."

Leon turned to the first officer that he saw, "Move the men back to the safety of East Fort, and prepare for a siege. Speak with Leando about the preparations. Any contact with the morags should be hit and run; do not again attempt to meet them on their terms; prepare to defend East Fort until I return." Spinning away he yelled for the Shadows, instructing them to carry Gaelnn to Gorath. They complied and quickly mounted. Holding the unconscious form of Gaelnn between them, they were up and away over the Divides streaking east toward Mero Woods.

How Gorath slipped down between the branches of the huge tree in the fading light of evening would always remain a mystery to Leon, but when they lightly set down, Queen Lea'Ah stood waiting for them. Somehow she had known they were coming.

She bowed her head to Leon, "High King Leon, my Liege, welcome once again to our home."

Leon squirmed uncomfortably, "Please, Queen Lea'Ah. The formality fails to sit right on me. Is there some way we can get around it?"

She smiled warmly, "Certainly, we will reserve the titles for times when others will expect them, but between ourselves, I will call you Leon and you shall call me Lea'Ah. Now, quickly, bring young

Gaelnn and follow me." She hesitated a moment, then turned to Gorath, "Please excuse me Gorath, but in the rush I neglected to mention how delighted I am to meet you. Perhaps we can find time to talk later."

"I WOULD BE HONORED, QUEEN MOTHER."

She turned and led Leon, followed by the scarlet clad Shadows carrying Gaelnn on a litter made of their cloaks. The path they followed led up living steps in the trunk of the tree, onto huge branches and finally into an airy, open room smelling of strange herbs. They laid him on a table as instructed and left the Queen Mother to her work, as she instructed.

Late in the following morning, as Leon sat staring out the window of his room in the tree, the Queen sent for him. He hurried up to the room where they had left Gaelnn. His friend lay staring off into space, tears slowly seeping down his cheeks onto the pillow beneath his head. "Gaelnn, you live," exclaimed Leon. Gaelnn's eyes didn't blink. There was no indication that he was even aware that Leon had entered the room. What Gaelnn was seeing was beyond the vision of the others in the room. Now and then a deep, soul rending sob would escape as he lay staring into his own world, assaulted by what horrors none knew or could even guess.

Leon turned to the Elven queen, "What?"

She led him out of the room, and quietly spoke to him in lowered tones. "He has retreated into a torture chamber of his own making, and I have not been able to draw him out. I have enriched his blood with the magic of the Elves. It will not harm him and should bring him great recuperative powers. Without it he would surely be dead by now, but it seems he has drawn himself into a private dungeon and there he stays. Something has to be done to bring him out of it: He has lost the will to live."

Leon stood staring at the beautiful Queen but not seeing her, his thoughts darting from one implication to another. What could he do to help his friend? How had he fallen this far? There had to be an answer. Consolingly, she laid her hand lightly on his arm. He nodded to her, then turned slowly to return and sit by Gaelnn, head in hands, searching his mind for an answer. Surely there was something he could do.

The sun was moving toward evening when Leon suddenly stood and walked from the room and hurried down to Gorath. "You know what has happened. Is there anything that you can suggest? Surely, something exists within your ancient wisdom that can help."

"I KNOW OF NOTHING FOR SURE. THE QUEEN MOTHER THINKS HE HAS LEFT HIS BODY TO SEEK OUT HIS OWN PUNISHMENT FOR THE WRONG HE HAS CAUSED. I KNOW OF NO ONE WHO COULD FOLLOW HIM. POSSIBLY E'ALAM MIGHT HAVE THE ABILITY … I JUST DON'T KNOW."

Leon studied Gorath as his pendant softly vibrated and he turned his thoughts to it. *"We can help you. You already have the ability."*

"Of course!" He exclaimed, "Perhaps you know of one other that has that ability, my great friend, just perhaps. I believe I have certain talents in that direction myself."

"FROM MY UNDERSTANDING, THERE IS ALWAYS A DANGER THAT WHAT YOU PURPOSE WILL CAST YOU BOTH ADRIFT IN HIS PRISON, YOU MAY NOT RETURN."

"I cannot simply stand by and watch him die! I must try something, whatever the costs."

"THE COSTS MAY BE THE LOSS OF VALOR'. BE CAREFUL TO KEEP CONSTANT CONTACT WITH YOUR BODY. I UNDERSTAND THAT THOSE WHO GO THE WAY YOU ARE SUGGESTING MUST MAINTAIN THAT CONTACT THROUGH A GOLDEN THREAD THAT STRETCHES ALWAYS BACK TO THEIR BODY. DO NOT LOOSE IT OR VALOR' WILL PERISH."

"Thank you for your advice, I must try and I must succeed."

He returned to the room where Gaelnn lay. He then instructed the Shadow guard to see to it that he was not disturbed. He sat down on the floor with his back against the bed and his legs crossed, and started going through the exercises that allowed him to meditate deeply. Meditation was the first step he had taken when visiting others in these out of his body experiences.

"Follow the thread of his life. Be sure to visualize your own as you go."

The thread he followed was pale, barely visible as it wound through a strange hell of Gaelnn's own making. Gaseous clouds of orange, red and black swirled around him. The rotten egg smell of sulfur nearly gagged him until he shut it out. He moved quickly along, following the pale thread, turning and twisting as though it were searching through the noxious gasses. Then he was on a path covered with sharp stones that shredded the boots on his feet. *"You don't have to walk his path, just follow it."* Promptly he mentally lifted himself to float just above the path. He saw blood on the stones and hurried on. Looking back his bright golden thread stretched along the way he had come. High cliffs rose on both sides of him as he entered a narrow draw following the pale thread that was Gaelnn's lifeline.

A terrifying lizard-like creature twice the size of a man leapt at him from the shadow of the cliffs. The Sword of VaLor' appeared in his hand. It flashed and sparkled in the dark swirling mists, bringing pure light into an otherwise dark and dismal surrounding. The beast fled back into the shadow from which it had come.

Leon continued to follow the pale thread over a sharp craggy mountain and down into a deep dark valley. He replaced the sword in its scabbard and drew forth his pendant, carrying it before him. The light was so out of place here that it gave him great comfort. The thread of Gaelnn's fading life led down into a crevice that smelled dank and moist. Sweat poured from his body, *"Calm yourself, observe without being a part of his nightmare."* He calmed himself and forced his body to ignore the conditions Gaelnn had made for himself. The path was steep and would have been slippery had Leon actually walked on it instead of just following it. Hideous laughter met his ears as he reached the bottom of the pit. In the heavy evil fog which filled the pit, Leon could see three figures walking menacingly around Gaelnn as he crouched on the ground in submission. Intermittently, they threw bolts of red energy at him. He jerked this way and that, like a rag doll being buffeted about by evil winds.

"Hold!" bellowed Leon. "Be gone! Leave us!"

The three, cowled figures turned to look at him through blood red eyes that glowed slightly in the dark of their hoods. Then, as one, they flung glowing balls of fire at Leon. He brought the pendant up and instantly, instinctively, imagined it reflecting the assault back at them. As the reflected energy touched them, they disappeared in a discordant harmony of shrieks.

Silence filled the pit, and then a heavy sob followed by the word, "Why?"

Gaelnn, his face ashen white, was looking up at Leon in a pleading way. "Leave me," he groaned, "Can you not see that I must die?"

"Nay Gaelnn, it is not to be that easy. You must return with me. There are battles yet to fight, and I need your skill and abilities as a leader."

"What? You have another army of loyal, valiant warriors that you wish me to lead to their deaths? Do not play games with me. Who would follow me now? I have failed you. I have failed VaLor', and I have disgraced my father's name. What would you have of me?"

"I would have you do for VaLor' what you were trained to do. If you must die, do it in battle, not cringing in pits of your own imagination. There are yet battles to fight and your duty lies with the armies of VaLor', fighting her enemies, not smothering yourself in self-pity. If you must die, do it like a man, killing morags."

"Who are you to call me to account?"

"I am your King, which is enough. But more important, I am your friend. Come. Take my hand. Live again. Avenge those who died at your side in that satro trap. You are guilty of nothing more than falling prey to Xzuron's mind tricks, just like Platen. You can yet regain your honor, and save the Chancellor from grieving over your loss. Did you think that no leader before you had ever led his men into a trap? Learn from it. And next time you will be the victor."

Gaelnn sat, staring at his friend. Then slowly he put out his hand to grasp Leon's. Leon thought of following his life line back and in the flurry of an instant they were floating, suspended above their bodies in the room of the great tree. Leon motioned Gaelnn to his body and watched as his friend slowly laid down into his nearly lifeless form. Then, Leon sat back into his own body.

Leon awoke from his trance, stood up and gently shook his sleeping friend. Gaelnn squinted hard, then opened his eyes.

The stone will guide and King will win,
In worlds without or worlds within

Excerpt from the prophesies of Orn the Seer

CHAPTER NINETEEN

The Gathering

Xzuron's huge tent pavilion was moved every other day so he could stay close to his advancing army. In spite of the constant moving he lived in great luxury, surrounded by expensive rugs, tapestries and furnishings, most of which tended to be dark in color as well as dark in content. The tapestries depicted scenes of evil or cruel acts, usually perpetrated upon the inhabitants of VaLor'. Gruesome statuary lined the heavy black walls of the tent and little light entered from the bright sunlight outside. Xzuron sat, lazing on his dark throne staring at a map of VaLor' which covered a large portion of one wall. Two of the ever-present satros were standing near the doorway, not too patiently awaiting the results of the trap Xzuron had set for the VaLor'ians.

Hesitantly, a well-attired morag entered the room. He bowed frequently as he approached the throne. Unlike most of his kind, he spoke. "Sire, I b-b-bare news of the b-b-b-battle."

"Speak up fool," purred Xzuron. "What is it you have to report?"

Finding that he was still alive, the morag relaxed a little and continued. "Sire, the attacking force consisted mainly of light cavalry, and a large number were eliminated. All would have been, had it not been for their leader ... and then that repulsive dragon that flew in at just the wrong moment."

Xzuron sat up straight, his eyes suddenly taking on a reddish glow, "Did you say Dragon?"

Once more fear covered the features of the morag, "Yes Sire, with men riding on its b-b-back. Huge it was. B-b-b-breathing fire and such."

"And?" Xzuron's voice was rising.

The morag could be seen to shrink as he strove to continue. "Sire, the leader of the attack killed one of your lieutenants. And one of the dragon riders killed the other. It was a t-t-terrible sight. Th-th-the main p-part of their army retreated under the p-p-protection of the dragon and ... and its riders."

Fire danced along the arms of the throne where Xzuron's hands gripped it. "How many men of VaLor' died?" His voice was acid and fire at the same time. His stare seemed to cut through the helpless morag cringing before him.

"The report was about two hundred dead and as many more escaped."

"Idiots!" screamed the sorcerer, "The plan was foolproof, yet these special fools proved they could ruin it anyway. Out!" he screamed casting fire at the retreating back of the hapless underling. "I am surrounded by fools!" Suddenly he grew cool and icy, "He comes to meddle in my affairs, this off-worlder who would be King. Well, we shall see." Turning to the waiting satros he screamed, "Pitch my tents in view of East Fort three days hence, or your power will be mine and you shall be ash on the plains of Maldor."

Bowing, his lieutenants backed from the room, red eyes gleaming under their hoods, hands clasped within their long sleeves.

E'Alam stood at the bow of the large raft as it plunged downriver. The Elves and Dwarves had quickly assembled rafts, piled them with well-secured supplies and arms, and headed down-river toward a meeting with the Dark Woods Elves. There were nearly three thousand warriors floating rapidly down the swift, turbulent waters of the West Catch River toward its junction with the East Catch River. A short distance after the convergence they were to join forces with the Elves of the Dark Wood and the Dwarves of New Home. The ride had been rough, but the rafts were well constructed and had held up to the challenge of the river's rapids. Now in sight of the convergence, the river picked up its pace, rushing as though it were anxious to join with its cousin from the east. With a final plunge the river of the West slid into the more placid waters of the slower moving East River, melding into the great river that would wind slowly through the plains of Maldor and past East Fort, four day's march but barely one day's float, to the South. E'Alam turned to watch as hundreds of rafts slid easily through the junction behind him, steering oars and paddles expertly guiding them through the plunge and then relaxing as they entered calmer waters. Ahead he could see the outline of the edge of Dark Wood. He directed the oarsmen to guide them quickly toward the left bank where he expected to find the waiting Elves and Dwarves. When the river ran into the woods, large ancient trees nearly spanned its width blocking out much of the light of day. The air was heavy with the smells of foliage, mosses and ancient bark. It was difficult to imagine that just a league east of the river the forest was gone; it had been devastated by Xzuron's army as it moved south. Toward the edges of the river the water moved slower and they drifted leisurely, in near silence, through the natural beauty searching the shore for signs of the waiting army.

"E'Alam!" The shout came from slightly ahead.

"There," pointed Kenanton, who was standing next to him on the lead raft. Within a few moments hundreds of Elves and Dwarves stepped out of the foliage along the river. As the flotilla came closer many rafts could be seen camouflaged with branches and leaves, moored to the bank of the river.

Kenanton motioned the oarsmen to guide the rafts toward the bank where willing hands soon made room, often tying one raft to another. They were led quickly, quietly back into the thick forest to a clearing beneath the branches of giant trees. This opening in the dense woods had become the main mustering area of a much larger camp well hidden in the surrounding thicket and dense overhead cover. There, the leaders of the gathering army met them. Fallon, Lea'Oen, King Dygor, and many more military leaders and advisors, including the King of the Dark Wood Elves, were gathered in the center of the clearing, seated at a long rough plank table that had been built to serve as a council table.

As soon as they were all seated, E'Alam stood. He had assumed the position at the head of the table and called for order. A hush fell over the gathering. "What is known of the enemy?"

Fallon stood. "We have sent the Rangers out into the plain to gather information and keep an eye on the movements of Xzuron's forces. Just before you arrived word came back that there had been a battle, and that it had resulted in what could have been a rout of our forces. The rout was only stopped by the appearance of Gorath and the High King. Exactly what happened could not be discerned without giving away the fact that our Rangers were watching their movements. It is clear though, that their army is now moving even faster than they were. In our estimation, they could reach East Fort within three days."

"What is your suggestion at this point?"

Fallon continued, "It is the intention of King Leon to allow them to come all the way to the walls of East Fort and then, while they are intent on the walls, we are to attack them from behind with all of the forces we can muster. At that point, they will have the Catch River on their left flank, the impossibly steep cliffs of the Divide range on the right, and our army behind. It should be quite a sight, but even so, it is all a ruse, since the King feels that the only sure way to stop Xzuron is to face him personally."

"No! He must not!" Allece cried out loud from the side of the clearing.

E'Alam turned to face her, "Child, it is for this purpose that he came, though he did not know it at the time. Now he has assumed the Sword and what was foreordained must be allowed to come to pass. Otherwise all of VaLor' shall parish."

She stood still for a moment with her hand over her mouth, then turned and fled into the woods.

E'Alam watched her go then turned back to those at the table. "We must be ready to do our part when the time comes."

Fallon turned from the vanishing image of Allece, "Perhaps the best place for you, friend Wizard, is in support of the walls at East Fort. They must believe that we are throwing all we have at them from the fort walls."

"I fully agree," replied E'Alam. "It approaches night, a perfect time for travel. So, unless there is something else that we should discuss I will have some food and depart." Elves bearing platters of food began to appear out of the dence woods. Soon the normal level of conversation resumed.

As the meal concluded and night began settling over the Dark Woods a large blue-gray falcon stretched eagerly skyward until it found the last rays of the setting sun. Banking south it hurried on with great strokes of its powerful wings.

Fallon sat staring into the embers of a small fire, the remnant of one of the many used for cooking earlier. It was not that he was cold. He sat there for a sort of comfort and inner peace that always seemed to come when he watched the dying embers of a campfire. For some reason he could not identify, he had inadvertently, become the spokesman for the assembled forces. With that came a lot of responsibilities. His tactical background was easily as good as the other leaders, but he had no blood ties to this land, and perhaps, that just might be the reason. As an outsider, and having no ties to any of the various factions, he could hardly look overly favorable on any particular group. Therefore, he might be depended on to make decisions regarding the coming battle without personal involvement. His youth didn't matter in this strange land where so many lived to such great age. The important thing appeared to be his training as a warrior, and of course, the years at his father's court did no harm. How had this all come about? Here he was, a displaced prince with no possible claim to greater title in this land, yet respected as though he were visiting royalty from a kingdom in the next valley. It had much to do with his association with Leon and E'Alam he was sure. He seemed, by virtue of his closeness with Leon, to have become some sort of intermediary when Leon was absent. He wondered where his friend was and how he was faring. Tomorrow he must start moving the army south if they were to arrive at East Fort in time to help. But would it be enough? Could anything stem the eventual success of the morag army? Would he be up to the task? There were too many questions, and too few answers.

A hand gently touched his shoulder. It was Allece. He motioned her to sit beside him.

"I'm sorry," she whispered, "It's just that I love him so. I know what he has to do must be done, but I fear to lose him."

"As do I," he assured her. "He is closer to me than my own brothers. There is a strange sort of kinship between us that I cannot explain. It has been there from the first day I met him in a small vale not far from the village where he grew up. He was the blacksmith's apprentice then, but there was a sort of essence about him that spoke of exciting things to come. I never dreamed it would lead to anything this strange. He was a fast learner and took to weapons as though he were bred for that alone. Later we found he was the son of a raider chieftain, which explained his light coloring and great size. I don't feel that he is really comfortable in his new role as High King, though perhaps he will grow into it." He sat quietly for a few minutes, "We should be off to our beds. Tomorrow we head south."

"Yes, thank you for understanding." She pressed his hand where it lay on his knee, then rose and walked purposefully into the shadows.

He started to rise, but stopped and sat staring deep into the coals, submersed in thought about the coming battle. The now familiar feeling of being watched settled gently over him and he looked up to see a softly inundating image of Leon floating above his head. "Leon, my friend, I had hoped you would contact me. Nod if you can hear me."

"Perhaps it might be better if I just spoke," the image grinned.

"Ah, yes. I had forgotten that when E'Alam appeared in this manner, he could speak quite plainly."

"I am not yet able to manage much of his wizardry, but this much I can do. For some reason it all comes easier in this land. How are things with you? Have the Dwarves and Elves assembled?"

"Yes, and we prepare to move downriver tomorrow, though perhaps the next day would be better since that would save us the necessity of setting up one more camp. We figure that Xzuron will get to the walls of East Fort in about three days, and we don't want to get there too soon. We heard from our scouts about a battle and how you had shown up astride the dragon. Perhaps you could fill me in on what transpired?"

The image shimmered in the soft glow from the embers of the fading fire. "There was indeed a battle. It seems Xzuron was playing mind tricks on our friend Gaelnn and convinced him to take on the whole morag army. Fortunately, he discovered it was a trap before he had committed the whole VaLor'ian force, but he and about four hundred mounted warriors were trapped and would have been annihilated had he not managed to kill the satro that was masterminding the trap. About two hundred managed to escape with a little assistance from Gorath, the Shadows and me. But in the fury of this whole mess, Gaelnn was seriously wounded. We had to take him to the Elf Queen to save his life, but he is recovering and we will soon be ready to travel. We will meet you on the way. As you suggested, I think you should move out the day after tomorrow."

"I'll pass your wishes on to the gathering first thing in the morning. I'm sure they will agree to one more day of rest and preparation before we start downriver. Take care of yourself. There are those here who are concerned for your safety."

Smiling, but looking slightly confused, the image faded. Fallon turned back to staring at the embers for a short while, then stood and walked off toward his bedroll.

Gaelnn's sword had been scorched and discolored when he had killed the satro, but the Elven magic had preserved it. Now, however, no degree of polishing would return it to its original luster. Still, its edge was keen and seemingly undaunted by the ordeal it had been through. The Shadows had taken it from his hand when they had rescued him and had faithfully carried it along. The Elven Queen's miraculous healing powers had left him well and anxious after only a day's rest, and now he stood ready to accompany Leon back to battle the morags, his sword, once more, comfortably in place at his side.

Leon walked down the beautifully landscaped pathway to where Queen Lea'Ah stood chatting with Gorath. By his calculations the morags would be approaching the North Fort walls today, and he wanted to be there before they had a chance to breech the walls. What he was supposed to do was still a mystery, but he felt as though it would all come to him when the time was right. Strange, he mused, how he had come to trust the sword and the pendant to guide him to the proper conclusions when he was called upon to act.

Gorath turned bright eyes toward Leon, "WELL, FRIEND. IS IT TIME TO RETURN TO THE BATTLE?"

"Aye, my trusty mount, and hopefully we will soon see an end to this threat to the land of VaLor'."

The flight back to the plains of Maldor was somewhat slower than had been the flight to Mero Wood. It was, in fact, quite pleasant. Leon found himself thinking of Allece, and seemed to see her dressed for battle and floating on some river. Strange, he thought, the tricks the minds of lovers play; for in the next instant her image filled his thoughts as she had been that night in the garden, beautifully clad in her blue gown. As Gorath topped the Divide Mountains his attention was drawn back to the present and the challenge that lay ahead. Gently they slid down the air currents until the Catch River came into view. Slowly, they banked south following the river. About a league beyond the river a wide swath of the plain had been trampled down to bare earth. It would be years before the grasses that had grown there so freely, would again cover the morag trail. They followed the river until it was joined by another small river rushing out of the Divides. There they saw the sight they had been looking for. Just south of the junction of the two rivers a flotilla of hundreds of rafts was heading toward a small forest where they obviously intended to camp. At the same moment, a large bat-like creature lifted up into the air from the far bank and headed south. With a great burst of speed, Gorath dove to intercept the tordaq and its evil rider. Just as Gorath was reaching out to grab the satro in his powerful talons, the satro saw them and banked sharply to the left. Then, screaming furious oaths, urged the tordaq into a greater burst of speed and headed north.

Gorath circled quickly and rushed to set his passengers down by the edge of the forest, saying as he did so, "I WILL BE MUCH FASTER IF I LEAVE YOU HERE AND PURSUE THEM BY

MYSELF. WE DON'T WANT THEM CARRYING THE NEWS OF YOUR ARRIVAL BACK TO XZURON."

"But will you be all right by yourself?" Leon asked above the whistling of the wind.

"DO NOT FEAR FOR ME, FRIEND. AS LONG AS THERE ARE NO MORE THAN TWO AT A TIME I AM PRETTY SAFE. I WILL SEE YOU AT THE BATTLE, OR BEFORE IF I CAN, BUT THE WAY THEY ARE MOVING IT MAY TAKE ME A WHILE TO CATCH THEM. QUICKLY NOW, I DO NOT WANT TO LOSE SIGHT OF THEM, THOUGH THEIR SCENT WOULD SURELY GUIDE ME." In the space of a breath, they were off and Gorath was again airborne, streaking after the fading figure of the tordaq and its rider as they fled northward.

Leon and the others turned and headed into the woods toward the river. They were barely under the canopy of leaves when the tall, familiar form of Flek the Ranger stepped into view. "Well, we meet again. Only this time, it is King Leon the Dragon Rider." Flek bowed his head slightly then returned the friendly warrior's clasp Leon extended to him.

Leon smiled broadly. "It is good to see you again. We had no idea you were waiting here in the woods."

"Hiding is the more appropriate word. We ducked in here when we saw the tordaq and its rider set down on the ridge on the far side of the river. That was two days ago and we have had to stay concealed until now. Glad we are that you brought the Dragon as reinforcement. Come. Let's go and greet the others. They should have landed their rafts by now."

That evening there were no fires. Tomorrow they would most likely engage the enemy, and they didn't want to give them any warning. Leon spent what was left of the day conferring with the leaders of the assembled force. There were Elfin archers and swordsmen, mounted Rangers, Dwarves thought to be the ultimate hand to hand combatants, and of course, the Shadows, not to mention, hopefully, one VERY LARGE Dragon.

The planning continued right up to dusk when a great commotion broke out from the direction of the deep woods, shouts of, "Hold! Let them through! Stand back!"

Into the clearing where the leaders had assembled marched row after row of skeletal warriors, ragged banners held high, bleached bones glistening in the fading light as they circled in and around the outer edge of the clearing until no more could enter. The mounted prince rode straight to Leon, halted a short distance away, dismounted and dropped to one knee. "What would you have of us, bearer of the Sword? We are yours to command."

"Welcome, Prince Antar. Please rise. You have come far. How have you kept your company from detection?"

The skeletal prince stood, his strange rattling voice answering, "We have no need of light, nor of rest, and so we moved by night. We followed the army of the sorcerer at a discreet distance, laying in wait for his reinforcements. I believe that is why the satro was watching from the far riverbank. He was probably sent to find out why no more morags were arriving. For the most part they lay upon the plains concealed from sight by the hands of my arms-men."

Leon stood for a moment looking at the strange sight surrounding the clearing: a skeletal army, weapons held firmly in fleshless hands, tarnished armor draped on bodies without muscle or sinew. He remembered his first sight of them, and noticed that the Shadows were ready to strike in his defense. "Stay your hands," he cautioned. "Your swords would be of little use here." Turning back to Antar, "You might provide just the sort of surprise we will need. Tomorrow we will attack the enemy from the rear, hopefully as they are engaged with the fort at their front. Our numbers are quite insufficient to carry the battle by sword alone; but possibly, just possibly, the addition of your special army will give us an edge. Continue on this night. Cross the Catch River, and prepare to attack their right flank when the war horn sounds twice, three successive times."

"As you will, my King." Antar turned and mounted. Then with a wave of his hand he led his companions back out of the clearing and into the night.

Allece kept well back in the woods, knowing that Leon would not approve of her being here. She so wanted to go to him, to feel his arms around her. But she knew her presence might endanger the mission. She knew he must not be worrying about her in the battle to come, and so she watched from a distance and melted away into the woods whenever he came her way.

Leon lay on his bedroll, staring through the canopy of leaves overhead into the star-studded sky. There was little sleep for him. His mind kept jumping about thinking of the battle to come and what his part might be. After all this time he still didn't know why he was here, what he was to do. He only knew he had to face the sorcerer of this he was sure. But then what? What special skill did he posses? How could he do what must be done when he didn't have the slightest idea what it might be. It wasn't that he was afraid, well at least not any more than any one else. The pendant had saved him numerous times, and it might have to do so again. The plan was simple. Xzuron had his personal pavilion close to the back lines of the hoard. Leon would punch a wedge into the back lines of the enemy, hopefully deep enough to reach the sorcerer's tents. Then, he would do whatever it was he had to do. Up until now the answers had always come when he needed them; he hoped they would continue to do so. He thought of Allece, careful not to call out to her for fear she would see him in her dreams and worry about him. In a way, he felt she was very near, at least in his thoughts. Finally he slept.

Earlier that evening, E'Alam stood watching from the high stone walls as the tide of gray slowly filled the plain before the gates of East Fort. The sun was setting, and the individual features of the morags were blending into one indefinable mass of seething, shifting gray flesh. Even the morags' armor and weapons blended together becoming gray and indistinguishable. They had stopped just outside of arrow reach, standing, waiting quietly as more and more morags filled the plain before the walls. They had pushed across the river at the ford without even slowing, in spite of the heavy hail of arrows from the earthen battlements the VaLor'ians had built there. At midnight the morags started a low rumbling hum, slowly increasing in volume until it seemed as though they were trying to shatter the walls with sound. Then in a split second it stopped and a sphere of pulsing red light rose into the air from the rear of the mass of gray and floated toward the walls. It came to a stop a short distance in front of E'Alam—within the sphere stood the master sorcerer Xzuron.

Xzuron turned a haughty expression to E'Alam, "Well, Wizard, are you ready to turn your puny army over to me, or would you rather die fighting a hopeless battle?"

E'Alam smiled, "Your little attempt to impress us has only shown us you are less sure than you pretend. Take your maggot army and return to the mountain that spawned you while you still have a chance."

Anger flooded the features of Xzuron. "Prepare to die then! For as the sun rises, so will the army of Xzuron. By this time tomorrow my morags will be feeding on the hearts of your wives and children." Swiftly the sphere returned to the spot from which it had risen. The morags stood, rank upon rank, upon rank, quietly waiting for dawn.

Gray death, in line on line will come,
Their numbers quake the hearts of some
Yet walls still tall and Wizards might,
Give strength and courage for the fight.

Excerpt from the prophesies of Orn the Seer

CHAPTER TWENTY

The Final Battle

Long before the first hint of dawn the rafts cast off into the current. Then the rangers left the protection of the forest and rode out onto the trail south, their horses easily matching the speed of the rafts as they moved down the river. The time for secrecy and hiding was past. Now they must move quickly, hoping for surprise. Soon the time for action would face them all.

Pink, red and yellow haze, and bits of cloud lightened the sky in the east as Leon's forces cautiously beached their rafts at the ford. A large segment of Dark Wood Elves continued to float on downriver to a point that would allow them to flank the enemy on the left. While they were still beaching their rafts the Rangers rode in. Quietly they formed their ranks and set out along the road to the Fort. By the time the sun had lifted an hour or two over the horizon they would be in position to strike.

E'Alam watched patiently as the sun began to peek over the horizon to the east. The beauty of the reddish hues cast in the sky that morning seemed at odds with the events about to transpire. He wondered where Leon was, but had no time to enter the trance state in order to seek him out. He, all of VaLor' for that matter, had placed their complete faith in the Sword and now all must trust in the prophecies to deliver them from Xzuron.

A low rumbling hum began to emanate from the mass of the enemy just as the first tip of the sun shown over the horizon. It grew in volume as the sun rose, getting louder and louder until some of the defenders on the walls held their hands to their ears. At the instant the full oval of the sun cleared the horizon a deafening shout, accompanied by a stamp of thousands and thousands of feet, blasted at their senses. The very rock of the walls quivered as though hit by an earthquake. Dust rose from the plain and flew up from walls and grounds within the Fort. Absolute silence followed for the count of twenty heartbeats; then the entire sequence began again. At the sound of the thunderous crash, cracks began to appear in the walls of the ancient fort.

Leando, displaying considerable alarm, hurried to E'Alam's side, "E'Alam, if this keeps up the walls will fall for sure."

The wizard nodded and waved him gently aside. Then, placing his hands on the parapet before him, closed his eyes and started mumbling words Leando could not identify. As the next thunderous noise came there was no response from the wall, but the first ranks of morags were thrown violently off their feet. For long minutes nothing happened, then two satros rose into the air floating on disks of power and poised just out of reach of arrows, waiting, and watching as the humming began once again. The great volume of noise grew and grew until it was again time for the climax. Then both satros launched bolts of energy at E'Alam the very instant he put up his protective force shield. A clap of unbearable noise similar to thunder rocked the walls of the Fort. New cracks appeared and the wall shuddered once again. In a flash of energy E'Alam attacked his attackers, but their combined power was too much for him to overcome. Gradually he withdrew his attack, and stood for a few minutes deep in thought. Then, he began again to cast the spell on the walls. This time, as the thunderous climax was reached and the satros launched their attack, he ignored it. Flames of energy reached him but a blue aura leapt to surround him as the blue crystal took over his defense. The flame deflected harmlessly back toward the satros. Again the thunder and again the walls held and ranks of morags were thrown violently to the ground. Xzuron's lieutenants floated back toward his pavilion and all was quiet for nearly an hour as the sun rose higher into the morning sky. The air at the fort was laden with dust and the acrid smell of fear-caused sweat, but all held their positions, prepared to die if necessary to defend the walls.

Two tordaqs rose from the midst of the morag army and flew toward the walls where they circled high above. Two more rose and placed themselves over other sections of the walls, satros rode easily upon their backs. Finally, the two satros on their floating disks of energy glided slowly over the heads of their army and halted; suspended near the front ranks. Again the humming started, unstoppable and deadly, as it approached the climax, and then the satros on the tordaqs launched fireballs and bolts of crackling energy onto the walls of the fort. Pandemonium erupted as men tried to dodge fire and flying bits of rock all along the walls. E'Alam could simply not protect the whole wall. Men were dying everywhere. The damage the flying satros did would not greatly disturb the solidity of the walls, but men were no match for this type of warfare. Sounds of the wounded and dying filled the air. Men were totally defenseless against this attack from above.

"Leando," E'Alam shouted, "get the men into the walls under cover."

Soon the defenders had left the walls for the security of the passages within, carrying their wounded with them; only E'Alam remained. Fire again rolled across the ramparts consuming the dead, the smell of burning flesh mixing with the dust. Then the tordaqs converged toward him, he knew he could not hold out against so much power. At least in the last war there had been several great wizards to carry out the battle. Now there was only him. The crescendo was building again and the satros were converging on him for the kill. He knew that if he fell so would the walls. He wondered where Leon and the Sword were; it seemed that they were the only hope now.

Without warning Gorath plummeted out of the glare of the sun smashing down two tordaqs and their riders before they knew what hit them. Landing easily on the walls he called to the wizard, "DO YOU MIND IF I JOIN YOUR LITTLE PARTY? I DON'T WANT TO SPOIL ANY OF YOUR FUN, BUT FIRE BATTLES JUST HAPPEN TO BE A FAVORITE SPORT OF MINE."

"Please feel free to assist wherever you like, I'm grateful for your timely arrival."

"IT'S JUST A LITTLE SURPRISE I WORKED UP FOR XZURON. THERE IS ANOTHER ABOUT TO STRIKE HIM FROM THE REAR."

The thundering noise of the battle on the walls helped to cover Leon's advance, allowing his forces to position themselves for the attack on Xzuron. Three Dwarfish wedges were formed with Fallon leading the center with his heavily armored knights and heavy horse to blast a hole into the center toward Xzuron's tents. As soon as they were slowed Leon would charge into the opening and head for the Sorcerer's pavilion. Formed on his right were Gaelnn and King Kanoor Stronghand and on the left, King Dygor. Elven archers and swordsmen followed. At Leon's signal the war horns sounded three double blasts and the battle was on. Xzuron was attacked from three sides at once by an army he didn't know existed. In minutes Fallon's heavy horse and the chanting Dwarves had broken well into the rear of Xzuron's forces, wreaking terrible vengeance in payment for the attack on their Catch Mountain home. Arrows flew into the surprised morags, and Elven swordsmen picked up the trailing edges of the wedges to finish the work started by Fallon's heavy cavalry and the Dwarves. Leon, swinging the Sword of VaLor', passed Fallon's knights and led at the point of his wedge, with skill seldom seen in the land of VaLor'. He fought as though he were invincible, and in many ways he was, for the stone protected him and his great skill and size overpowered the enemy even though they were most often larger than he. Leon's wedge moved slightly faster than the others, and gradually the side wedges worked toward the center, opening a huge pie shape in the ranks of the morags into which poured Elven archers raining a steady stream of death into the enemy. The morags at the rear seemed to be without direction and soon they were turning toward their own kind, fleeing and bunching tighter and tighter together to avoid the unfailing blades of the fierce Dwarves and the scarlet clad Shadow warriors that led them, especially the tall blond with his invincible sword. Leon broke through into a clearing where a large tent pavilion stood at its center. The resistance had grown stronger just before the clearing, and now he faced a squad of particularly large and fierce looking morags. Shouting encouragement he smashed straight into the center of their formation, cutting through like a scythe through straw.

Floating above the tents a bubble-like sphere awaited his arrival. Standing within the sphere Xzuron glared at Leon, his cruel voice seeming to cut with ease through the noise of the melee surrounding them, "So this is the fool who would be King. Well, little King, today you shall learn how to die, as will those who have supported you. Your trinket of a sword will not stop a sorcerer's power." With that Xzuron launched a stream of pure bright energy straight at Leon. In a seemingly futile but instinctive movement Leon swung the sword of VaLor' up before him with both hands, expecting to die. The energy smashed into the sword…and was instantly absorbed…the sword grew warm in Leon's hands…it vibrated … it pulsed. A sucking noise began to mix with the sizzle of energy, the smell of ozone and the background clamor of battle. The Shadow guard quickly moved to surround him, giving him the cover of their blades. Leon stared at Xzuron. He could see that sweat had broken out on the sorcerer's face, and still the sword drained and sucked. Fear now began to flash across the evil features. Then, it set in hard. He was trapped. The sword was draining away his life's energy and he could not stop it. The sphere began to fade. The sorcerer settled to the ground. Suddenly there was silence all around the clearing. The morags stopped fighting and stared in wonder and confusion. Xzuron started to age before their eyes. Then his eyes sharpened and he turned toward his troops and stretched his left hand toward them. In that instant a few disappeared in a puff of gray dust and he seemed to gain strength. Steadily, more and more of his followers evaporated into dust, and he could be seen to grow stronger with each one. Xzuron grew younger again right before the eyes of the onlookers, strengthened again by drawing out the life energy of those he had created. The Sword's vibration weakened and Xzuron's eyes plainly said that now he had regained enough control to break the energy draining power of the Sword. His evil features began again to show disdain for those around him.

A great rattling, crashing turmoil smashed through from the right flank, and just for an instant the sorcerer's concentration slipped. And the Sword took over again. Again he started to age. Again he reached into his morags for strength.

The sword sucked with even greater force than before. Leon began to become aware of spells, not only spells, but more. He grew aware of, the mind that had created the morags. He knew how Xzuron had infused them with life, had given them living energy that he had taken from the earth itself. He began to see that the earth had a great supply of life energy, if you but knew the secret of how to steal it. Still, the Sword sucked a steady stream of energy. In his mind Leon saw the great caverns in mount Orag, saw the making of the satros and the control that Xzuron had over them through the red stones that they wore around their necks, saw the re-populating of the tordaqs, saw the mate of Xzuron and her infant son. He knew the secret of the sphere that floated, and he became aware of the feeling of power that filled the being of the man before him.

Xzuron's army was rapidly evaporating into gray dust. Now they were disappearing in great swaths, all in total silence. The sorcerer seemed to grow stronger, younger. His face once more took on an expression of confidence. With his army almost gone he made a great, visible effort to break the contact with the sword, but the sword held him fast and once more he began to age before Leon's eyes. Fear again replaced confidence as the last of his followers; morags, and the satros disappeared from the plain before the walls of East Fort.

Leon was steadily gaining knowledge and power from his enemy, through the link provided by the sword. Vibrations traveled throughout his body. He was warm and vibrant, his confidence increased as never before. The acts of E'Alam began to seem simple and easily accomplished. His body continued to hum and vibrate to the frequency of the sword. He felt full to the point of bursting with power and knowledge. No longer was he an apprentice. He had gone beyond apprentice, beyond Wizard…to Sorcerer. Still the Sword sucked.

Xzuron grew bent and wrinkled, then frail beyond comprehension. He began a soft high laugh. Finally, looking straight at Leon he said, in a hate filled screeching voice, "Now the price is yours to pay," then he dissolved into a small pile of ash. The sword stopped pulsing. All around them the thousands upon thousands of morags were gone, dissolved to a light gray dust that covered the plain, there to remain for months before being blown away or dissolving into the ground.

Only VaLor'ian warriors remained on the plain before the fort as rider-less tordaqs disappeared into the northern sky.

Gorath turned to E'Alam, "IT WOULD SEEM THAT OUR YOUNG KING HAS SUCCEEDED IN HIS QUEST. I BELIEVE HE IS GOING TO HAVE NEED OF US NOW MORE THAN EVER. WOULD YOU CARE TO RIDE THIS OLD DRAGON DOWN TO SEE IF WE CAN BE OF ASSISTANCE?"

E'Alam bowed grandly, "It would be my great honor." He mounted Gorath's back and they drifted off toward the battle scene in the distance.

Leon turned to look to his people. Dead and wounded lay in what had been the fighting wedge, now healers worked frantically to save those who could be saved, and warriors knelt to morn those who had died. Three of the Shadows had found the death they had sought fighting beside Leon up to the end. The others stood at his side still ready to protect him from any unknown danger.

Gaelnn approached and Leon took him by both hands and said, "My friend, you have fought well and more that justified my faith in you, thank you."

Gaelnn smiled, "No, thank you, for you gave me back my life and my honor."

A stone's throw away stood the skeletal army of Prince Antar. They moved forward to stand before Leon. The strange rattling voice spoke, "High King, have we done as you would have us do?"

Leon Smiled, "Aye, and now I can give you your promised reward. Come before me."

Antar dismounted and knelt before Leon.

Leon raised the Sword of VaLor' and placed it over the head of the Prince and willed that the prophecy should be fulfilled, and so it was. A flow of power gushed out of him into those before him, and in a moment Antar and his whole army stood alive and well, resplendent in shining armor. Leon knew that as this had been done, the lost kingdom of Antar had once again appeared on the banks of the Deep River from which it had disappeared at the treacherous but valiant death of Antar and his army. He knew it was so, and so it was.

Gorath settled down close to Leon and E'Alam dismounted. The Wizard turned to Antar, "Hail, Antar, now you may return to your home in peace and with honor."

Antar saluted the Wizard with his right fist over his heart, "It would seem, son of Wizards, that you were quite right in your assumptions regarding our new King. For as it was written, so it is." He then turned to Leon, "My Liege, with your permission we would take our leave. Once more we need travel the trail over the Divides that we may again see our homes."

"Indeed," replied Leon, "go with my blessing and our thanks, but your trip might be made easier if you ride the river to Val. We would then be better able to provision you, and you will need provisioning now. As a matter of fact you still look a little gaunt."

"You are quite right, my King, I feel a bit like, all skin and bones, but at least there is skin, and it will feel good to fill it with food once again."

In short order, Antar and his men were on their way to East Fort, escorted by the feathered Shadow, who, even though he now wore the crimson of Leon's private guard, still wore his many feathers.

The sword to save the land he'll raise,
While seeks he not, the crown nor praise.
And Antar's sons called forth shall fight,
The south bound hoards of evil might.
Then gain the treasure they have sought,
And end the curse by battle fought.

Excerpts from the prophesies of Orn the Seer

CHAPTER TWENTY ONE

The Magic

As Leon stood watching Prince Antar depart, Jerome came hurrying up followed by other squires carrying a litter. "Jerome, your help with our fledgling corps of knights did well, and I am grateful for their help in the battle."

"My King, my friend, I fear I bring sad news. Allece fought in the battle and is severely wounded,"

Leon rushed to the litter. The bearers laid it gently on the ground. Blood stained her torn tunic. He could see bandages through his sudden tears. Her face was ashen white from loss of blood. His voice stuck in his throat as finally he stammered, "How ... how did this happen? She was supposed to be in Val." He fought to hold back tears, "E'Alam, can you help? I am full of new knowledge but I know of nothing that can help her."

E'Alam leaned over her still form, "This requires a greater skill at healing than I possess."

Leon stood. A great rage was building within him. Energy crackled all about his being, anxiously waiting to lash out, to crush, to burn, to destroy. All those about him stood well back except E'Alam and Gorath.

Leon groped within, touching his new power, caressing it, being drawn into the power, becoming one with it, seeing all that surrounded him as insignificant, he tasted the power. Without her, power was all that mattered. And he was power.

As those about watched; Leon's countenance changed. His eyes and features became first, indifferent to the others, then gradually hardened into contempt, and finally hate.

Leon looked around, "Why do I need you, you are as nothing. I could burn you all to stubble in an instant."

"True," replied E'Alam. "Listen to yourself Leon, you are beginning to sound like him," he pointed at the dust of Xzuron. "Take hold of yourself. Deny the cravings that draw you to the darkness. You now have great power. Use it justly; seek the spirit of the stone."

"Stone," he shouted, "I need no stone." So saying he whipped the chain from around his neck and flung it upon the ground.

"Such foolishness!" screamed Leon, visibly losing all control to the power.

Fallon stepped forward pleading, "Leon, my friend, remember who you were and where you came from."

"King!" shouted Leon, "Who are you to speak to me thus! I, Leon the great, the slayer of Xzuron, the heir of Xzuron, nay Xzuron himself am I."

Fallon bowed low in a great show of courtly grace, inconspicuously reaching into his cloak for a small leather bag, and as he swept back up he flung the contents full in Leon's, rage contorted, face. In an instant Leon's Sword came up for an attack ... Then his eyes cleared, his face softened, he dropped the Sword and fell to his knees sobbing by the side of Allece's litter. Slowly he reached out for his pendant and replaced it about his neck.

"LAY THE SWORD UPON HER BODY GOOD KING, AND PLACE YOUR PENDANT AGAINST THE STONE IN ITS POMMEL, THEN THINK OF HER AS SHE WAS. DO NOT USE THE SORCERER'S POWER, REACH INTO YOUR MIND AND HEART."

Through tear filled eyes Leon sought the Sword, which lay next to him on the ground. Eagerly he picked it up and gently laid it on Allece's still form. He then leaned over her still form and placed the pendant stone, now hanging around his neck against the large blue stone in the pommel of the sword, and remembered her standing full of life and love in the gardens of the palace of Val. A blue cloud formed around her. At first it was thick like fog. Gradually it began to clear. Slowly, ever so slowly, her coloring began to change from the pallor of near death to the pink of health. Her eyes opened and her arms came up to encircle his neck. In that instant he knew real power, the power that mattered, the power of love, and yes of friendship, of people caring for people, of valiant warriors defending their homes and families at whatever the cost, the power of being, the true power of the Stone.

Leon removed his pendant from the pommel of his sword and set the sword aside, helping Allece stand. Then, looking to his friends who had once again moved in close to him, he asked, "How will I prevent the madness from returning?"

"THEREIN REMAINS YOUR ONE LAST CHALLENGE. I CAN TEACH YOU HOW TO DISPEL THE ENERGY YOU

HAVE STORED UP, BUT IF YOU CHOOSE TO REMAIN HERE IN VALOR', THE SORCERER'S CALL WILL ALWAYS BECKON YOU. I BELIEVE IT WAS FOR THIS REASON THAT THE STONE CHOSE YOU, AN OFF-WORLDER, TO CARRY THE SWORD. YOU CAN RETURN TO THE WORLD OF YOUR BIRTH. THERE YOU WILL STILL POSSESS THE KNOWLEDGE OF THE SORCERER, BUT YOU WILL HAVE BLOCKED YOUR ACCESS TO THE EVIL AND DEPRAVATION OF THE DARKNESS. AS YOU ARE NOW AWARE, ALL POWER HAS A POSITIVE AND A NEGATIVE INFLUENCE. THE SORCERER FOLLOWS THE NEGATIVE SIDE WHILE THE WIZARD FOLLOWS THE POSITIVE. AS IN ALL THINGS, THIS MUST BE YOUR CHOICE. BUT I WOULD ENCOURAGE YOU TO MAKE YOUR DECISION QUICKLY WHILE THE EFFECTS OF THE ELVEN DUST STILL HOLD YOU IN CHECK."

Leon looked worried, "What of Allece?"

"AS WITH YOU, IT IS HER CHOICE. LIVING IN YOUR WORLD IS AS POSSIBLE FOR HER AS IT IS POSSIBLE FOR PEOPLE FROM YOUR WORLD TO LIVE HERE.

Leon turned to Allece, "What say you?"

She smiled, and squeezed his hand. "Oh, you won't get rid of me that easily. Of course I would choose to go with you, wherever you go"

Leon beamed, "Then let us do what we may for those here who need our help, and hurry to the fort."

In a matter of just three hours Gaelnn, Fallon and D'Nee escorted Leon and Allece to the small chapel. Allece was resplendent in a borrowed gown, while Leon still wore his battle soiled scarlet attire sparkling with Elven dust. After they were married they were presented to the assembled army where they were cheered, and honored. The Stone would surely bless their union.

Leon promptly assembled the council of VaLor' and spoke to them. "Since I must leave this beautiful land, it is my wish that you accept Prince Fallon to stand as King in my stead." A chorus of approving O's! and Ah's! followed. He continued, "The prophesies, as you know and I have just become aware of, call for an off-worlder to continue to rule. This more than any other thing seems to explain why the Stone called my friend, and would be brother, to travel here with me. Since there is little time for me, I ask for your support in this my final request as your King." One after another the entire council rose in support, until all in the room were standing.

Leon then turned to his Shadows, "Please escort Prince Fallon into the chamber". While the Shadows were gone from the room the council members returned to their seats and waited with visible impatience.

The resounding voice of the door guard sang out, "Prince Fallon, companion to the High King of VaLor'."

Into the room strode Fallon surrounded by the scarlet clad Shadows.

Leon stood, "Come my brother and stand with me."

Fallon approached smiling. "What would you have of me, my King?"

"Would you serve this people?"

"Aye, my Lord King, in any way that you choose."

"And if it be their choice?"

Fallon nodded, "Yes Sire I find them a gallant people worthy of all that I might be able to give them. What is it you wish? Is there yet another Quest?"

"I wish, that you would have the prize your birth denied you. Please kneel." Fallon knelt, a little confused. Leon placed his sword point down on the floor, then placed his left hand on the pommel stone and placed Fallon's left hand on his own, then "Please raise your right hand." Fallon did so. "Prince Fallon, with the full support and under the direction of the entire council," he paused. Then, removing his crown, he placed it gently on Fallon's head, much to his friend's surprise, "I crown you King Fallon High King of VaLor'."

A cheer broke out from the assembled councilmen. Fallon still knelt, stunned.

"Rise King Fallon, and begin your own personal quest," and then in a quieter voice, "and as a small bit of advice, I would strongly suggest that you keep Leando and Gaelnn as your advisors." Then he whispered, "A Queen from the Plains of Planor could only strengthen your subjects' respect for you."

At that Fallon smiled broadly and stood.

Gorath glided silently down the air currents, and settled just outside the gates of the Blue Keep of VaLor', in the dimming rays of the setting sun. E'Alam, Allece and a heavily bundled Leon, bundled to hold the Elven dust on him during the flight, dismounted from the mighty Dragon's back.

"E'ALAM WILL ESCORT YOU TO YOUR OWN WORLD. HAVE YOU DISCOVERED THE WAY TO RID YOURSELF OF THE SORCERER'S POWER?"

"I believe so," said Leon. He walked over to the edge of the hill upon which the Keep stood, faced east and placed the tip of the Sword of VaLor' into the ground and willed the earth to receive that which had been stolen from it. A draining sensation filled his being. He nearly called it back, but he knew that which he did must be done. Long minutes passed; the draining ceased. He felt empty and weak, but more right than he had felt since the battle with Xzuron. He turned back to his friends, "It is done."

Before his eyes Gorath started to shimmer and diminish in size until a four foot, eight inch sprightly looking middle aged Dwarf with a heavy grey beard that hung to his waist, stood before him. "Now my young friend, if I may have the Sword?"

Leon placed the Sword in its scabbard, removed both and handed them to the Dwarf, somehow knowing it was right.

As the Dwarf touched the Sword it too shimmered, elongated and resolved into a staff with a large blue stone at its top, it was much taller than the Dwarf who held it. "I am E'Gorath, high wizard of the eight worlds of the Lodestone. We shall surely meet again E'Leon, for now Wizard you are, and the title fits you well. It was I who saw the last great battle, and I shall see the next. E'Alam will return to his own world Sithia, and to his ongoing guardianship of others. You, E'Leon, will watch after Angar, your home world. Enjoy your time with your lovely bride and await the call of the Stone. E'Alam, you have fulfilled your part well. I look forward to our next meeting at the inn in Downfelt."

E'Alam smiled, "That will be a pleasure, as always, Master."

E'Gorath continued, "This is the conclusion of but one small part of the prophecies, those that pertain to VaLor', and I must return to my people and to my home within the mountain of my ancestors and again await the call of the Stone."

He turned again to E'Leon, "Finally, after you have been away for a few years you may return to VaLor' for short visits, not to exceed two weeks. Should a sword such as this be needed again, I'm sure you have gained the knowledge to construct a very effective staff-sword on your own."

E'Leon nodded smiling, the knowledge crystal clear in his mind.

Once again the shimmering began and Gorath the dragon, Staff in right front claw, leapt into the air and headed swiftly south.

E'Leon turned to E'Alam, "One thing that has given me pause is the question as to why you chose to have me physically make the trip from the Blue Keep on Ganor to Old Home, but I think I have finally figured it out. The question came to my mind about the time I was climbing those endless stairs in Old Home when I suddenly remembered that you had brought Jerome to Valor' in a sphere, why not Fallon and I. Now it seems obvious, the prophecies had to be met in their own time and undisturbed by human interference and Jerome and Snowball were not a part of the prophecies."

E'Alam nodded, "One of the greatest destroyers of prophecies is humans trying to help out and make them hurry or change.

Now we had better get moving." E'Alam guided his two, still slightly confused companions into the Blue Keep.

The Sword VaLor' its power born,
Of Royal hands twixt worlds torn.
Twill save the land and bring back life,
To Comark dead of war and strife.
Then King shall rule though not alone,
Must heed the call of earth and Stone.

Excerpts from the prophesies of Orn the Seer

Throughout the Plains of Comark, long dormant seeds felt the return of the land's stolen life and found joy in beginning again their long interrupted cycle of growth. In a few days the plains would be covered with vibrant new vegetation, eager to make up for years of starvation. Finally, life had returned to the Plains of Comark.

5526 AS, ANGAR

Leon came awake with a start. His pendant was vibrating so insistently that it woke Allece. The whole Keep seemed to be humming. They sat up in bed knowing that the time had come for him to once again answer the call of the Stone.

THE END

GLOSSARY

A.S.	After Stone, After the Lodestone was set in the Keeps
Allece	Lord Leando's Daughter
Antar, Prince	Long dead skeletal prince
Blue Keep	Medieval type castle, Home of the Lodestone
Downfelt	Small village in middle VaLor'
D'Nee	Daughter if the Over Chieftain of Planor
Doran,	Prince, Son of Dwarf King of Old Home
Doranon	King of Dwarves of Old Home
Dygor, King	King of New Home Dwarves
E'Alam	Wizard, Pendant bearer, Knight of the Stone
Fallon, Prince	Once Squire to Sir Galan, now Leon's closest friend
Flex	Ranger, huntsman, for crown of Val
Galan, Sir	Knight of a Southern realm, Leon's Arms teacher
Gaelnn	Son of Lord Leando, the Chancellor of Val
Grotto, the	Cavern home of the Pendants, until it calls a bearer
Guardian	A Knight of the Stone for that area
Gathor	First advisor to King Doranon of Old Home Dwarves
Jerome	Fallon's Squire
Knight of the Stone	A Pendant bearer, Warriors for the Stone
Kemper	One of Leon's boyhood friends
Korshan	Sorcerer in Sithia, eighth World, evil seeking power
Kortox	Combination of Korshan and the demon Thantox

Krantor	Over Chieftain of the Clans of Planor, Horse warriors
Lea'Ah	Queen of the High Elves
Leando, Lord	Chancellor of Kings palace on Val
Lea'Oen	Prince, Son of Lea'Ah, Pendant bearer
Larkin	Village smith and foster father to Leon
Leon	Orphan who becomes a pendant bearer
Leonetta	Leon's Mother who died early in his life
Mae	Wife of Larken the smith on Ganor
Mia	Wife of Tidus, staff of Keep on world of Ganor
Mt. Orag	Extinct Volcano, Home of Xzuron the Sorcerer
Nelmar	King of the High Elves
North Fort	Built after the big war to hold back sorcerer's armies
Orn	Ancient Prophet and seer
Plain of Cormac	Three hundred year old Battle field
Raiders	Viking like warriors from the North
Satros	Once human captains of Xzuron's armies
Sean	Youngest of Leon's boyhood friends
Sithia	Eighth Sister World, now held by Kortox and his demons
Snowball	Fallon's white war horse stallion
Tad	One of Leon's boyhood friends
Thantox	Demon Lord of the void
Tidus	House staff for Keep on Ganor
Tordaq	Huge bat-like mounts for Satros
Val	Capital city of VaLor'
VaLor'	First world of the Sister Worlds
Valorians	People of VaLor'
Windwalker	E'Alam's special mount on VaLor'
Xzuron	Evil sorcerer, nemesis on VaLor'

THE LODESTONE SAGA

BOOK TWO
THE TIARA OF THANN

ROBERT LOUIS ENGLEMAN

CHAPTER ONE

Trechery

5507 AS, ROYAL PALACE, THANN

Gloreena Kin Olomon surged up wide steps toward the royal chambers, her beautiful face marred only by an expression of visible cruelty, set off by her waist long coal black hair, accentuated further by her black robes billowing in the wind caused by her passage. Ebony feathered fringe fluttered in rhythm with her movement. A blood red pendant glowed brightly where it hung between her breasts on the outside of her flowing black gown. Reaching the landing of the royal suite she nearly growled with pleasure as she watched the king fall beneath the rain of her warriors' swords, hammered down by the sheer weight of their numbers. Near the door to the royal chambers her beautiful blond sister struck back with fire and bolts of energy, throwing fear into her attackers. Gloreena cursed and cast a bolt of pure energy at her unsuspecting sister who barely averted the bolt as she turned to face the greater danger…. Gloreena. In that split second of distraction, a blood red crossbow bolt pierced the Queen's heart. Blood pumped out in a gush. She turned and gestured at her assailant. Then she slid slowly to the marble floor, looking back at her sister through slowly glazing eyes. A faint smile touched her lips. With a fleeting look of approval Gloreena stepped over the form of her now dead brother-in-law, the king, and unknowing father of her own child. She smiled about that. Her spell had fooled them both, and she hadn't even had to touch him. She smiled; magic was wonderful. His body now lay stretched across the top steps, lifeless hand still gripping the ornate 'Sword of State'. Blood soaked his nightclothes and dribbled like red honey down the glass-bright, marble steps. Nearly a dozen of her raiders lay scattered about him, but the surprise had been complete. Neither he nor the palace guard had a chance to set up an effective defense. In the distant corners of the palace the battle could still be heard as resistance was eliminated. All of those who had stood by the royal family would be killed. The Queen lay still, her hand vainly clutching the shaft of the enchanted crossbow bolt that had killed her. Her blond hair surrounded her face like a disheveled halo, and her gray eyes were fixed in an unending stare into the eternities. Gloreena's second in command stood to the side frozen forever in stone, a last evidence of the Queen's power and her final spell. He still held the crossbow that had been his last weapon. His loss was of little concern. The smell of blood, sweat and opened body cavities made the air thick and strangely sweet. Kortox would be pleased. She breathed deep, paused just long enough to kick the body of her sister, nod her head in satisfaction, then hurry into the royal chambers. Seconds later Gloreena's screech could be heard throughout the castle. She ran back onto the stairway.

"WHERE IS THE BRAT!" Gloreena screamed at the top of her lungs, her gray eyes flashing. Then she heard fighting from the top of the tower. She turned and sprinted on up the stairs. She had to find that baby! Only its death would eliminate any challenge to her rule. She could hear battering above. Someone must have closed and latched the door because her soldiers were trying to smash it down. Suddenly, there was a blinding flash of light from the top of the stairs followed by the deep rumble of cascading stone and dust, then … deep silence, interrupted eventually by cursing and moaning.

About the Author

Robert Louis Engleman is a retired electrician who found pleasure in reading science fiction and fantasy novels from a time, well before TV, while he was in his early teens. When he was eighteen, and still in the army, he wrote his first full length novel. That was actually well before computers believe it or not. The arrival of computers simplified the process greatly, and retirement gave him the necessary time. This book is one of a series of fantasy and science fiction novels that he has called the Lodestone Saga. He lives on a small ranch in Washington State and raises horses, (three, at present), dogs (one, at present) and plays servant to cats (three, also at present). He enjoys horseback riding, skiing, and sailing. He hopes that you'll find even a small portion of the pleasure reading his stories that he had writing them.

www.ingramcontent.com/pod-product-compliance
Lightning Source LLC
LaVergne TN
LVHW021656060526
838200LV00050B/2381